Finding Miracles

Finding Miracles

JULIA ALVAREZ

EMBER

This is a work of fiction. Names, characters, places, and incidents either are the product of the author's imagination or are used fictitiously. Any resemblance to actual persons, living or dead, events, or locales is entirely coincidental.

Text copyright © 2004 by Julia Alvarez
Cover art copyright © 2018 by Ana Juan

All rights reserved. Published in the United States by Ember, an imprint of Random House Children's Books, a division of Penguin Random House LLC, New York. Originally published in hardcover in the United States by Alfred A. Knopf, an imprint of Random House Children's Books, New York, in 2004.

Ember and the E colophon are registered trademarks of Penguin Random House LLC.

Visit us on the Web! GetUnderlined.com

Educators and librarians, for a variety of teaching tools, visit us at RHTeachersLibrarians.com

The Library of Congress has cataloged the hardcover edition of this work as follows:
Alvarez, Julia.
Finding miracles / Julia Alvarez
p. cm.
Summary: Fifteen-year-old Milly Kaufman is an average American teenager until Pablo, a new student at her school, inspires her to search for her birth family in his native country.
ISBN 978-0-375-82760-0 (trade) — ISBN 978-0-375-92760-7 (lib. bdg.) — ISBN 978-0-307-43333-6 (ebook)
[1. Adoption—Fiction. 2. Central America—Fiction. 3. Schools—Fiction. 4. High schools—Fiction.] I. Title.
PZ7.A48Fi 2004
[Fic]—dc22 2003025127

ISBN 978-0-399-55548-0 (pbk.)

Printed in the United States of America
10 9 8 7 6 5 4 3 2
First Ember Edition 2018

Random House Children's Books supports the First Amendment and celebrates the right to read.

for the *milagritos*,
who have brought more light
into our lives

—especially
for lizzi,
nuni, lauri

and to the mothers & fathers,
lost and found,
the wrenching loss,
the amazing gift

Part One

Part Two

Part One

I

Allergic to Myself

I TOOK THE CLASS where we wrote stories with Ms. Morris. It was a three-week elective we could do on the side with regular English class. I did it because, to be truthful, I needed the extra credit. I've always had big problems with writing, which I'm not going to go into here. I knew my English grade, a C, was rapidly gyrating into a D. So I signed up.

"Stories are how we put the pieces of our lives together," Ms. Morris told us that first class. The way she talked, it was like stories could save your life. She was like a fanatic of literature, Ms. Morris. A lot of kids didn't like her for that. But secretly, I admired her. She had something worth giving her life to. Except for saving my mom and dad

3

and sister, Kate, and brother, Nate, and best friend, Em, and a few other people from a burning building, I didn't have anything I could get that worked up about.

"Unless we put the pieces together we can get lost." Ms. Morris sighed like she'd been there, done that. Ms. Morris wasn't exactly old, maybe about Mom and Dad's age. But with her wild, frizzy hair and her scarves and eye makeup, she seemed younger. She lived an hour away near the state university and drove a red pickup. Occasionally, she referred to her partner, and sometimes to her kid, and once to an ex-husband. It was hard to put all the pieces of her life together.

Ms. Morris had this exercise where we had to jot down a couple of details about ourselves. Then we had to write a story based on them.

"Nothing big," she said to encourage us. "But they do have to be details that reveal something about your real self."

"Huh?" a bunch of the guys in the back row grunted.

"Here's what I mean," Ms. Morris said, reading from her list. She always tried out the exercises she gave us. "The morning I was born, I had to be turned around three times. Headed in the wrong direction, I guess." She looked up and grinned, sort of proud of herself. "Okay, here's another one. When I was twelve, an X-ray discovered that I had extra 'wing bones' on my shoulders." Ms. Morris spread her arms as if she was ready to fly away.

4

The *huh* guys all shot a glance at each other like here we are in the Twilight Zone.

"So, class, a detail or two to convey the real you! Actually, this is a great exercise in self-knowledge!"

We all groaned. It was kind of mandatory when a teacher was this kindergarten-perky about an assignment.

I sat at my desk wondering what to write. My hands were itching already with this rash I always get. Since nothing else was coming, I decided to jot that down. But what came out was, "I have this allergy where my hands get red and itchy when my real self's trying to tell me something." For my second detail, I found myself writing, "My parents have a box in their bedroom we've only opened once. I think of it as The Box."

Ms. Morris was coming down the rows, checking on our progress. "That's great!" she whispered when she read over my paper. Now my face, along with my hands, turned red. "You could tell an interesting story with just those two facts!"

"I made them up," I said a little too quickly. Oh yeah? All she had to do was look at my hands.

"Then write a story about a character for whom those two facts are true," Ms. Morris shot back. You couldn't get around her enthusiasm, no way.

I felt relieved when music sounded over the loudspeaker for the end of the period. That's a telling detail about our school. Instead of bells, we get music, anything from classical to "Rock-a-bye, Baby" to rock. I guess we're free spirits in Vermont. Bells are too uptight for us.

I ended up writing some lame, futuristic story about this girl alien whose memory chips are kept in a box that she can't open because her hands need rebooting. Some idea from a late-night movie Em and I had seen on TV at her house, where her parents have a dish and get all the weird channels.

I could tell Ms. Morris was disappointed that I didn't write about my own life. And though my hands kept breaking out in rashes, trying to tell me *Milly! It's time!*, I wasn't ready yet to open my box of secrets.

But sometimes, like with my allergies, it takes an outside irritant to make you react. My outside "irritant" showed up the next day in Mr. Barstow's class.

He stood in front of us, head bowed, so you couldn't really see his face. His skin was golden brown like mine gets in the summer after a few weeks in the sun.

Mr. Barstow, our homeroom/history teacher, was introducing him: Pablo something something something—he must have had about four names. "Let's give our classmate a warm welcome!"

Warm welcome was right. It was one of those freezer-compartment January days when even people who love winter have to ask themselves, Am I out of my mind? I wasn't

6

one of those people, winter lovers I mean. But from time to time, I had my own reasons to ask myself, Milly, are you out of your mind? Loving winter was not one of them.

"Hey, class, come on. You can do better than that!" When he wasn't teaching World History or being our homeroom teacher, Mr. Barstow was the football-basketball-baseball coach. He could work up a crowd. He had less luck with ninth-grade homeroom in the middle of winter.

We managed a lukewarm applause.

Pablo wasn't dressed for cold weather at all. He had on a short-sleeve khaki-colored shirt and a pair of new jeans that looked like they'd been ironed. Nobody at Ralston High wore jeans that were one, new; two, without a rip or tear; three, ironed. He looked so awkward up there. My heart just automatically went out to him.

Mr. Barstow was going on about Pablo, how he had two older brothers, how his parents were refugees. . . . I shifted into classroom cruise control . . . coasting along . . . not paying attention. . . . But then Mr. Barstow said something that made my hands begin to itch and my face darken with self-consciousness.

Em, my best friend, sits one row over and three seats in front of me. I could see her shoulders tense up. She was going to turn around any moment. *Please, Em,* I thought, *please don't!* I just couldn't stand her drawing any attention to me.

7

But if Em looked my way, I never knew. I stared down at the graffiti on my desk until it began to swim under my eyes, reorganizing into the shape of the country where Mr. Barstow had mentioned Pablo was from.

Besides Em, I hadn't told anyone in this room that it was the place where I came from, too.

"Hey, Milly." Em put down her lunch tray across from me. Today, Em was having a plate of green salad, a couple of carrot sticks, and an apple. Em was forever trying to lose weight, which wasn't easy, as my sister, Kate, would say, because *where* was Em going to lose weight, please? The only answer really was her hair. Em's Tinkertoy skinny, but with very thick bundles of curly, strawberry blond hair.

Besides the rabbit food on her tray, Em also had three bottles of spring water. She had read somewhere how human beings need to drink eight glasses of water per day. Almost every period, Em had to ask permission to go take a leak. A lot of kids at Ralston thought Em was on drugs. But really, Em was addicted to nothing more than H_2O.

"I think he kind of looks like Brad Pitt." Em had sat down and was heading straight for the subject I was hoping to avoid. It's what I loved and hated about my best friend. "I mean, a very tanned Brad Pitt."

"Who?" I said. I couldn't let on, even to Em, that Pablo had been on my mind all morning.

"You know who." Em was staring at the bouquet of lettuce on her fork. "But boy, does he need some help with his wardrobe!" Em giggled, then stuffed her mouth full of lettuce. She ate her vegetarian food like a carnivore.

"Well?" Em swallowed quickly, ignoring her rule about chewing each mouthful I don't know how many times. "Don't you think he's cute?"

I shrugged. "I couldn't see his face, he was looking down the whole time."

Em leaned toward me and whispered, "Look now. He's over there with Jake."

I glanced over at the cafeteria line. Pablo was standing beside one of our close friends, Jake, who was scanning the room for a place to sit down. Our lunchroom is about as segregated as the pre-civil-rights South. The in-group always claims the booths, close to the food. We borderliners get the long tables by the recycle bins.

Oh please, don't ask them over, Em, I was thinking. Just having Pablo nearby was like shining a spotlight on a part of my life I had avoided for so long.

But telepathy with my best friend did not seem to be working today. "Hey, Jake!" Em waved for the boys to come over.

At first, Jake must not have heard her in the commotion in the cafeteria. But Em kept waving until Jake

9

connected with her and nodded. He turned to Pablo and jerked his head in our direction to show where they were headed through the lunchroom crowd.

I looked down at my tray, a half-eaten burrito, a bag of chips, a brownie, a Coke, and the bottle of water Em insisted I drink. ("What good will it do me to be alive at ninety if my best friend'll be long dead by then?") There was no way I was going to be able to wolf it all down in the minute it would take . . .

"Mind if we join you, ladies?" Jake was asking. Sometimes Jake puts on this act like he's someone from our parents' generation, which is funny since Jake looks younger than most anybody in our class. He's on the short side, with freckles on the bridge of his nose and bright blue eyes and just the slightest smirk, like he's about to crack a joke or something. "Pablo, these are two of the coolest ladies in our class."

Right. Only a borderliner could say that about two other borderliners.

Pablo smiled shyly and slid in beside Jake. He *was* good-looking, in a way you don't see around Ralston, dark and foreign, out of place. Maybe he'd only be here a few weeks before his family went back or moved away.

Em started peppering him with questions. What did Pablo think of the food? Ralston High? The United States of America? Pablo looked confused, like maybe he didn't understand much English. Em knew that I could speak some Spanish. I hoped—*telepathically contacting Em, telepathically contacting Em*—that Em would not offer my services.

This time, telepathy worked with Em, but not with Jake. "Hey, Mil," he piped up. "Aren't you, like, good in Spanish?"

Why was Jake asking me? I shot Em this look. Had she betrayed my secret?

"Aren't you in Advanced Spanish?" Jake persisted.

"But I'm not that good," I managed.

"You've got to be better than me." Jake shook his head at the state of his Spanish. Then, in his parents-throwing-a-barbecue-in-the-backyard voice, he added, "Pablo's coming over after school. Why don't you ladies join us and we'll play some pool, raid the fridge, whatever." Jake's mom is a caterer who's been written up in magazines. She sometimes brings leftovers home.

"Sure we'll come," Em offered for both of us.

"I can't," I said. "I have to . . . Mom asked me to help Nate. . . ." I was drawing a blank. What could I say my little brother needed help with? "Nate's got this project . . . on the solar system—" My lie was lost because just then two more of our friends, Dylan and Will, had joined our table. Jake went through a new round of intros. "These are the two coolest dudes in the school." Jake had a way of making everyone feel important. He was always saving the whales or getting us to recycle or pay attention to the people of the

Third World. Pablo was probably his new cause. Em once teased Jake, saying, "If you were a car, you'd be full of bumper stickers."

Jake had come back with, "And if you were a car, Em, you'd be full of gas." Everyone laughed, but Em was upset because she wasn't sure Jake wasn't putting her down. That night we must have spent over an hour on the phone analyzing what exactly Jake might have meant with his remark.

While everyone talked, Pablo sat by, looking at whoever was speaking, trying to follow the conversation. Then, just like that, he was staring at me, not like he was hitting on me, but like he knew me. I told myself I was being paranoid. Even though we were both from the same country, we had nothing obvious in common. We didn't look at all alike. My hair's light brown, my skin a pale olive like some French Canadians' in our town, except, like I say, in the summer, when I tan real dark. My eyes are actually the only unusual thing about me—they're this golden color with brown speckles in them like pieces of amber with fossils inside. The point is: I totally pass as 100 percent American, and as un-PC as this is going to sound, I'm really glad. The last thing I want is people staring at my family and asking, "Oh! Where'd you get her?" My parents' friends, the Hopkinses, adopted Mimi from China, and they are forever getting comments like that. So if Pablo was staring at me, it was not because I looked like one of his people or anything.

12

So why are you looking at me? I wondered.

As if to answer my question, Pablo leaned across the table. *"¿De dónde eres?"* he asked. Where was I from? It was so noisy at our table that for a moment I doubted whether I had heard him correctly. But he repeated himself, *"¿De qué país?"* From what country?

I did something I still feel bad about. I shrugged as if I didn't understand a word he had said.

But Pablo kept staring at me like he wasn't convinced. The rash on my hands was itching horribly. I had to get out of there fast. So I pulled an Em. I drank up my bottle of water in practically one gulp and dashed off to the john. I don't know why I thought I had to *prove* I had to go to the bathroom.

Em came in just as I was locking myself in my stall. "Hey, what's going on? Are you all right?"

"Why?" I managed, trying to make my voice sound as normal as possible.

"The way you ran off. It's like you'd seen a ghost or something."

I have! I felt like saying. Instead, I said, "It's my stupid period." I hoped Em wouldn't remember the tampon I'd borrowed from her a week ago. She had everything in that backpack.

Em flushed. "You sure you can't come over to Jake's?"

"I can't, Em. I've got to go home and help Nate."

"Oooh, poor baby," Em wailed in a show of feeling bad

13

for me. "I think I'll go by for a little while anyhow." She was at the sinks now. By the way she was spacing her words, I could tell she was looking at herself in the mirror. "Call me tonight, okay? You sure you're okay?"

"Raindrops Keep Falling on My Head" sounding for sixth period drowned out my "sure."

All afternoon, I couldn't stop thinking about what had happened. I felt like an awful human being. I also felt mad. Why was this Pablo guy singling me out? Everyone else just assumed I was from here. Or did they? Had Jake asked me about knowing Spanish because he knew I took Spanish or because he *knew*?

I dragged myself through my afternoon classes. I was so glad that I'd already had Spanish in the morning. I don't think I could have tolerated even hearing the language. Just thinking about all this stuff was making me itch like crazy.

When the last song played (some march with trumpets), I rushed out with just a wave to Em. I couldn't wait to get home and hide under my covers. Actually, I'd have to figure out a way to convince Nate that he didn't want to go out with his friends today. We live in too small a town, and Nate couldn't be seen in public *and* be working on a project on the Milky Way at the same time. I had an afternoon of stupid video games with an eight-year-old ahead of me.

* * *

On the bus, I stared out the window at the wintry Vermont countryside: gray sky above and gray snow below, blah on blah. My breath was misting up the window. Had Em been with me, she would have drawn a smiley face to make me smile.

But I was glad to be alone. My sister, Kate, hardly rode the after-school bus anymore. She always had some extra-curricular activity, chorus, yearbook, debate club. Kate's my same age, but a grade ahead of me. (Her birthday's the 9th of April, mine's the 15th of August, or so it was decided. We're both turning sixteen this year.)

Sometimes a new acquaintance will do the math and start asking questions. How could Kate and I be sisters and be the same age but not be twins? One time, I questioned Mom and Dad about how much everyone we knew knew. They exchanged a glance.

"We've just told a few friends," Mom said, then hesitated. "Honey, I hope you know there's nothing to be ashamed of. Children come to families in different ways."

That inspirational stuff always sounds great, but it doesn't take the feelings away. I wanted to be just another Kaufman. Was that so hard to understand?

"It's private, that's all," I tried explaining.

The funny thing is that Kate looks more Latin than I do. She's got our grandmother Happy's chocolate brown eyes and brown-black hair (Grandma's is from a bottle now) and olive skin that was common, Grandma says, on her

15

mother's side, before they all got wiped out in the Holocaust. Grandma Happy actually has a lot to be sad about. But that's a whole other story.

Kate is also smart. I should know. We shared a room for years, before I begged for my own attic cubbyhole, where I didn't have to watch Kate put together a report the night before and come home a week later with an A. Meanwhile, I was lucky if I could hang on to a B minus with some assignment I'd struggled over for weeks.

For a long time, I actually thought I was stupid. All through grade school and middle school, I had to have special lessons. I just couldn't seem to put letters together into written words and sentences. And I used to get such headaches! I was totally convinced that I had a brain tumor. Once, I overheard Mom talking to one of my tutors. He was saying how he'd read some article about children adopted from the Third World having learning disabilities. "When you think about the traumas many of these kids have been through, it's a miracle they even survived."

Was he referring to me? Was I a *survivor*?

How could I claim credit for something I couldn't even remember?

The bus had stopped.

"Earth to Mil, Earth to Mil," Alfie, the driver, called

16

out. Alfie's an ex-hippie, a favorite of Em and Jake and me. His conversation is sprinkled with misquotes from old sixties songs. Em's theory is that back in his Woodstock days, Alfie fried his brain with drugs, and his memory cells got all jumbled up. "You gotta get out of this bus if it's the last thing you ever do," Alfie sang.

Very funny, I thought as I filed by, not giving Alfie my usual smile on my way out. He knew something was wrong and started improvising on "Hey Jude" in that soft, throaty voice of his: "Hey, Mil, don't be a grouch, take a bad day and make it happy . . ." On and on as I went down the stairs. You couldn't give Alfie a dirty look. He was just too nice a guy with his bandanna and ponytail and pretend-gruff face. So I did the only thing I could think of. I turned around and gave him the peace sign.

He flashed me one back. His came with a smile.

Mom was home, talking to Kate on the phone, coordinating picking her up later from chorus. I searched the house. No Nate.

I rushed into the kitchen just as Mom was hanging up. "Where's Nate?"

I must have looked panicked, because Mom's hand was at her heart. "What do you mean, 'Where's Nate?' "

"Nothing." I tried to calm my voice. "I was just looking for him, that's all."

"Honestly, Milly. You scared me to death." Mom was annoyed.

"I'm sorry," I mumbled. "I was just looking for him to help him with his project." Lie twice told. How deep was I going to dig this hole? "Where is he?"

"It's Thursday, honey." Mom was now watching me closely. We all know schoolwork is not a strength of mine—it wasn't likely that I'd be helping my brother with any project. "Nate has hockey practice."

Hockey practice! There wasn't a more public place in winter in our town than the Ralston Rink. By tomorrow, everyone would know I was a big liar. I slumped down in a chair just wanting to cry but telling myself I couldn't because then I'd have to explain why.

Mom sat down at the table across from me. She had on what Kate and I call her therapist look. I *understand*, it says, before you've even told her what's wrong. "Everything okay, honey?"

"I just wanted Nate to be home, that's all."

Mom sighed. "I know how you feel." Mom had taken afternoons off from her busy practice as a family therapist to spend quality time with her family. ("Walking the talk," she called it.) But suddenly we were all so busy that what she did was spend time sitting in her car, waiting for Kate to come out of choir or for Nate to finish his sports practice, and until recently, for me to come out of some special tutoring lesson.

"I was about to make some cookies. Want to help?"

18

I shook my head. I was feeling too low to do anything useful. The only thing I would have agreed to was if Mom had suggested, "What do you say we bury you under the snowdrifts in the backyard and dig you up once everyone you know has graduated from Ralston High?"

"Roads were terrible today." Mom talked, her back to me, as she mixed ingredients at the counter. "I stopped at Sterlings on the way home, hoping I'd find something for Happy's birthday. Nothing." Mom was trying to draw me out. First she'd offer a little of her life, then slip in a question about mine. "How was school today?"

"Fine," I said. "I mean it was interesting." And then, I don't know what got into me, since I was trying to avoid the subject. But suddenly I heard myself saying, "There's a new guy in our class, Pablo." I mentioned how his family were refugees, how he probably didn't know much English, and then I slipped in where he was from.

Mom reacted with the same tensing up as Em had in class when Mr. Barstow mentioned Pablo's native land.

Mom turned around, her hands all greasy from buttering the cookie sheets. Her eyes were like two wide-open doors. "Milly, honey," she began, coming toward me. "Is that what's going on?"

Yes, no, yes, no, my head and heart were having a shouting match. Yes, I wanted Mom to hug me. No, because if she did, I knew I'd break down sobbing.

I guess I opted for no, or maybe the shouting inside was

just too loud and confusing. I bolted out of the kitchen and upstairs and ended up under the quilt Mom made me last year with fabric pieces I'd picked out. Which made me feel even lousier about rejecting her.

The thing about feeling sorry for yourself is that after you do the whole funeral scene in your head—everyone saying how great you were, how sad that you had to die so young—you want to be alive again. Mom called up that she was going out for a sec to pick up Kate and Nate. I knew she was "giving me my space," but I kind of wished she had come up and given me a second chance to be a nicer human being instead.

When I heard the car pulling back into the driveway, I felt a flood of relief and happiness. But I didn't go running down the stairs to greet everyone. Instead, I waited, too proud to show how desperately I needed my family around me.

"MILL-L-L-E-E-E!" Nate called up.

I pretended not to hear. But when he didn't call up again, I opened my door and called down, "What?"

"Hey, Milly-the-pooh, come on down." It was Kate. I wondered if Mom had had a talk with them.

Down I came, trying to figure out what look to put on my face when I entered the kitchen. I felt I owed Mom an apology, but then, if I said anything, Mom being Mom, we would have to have a talk about it.

"Milly, you should have seen this goal I made!" The minute I came in the room, Nate launched into the story of his triumphs at practice. He raced around the kitchen, batting an imaginary puck. Kate rolled her eyes at me.

Nate swung and almost knocked Mom over as she was taking a cookie sheet out of the oven. Mom almost swore, but in the end all she said was "foul!" Kate and I laughed. There was no way Mom would ever say the f-word. She was raised Mormon, and even though she'd been quite the rebel, leaving Provo to go to college in the East, joining the Peace Corps when she graduated, marrying a Jewish boy, there was still a prim part of Mom who thought Chap Stick was enough "makeup" and said excuse me every time she sneezed.

Mom brought the cookies to the table, sailing the plate in the air with a flourish, like a fancy waiter. Nate lunged but missed. "Come on, Mom!" he wailed impatiently.

Mom set the plate down in front of me. "Milly gets first pick."

"Why?" Nate asked, instantly adding "no fair!" before Mom could even reply.

"Because . . . I risked Milly's life making these cookies!"

Even I looked startled.

"I left the oven on," Mom explained, pulling up a chair beside me. "What if I'd burned the house down? What if something had happened to my baby?" She squeezed my hand, which actually made the itching feel better.

21

Nate was grinning. He loved it when someone else got to be the baby in the family.

"I saw Em after school," Kate said between nibbles of her cookie. She was turning the lazy Susan at the center of the table round and round. Any minute Mom was going to tell her to quit, that this was the third lazy Susan in the last year. It was Kate's nervous tic, an inconvenient one, I often thought, as you couldn't exactly carry a lazy Susan around with you. Mine was much more portable: skin rashes. "She was headed over to Jake's."

"Yeah?" I asked nonchalantly.

"There was some hot-looking guy with her. She said he was someone new in your class."

Hot-looking? What about his hair? What about his clothes? I could feel Mom extra quiet beside me.

"Em said he's older but was put back until he catches up."

"Where's he from?" Nate asked.

Kate shrugged. "I didn't ask."

I didn't volunteer. Neither did Mom.

After dinner, I took the cordless up to my attic room. Em and I usually talked at least once every night, sometimes more if the line was free. We are all heavy users at our house. Except Dad, though sometimes he has a bunch of phone calls to make about private jobs he takes on when the local contractor goes into his seasonal slump.

22

Em reported that she had had a great time at Jake's. Dylan and Will had come over. *And* Meredith! I felt a pang of jealousy. Meredith had been Em's best friend before Em and I became best friends. It wasn't that Em dumped Meredith to be close to me, but just that they saw very little of each other now that Meredith was at Champlain Academy, the private school one town over. "I wished you'd been there," Em was saying, as if she could sense that I felt left out. "Everyone missed you so-o-o much."

I felt better knowing I'd been missed, even if Em was exaggerating. "So how was Pablo?" I ventured.

"What do you mean how was he?"

What I meant was, had he said anything about the awful classmate who pretended not to understand him. "I mean, did he talk any?"

"Mil, he hardly speaks English, how could he talk to us? Well, actually, take that back. Meredith tried talking to him in Spanish." Meredith's family had lived in different Latin American countries when she was growing up. Her dad used to be some reporter specializing in Latin America, until he took a job teaching journalism at the university. "Meredith told me later that he actually knows a lot of English. I guess he's just really shy."

Oh yeah? Pablo didn't seem to have that problem with me.

"How did Nate's project go?"

"What project?"

23

"Mil, the project you had to go home to help him with!"

That's the problem with lying. You have to remember stuff that didn't happen so you can report on it when asked. "Oh, you know, the usual. 'The Earth is a planet revolving around the sun.' Hey, my dad needs to use the phone." Dad was standing at the door, waving a hand that he'd be back. But Em had already hung up. "It's okay, Dad, I'm done. Really."

Actually, Dad didn't need to use the phone, but could he come in? "Nice place you got here." He was looking around, like my room was for rent or something. Dad had been the one who had redone the attic just the way I wanted, putting in the seat at the dormer window and a skylight, which had not been easy to do on our old roof.

Dad tested my book stand. "Hmm," he worried. "I should probably bolt this thing to the wall. It could fall on you if you leaned over to get a book from the bottom shelf." Dad demonstrated. (The stand did not fall over.) I love Dad, but he has got to have the worst worst-case-scenario imagination going. Not that you can tell just looking at him. Dad's got these cowboy looks, tall and lanky with a strong jaw, like no problem, he can handle any outlaw possibility in the world. But he worries! My New York cousins say he's got a Woody Allen mind trapped in a Clint Eastwood body.

24

Dad was now kneeling in front of the stand, rocking it back and forth. "What I could do is reinforce . . . Nah, wouldn't work."

I sat down on my bed and waited. "It's fine, really it is."

"Well, anytime you need it bolted down, okay?" Dad stood and looked around for anything else he could offer to do for me.

Mom had obviously suggested Dad try talking to me. But Dad is not a big talker that way. Oh, he can discuss wall joints and two-by-fours and whether you want paneling or drywall. I think that's why we gravitate toward each other. We have a certain understanding that words are not always the best way to communicate about the things that matter deeply to us.

"I guess I better be heading back to my dungeon." Dad's workroom was in the basement. He had trudged all the way up three flights of stairs to "talk" to me. His current project was a cherry footstool for my grandmother, Happy, whose birthday was always a big deal. This would be her seventieth, so an even Bigger Fuss would be expected.

"Dad." I called him back as he was turning to go. "I did want to ask you . . . about when you . . . you got me."

"Sure, Mil." Dad waited.

"This new guy in my class." Dad nodded. So Mom had said something to him. "He and his family are refugees. Mr. Barstow explained about Latin American dictatorships disappearing people and stuff."

Dad shook his head the way people do when they feel bad about the state of the world. He often said he couldn't bear the thought of how many people were living subhuman lives under oppressive regimes.

"Is that what might have happened like . . . to my birth family?"

Dad sat down on my bed. Suddenly, he looked so tired. "You know, honey," he said, his voice sad and gentle, "we don't really know."

"How about my papers and stuff?" Maybe there was more information in The Box they kept in their bedroom? My hands had begun their tingling. Conversations like this always set my allergies off.

Dad was shaking his head. "I wish there were more answers for you," he said when my face fell. "Maybe, who knows, maybe your birth family opposed the government and maybe . . ."

"It's okay, Dad," I said. We both knew *maybes* didn't add up to a story I could hold on to.

"I hate for you to lose sleep over this, sweetie." Dad was already worrying about me. "Maybe it'd be good to get to know this new guy?"

"What for?" I snapped. I knew I sounded defensive. I didn't want people pushing me to be friends with some stranger just because we'd been born in the same country.

"He might help you figure out some things." Dad shrugged, as if to say *but what do I know?*

I was scratching madly now. Dad looked down. My hands were covered with an angry red rash.

"Just my allergies again," I explained. The doctor had said that my system was probably supersensitive to American allergens. Stress didn't help any.

"Calamine," Dad pronounced, like that would solve all my problems. Moments later he was back with last summer's bottle.

That night, I went to bed, my hands soothed by that pink lotion. But I still couldn't seem to fall asleep. I felt itchy *inside*, as if I was allergic to myself. Actually, Dad had offered a solution for that, too. But I wasn't ready yet to try the friendship cure.

2

Command Performance

WHETHER OR NOT I wanted to hang out with him, Pablo had been taken up by my friends. It seemed like I could not get away from him.

He even turned up one day in Mrs. Gillespie's Advanced Spanish class. The minute he stepped in the door, his eyes found my eyes.

"¡Hola, clase!" Mrs. Gillespie began. Today we had a special guest! Mrs. Gillespie went on to explain that Pablo Bolívar had recently joined the ninth-grade class at Ralston. We were to go around the room, introduce ourselves, and tell our visitor a little something about ourselves.

I felt my heart sink. Meanwhile, my hands were burning up. Actually, I wished they would burst into flames. That

28

was the only way I was going to get out of this room fast enough.

I sat paralyzed like one of those animals Dad sometimes surprises at night in his headlights. Up and down the rows we went, my turn getting closer and closer. I heard every name, every boring or cute detail . . . and then, I was next. I opened my mouth but nothing came out.

"Milly?" Mrs. Gillespie reminded me.

"*Ya yo conozco a Milly,*" Pablo spoke up. He already knew me. He shifted his gaze to Andrea, sitting behind me. The introductions moved on.

I felt a flood of relief and confusion. Had Pablo tried to save me from embarrassment or was he saying that I wasn't worth getting to know?

What do I care what he thinks of me? I kept asking myself. I felt bad enough about myself.

I started avoiding everyone. Soon as school was over, I'd rush to the bus before Em could hook her arm through mine and tell me "our" plans.

I should have talked to Em. But every time I tried, I'd get the same stage fright I'd gotten in Spanish class. Nothing would come out.

What was there to say anyway? That I felt helpless and adrift not knowing my story, who my birth parents had been, why they had given me up? That the longing hurt too much and I was afraid of falling into a big black hole of sadness?

I remembered this myth we had learned in Spanish about a woman called *la llorona,* who cried and cried for her lost children. She had drowned in her own tears—at least in the version Mrs. Gillespie had told us.

I didn't want to end up a basket case that everyone wanted to give away *again.*

"What's going on?" Em finally asked me during one of our nightly calls. Something had changed, but she couldn't put her finger on it. "Are you mad at me for something?"

"Oh, Em," I reassured her. "It's just that my grandma's birthday's coming up, and she's decided to have it here. Mom is a wreck, so I'm helping her out."

"Happy?"

For a moment I thought Em was asking me how I was feeling. But no, she was just confirming that my rich and impossible grandmother, Happy, was going to be here at the end of the month.

Maybe because I was home-based these days, I actually started looking forward to my grandmother's birthday this year.

Usually we drove down to Long Island, where Happy put

us up at the local Sheraton. Some renovation was always going on in her mansion that made staying with her "inconvenient." Dad's sister, Aunt Joan, would come out from the city with her husband, Uncle Stanley, and our three wild and crazy cousins, Bee, Ruthie, and Nancy. Command performances, Mom called them. I mostly stayed out of the way. Happy was always polite to me, asking how my studies were going. (Mom and Dad *swore* they hadn't breathed a word about my learning problems.) But I always got this feeling that Happy thought about me different from the others. Once when I told her I didn't like math, Happy had given me this look. "Poor dear," she remarked. "Mathematics has always been a Kaufman strong suit."

This year, for her seventieth, Happy said she wanted a relaxed family gathering in Vermont. Mom flipped at first. Happy would be looking at everything with her super critical eye. Our house is one of those redone-ramshackle houses (Dad's specialty), nothing fancy. Dad's a carpenter; Mom, a part-time therapist—put their two incomes together and even this old house is more than we can afford. If it weren't for Happy's handouts, it wouldn't even belong to us.

From the basement and the backs of our closets, we began to dig out stuff Happy had given us over the years: the silver napkin rings with our monograms; the dozen framed photographs of Happy with important, famous people; the crystal decanter and matching glasses; the gaudy menorah from Israel. (This we really couldn't use. Dad's a

31

secular Jew, as he calls himself, with Mom always putting in "and a sexy one, too.")

A couple of nights before they were all to arrive, Aunt Joan called up with the latest bulletin. Happy had told her that she had some things to "discuss with the family."

"Oh boy," Mom said, rolling her eyes. "Wonder what bomb she's going to drop."

"Let's be positive," Dad suggested.

"You're kidding?" Mom said, looking at Dad with disbelief. Optimism was not Dad's strong suit. But she kept her mouth shut. After all, Happy is Dad's mom.

"I think it's great Happy's coming here," Nate piped up. Nate's the only unconflicted person in our family when it comes to our grandmother. The truth is, Happy dotes on her only grandson. She's obviously grooming him to be the son her son never turned out to be. And Nate's just Nate around her. Spilling over with eight-year-old enthusiasm and puppy-dog affection. Happy eats it up. "Maybe she'll come and see my game, you think?"

"I doubt it, honey," Mom said, not wanting Nate to be disappointed.

"Oh, let's wait and see," Dad reminded Mom. Last summer, Happy had come up for the Cub Scout sing-along, at which sixteen little boys sang campfire songs off tune for over an hour.

"I'm with Mom." Kate was legitimately spinning the

32

lazy Susan, looking for the salt shaker. "Her Highness is not going to hang out at some freezing rink in her mink coat."

At this image of Happy in her furs, surrounded by screaming fans, we all burst out laughing.

All except Nate. He was looking from one to the other, his bottom lip quivering. "I don't know why you guys have to be that way with Grandma." Nate bowed his head, ashamed to be seen crying. Huge cartoon-type tears were falling on his broccoli stir-fry, which he hadn't wanted to eat anyway.

What Nate didn't realize was that it wasn't us down on Happy, but the other way around, Happy down on us.

Or really, it was Happy never being *happy*. Talk about irony. Her real name was Katherine, but as a kid no one could make her smile. Thus the nickname. (My gossipy Aunt Joan was the source of most of our Happy-as-an-unhappy-child stories.) Happy was an only child of really rich parents, *the* Kaufmans of Kaufman Quality Products: "K Is for Quality from Burners to Wrappers." Kate and the cousins used to do a performance of the jingle for Happy when we were little kids. I'd get my usual stage fright and stand there, my mouth hanging open, my hands itching like crazy. "This one just is not a ham, is she?" Grandma would laugh, shaking her head at me.

Anyhow, Happy's father was this genius who invented everything from burner bibs (it really isn't worth knowing what those things are) to two-ply toilet paper and, of course, Happy Wrap, named after Happy. ("Seal in the Freshness, Bring out the Smiles.")

Happy's mom was the real sad story. She had come to America from Germany way back in the 1930s as a nanny, but the rest of her family stayed and later perished in the Holocaust. Happy's mom never ever talked about it. Instead, she drank too much, and as it turns out, took lots of pills that didn't agree with the drinking. She died of an overdose soon after Happy came out—as a debutante. I guess with grandparents you don't really have to say that.

Happy married Grandpa Bob, who legally changed his last name to hers. If I didn't know Happy, I'd say one big step for feminism. She had Dad, then Aunt Joan, then got divorced. Grandpa Bob died when I was four. Happy remarried three times but never had any more kids. She was like a Queen Bee, discarding husbands. Right now there was no one—that we knew of anyhow. But they crept up on you, Happy's marriages and divorces. As a matter of fact, we wondered if the news she wanted to discuss was a fifth husband?

The night before Happy was to arrive, there was a knock at my door. "Just us," Mom and Dad chimed when I asked, "Yes?"

Oh no, I thought. When your parents are at your door together, you know it's more than a friendly visit. I put my hands under my covers so I could scratch them out of sight.

Mom and Dad sat on either side of my bed. It reminded me of the day way back when I was a little kid and they had told me.

"Milly, your mom and I, well, we've noticed . . . ," Dad began. Suddenly, he looked helpless and flashed Mom a conversational SOS.

"We've noticed a change," Mom picked up. "Is something bothering you? At school? This new boy—"

"You guys!" I said, exasperated.

"You've always chosen to be very private about this," Mom continued quietly. "But it might be good to talk about it, don't you think?"

"Children come to families in different ways." Dad always quoted Mom when he didn't know what to say during a heart-to-heart. Somehow it didn't annoy me as much when Dad said things as when Mom did. "We couldn't love you any more if you were . . ." Dad's voice got all gravelly.

For a minute my own sadness fell away. "Are you okay, Dad?"

Mom reached over and squeezed Dad's hand. When he didn't say anything, Mom explained that Happy's visit was stirring up stuff for all of us. "Dad's probably just feeling a little sad about his own mother. Happy's never made it easy for him."

35

I knew the whole story. I mean, I had lived a lot of that story. Happy being furious with Dad for leaving the family business and going off to the Peace Corps. Then even more furious when Dad came back three years later with a non-Jewish wife, a baby daughter, and a sickly, foreign orphan girl. His stock went up briefly when he rejoined Kaufman Quality Products, then plummeted again when he quit and we moved away from Long Island to a state where you couldn't buy a decent bagel. Periodically, Happy would try to pressure Dad to come back to Kaufman, and when he refused, she'd issue some threat. In fact, one of Mom's theories about the birthday weekend was that Grandma was coming up to deliver her latest ultimatum. Recently, she'd approached Dad again about joining the family business, and Dad had again refused. "Get ready for the next disowning!" Mom had joked, out of Nate's hearing that time.

"Grandma doesn't really mean it, Dad," I tried consoling him now. No matter how pissed Grandma would get, she always took us back. And she never stopped sending checks in the mail, which Mom and Dad couldn't accept but ended up cashing because we needed the money. "I mean, I got thrown out once, and that was that." I was trying for a joke, but the minute I said it, it didn't sound funny at all.

Mom was looking surprised. "Honey, you weren't thrown out. It's just someone couldn't keep you—"

"What's the difference?" I guess the pain showed on my

36

face. Mom put her arms around me while I struggled not to cry.

"You see why," I managed, "why it doesn't help to talk about it? Why I just want to forget about it?"

My parents didn't look convinced, but they nodded.

"What do you think?" Dad asked, like I was some fashion consultant. We were in the mudroom, waiting for Happy's caravan to arrive from New York.

"Truly awesome, Dad."

Dad took a second look in the mirror. He was wearing his nice chinos, the L.L. Bean shirt we'd all pitched in to get for him for Christmas, and a beige cashmere cardigan that still smelled of mothballs. A gift from Happy. *Davey,* the monogram read. A nickname Dad dislikes, to put it mildly.

"I guess this is as good as it's going to get." Dad shook his head at his reflection. His hair was thinning in back, his face seemed more lined: he had that tired look middle-aged people always seem to have. "The truth is, you've got an old fart for a dad."

"Dad, you're like forty-five. That's young these days." Of course, I didn't for a moment believe it. Forty-five was old. By then, I better have stuff figured out. But could that ever be for me? My whole life lay on top of a mystery that, like Dad said, no one knew much about.

Dad was now looking me over. "By the way, you're the one who looks great."

It was the top, I swear. I'd gone shopping with Em for a present for Happy's birthday, some token gift, because really, as a fifteen-year-old on a ten-dollar-a-week allowance, earning five bucks an hour for occasional baby-sitting, what can I buy a multi-millionairess? I ended up using the money on this top at Banana Republic. The minute I tried it on and saw the impressed look on Em's face, I knew the top was perfect for me. The golden wheat color brought out my best feature, my eyes. Its snug fit actually *gave* me boobs and curved in toward the waist, announcing a figure!

As for Happy's gift, I ended up making her a homemade birthday card with a corny poem I found on a Web site about grandmothers. Relatives always act like stuff you make them is what they really wanted anyway. As I wrote out the poem inside the card, I actually got teary-eyed. Maybe it was suddenly realizing that Happy was my *only* grandparent. (Mom's parents had both died in a car crash when she was in college.) I wanted—strike that: I *needed* all the family I could get.

I guess it was a lame excuse: using the money for my grandmother's birthday present on myself. But part of my motivation for buying that top was to please her. I wanted to look good. I wanted Happy to approve of me, to be proud that I was part of her family.

* * *

Happy walked in the door, shaking herself out like a wet dog. "Brrr, it's cold up here."

Oh no, I thought. Was she complaining already? I wanted everything to turn out perfect for her birthday with us. After Mom, I think I was the most invested in this visit.

On either side of her, Uncle Stanley and Aunt Joan were like her personal valets, taking her coat, agreeing that it was freezing. It was a second or two before I realized that a third person had slipped in with them, a quiet, pale man, very formal in a suit and tie and kind of nervous, like a person who knew he didn't quite belong. Mr. Eli Strong, he was sort of introduced. I say *sort of*, because just then the cousins burst in, loaded down with packages and shopping bags, hugging and kissing, lifting their eyebrows suggestively at Happy's mystery guest, and then exploding into laughter.

Poor Mr. Strong—I sure hoped he had a strong personality and wouldn't get scared off by our noisy reunion. Entrances and exits were big in this family of command performances. Everyone was talking at once: mostly terrible-weather-on-the-road stories. I don't know why it is that people who drive up from the city in the winter always make it sound like they just survived a dangerous trek. It's only Vermont, not the North Pole, for heaven's sake.

Happy was looking at Dad, nodding appreciatively. "That sweater was made for you, Davey." All members of the Vermont Kaufman family over eight struggled to keep straight faces. "You do look a little tired, though. Have you lost some weight?"

Now it was Kate's turn. "Katherine, dear!" Kate's smile tightened. Kate hates the name Katherine, but who was going to tell Grandma that her namesake didn't like being called Katherine? "You are looking lovely, as always, but that hair needs a good trim. Next time you come down to New York," she added, as if poor Kate couldn't get a decent haircut in Vermont. "Sylvia, how are you, Sylvia?" No time for Mom to reply because just then, Nate came bounding straight into Grandma's arms. After a long hug and a dozen kisses, Happy held Nate at arm's length to take a better look at him. "My, my, how you've grown! Soon we should be thinking about a prep school for him," Happy mentioned to Dad. Nate looked panicked and glanced over at Mom, who shook her head imperceptibly. No, he did not have to go to boarding school like Harry Potter.

Finally, Happy caught sight of me at the edge of the group. "Milly?" she questioned. "Could this really be Milly?" It was not her phony millionairess-at-a-cocktail-party act, but the genuine article: Happy Kaufman was impressed.

I followed Nate's lead and gave my grandmother a warm hug and kiss. "It's great you decided to have your party here, Grandma. Happy birthday!"

It was meltdown. Happy was smiling widely, *happily*. Seconds later, she took Nate's hand and slipped her other

40

arm through mine and allowed us to escort her into our humble abode, whose mortgage she, of course, had paid for.

Dinner was Mom's solo performance . . . almost. She had knocked herself out making filet mignon—something she never makes in our on-and-off vegetarian family on a budget. We also had these creamed potatoes called potatoes dauphinois, a spinach soufflé, and homemade French bread. She threw in the towel at being Martha Stewart and called Jake's mom and ordered a Gâteau Roland (just a fancy name for a chocolate cake—everything seemed to have French names tonight). Happy assumed Mom had made the cake—and Mom just . . . well . . . she didn't try to correct the wrong impression. Poor Mom really needed this moment of glory. I could see her finally relaxing after weeks of being on edge. She even asked Happy how the renovations at the house were going. The answer could last an evening.

Meanwhile, Dad was grilling poor Eli Strong in this kind of suspicious tone of voice. "So what is it you do, Mr. Strong? Law? What kind of law? Estate law, I see."

"Children," Happy broke in. She spoke now to the whole table. It was odd to hear grownups called children. "Mr. Strong is my estate lawyer. And he very kindly agreed to accompany me here so we could discuss some matters privately after dinner. Just the children," she added. Everyone understood she meant Dad and Aunt Joan. Her *blood* children. Another word, like *adopt,* that makes *my* blood run cold.

Nate, the only person present who could get away with asking, blurted out, "So are you gonna get married, Grandma?"

Grandma looked at him a moment as if he had dropped in from outer space. "What on earth for? I've got enough problems already!" She glanced pointedly at Dad, then threw back her head and laughed. We guessed it was a joke and joined in.

After dinner, Happy and Dad and Aunt Joan proceeded into the family room with Mr. Strong and shut the door. Uncle Stanley played video games with Nate while the rest of us cleaned up in the kitchen. Then the cousins trooped upstairs to my attic room, where we would all be sleeping. Kate had ceded her room to Aunt Joan and Uncle Stanley. Grandma had decided she'd be more comfortable at the local inn, where Calvin Coolidge or some such person had once stayed. (Why does it matter that some long-dead famous person slept on your bed? It's downright creepy, if you ask me.) Mr. Eli Strong had a room there as well. "*Separate* rooms," the cousins chimed in meaningfully.

We talked for hours, first with the lights on, all of us piled on my bed; then in the dark, everyone tucked away in sleeping bags and on air mattresses. I felt bad for poor Nate, the only boy. He had tried to worm himself into our cuz-coven, but we couldn't risk it. He was bound to repeat something he heard—and my crazy New York cousins were full of wild stories and theories. They had all been in therapy for years and had a running commentary as to what was "really" going on in our family.

At one point in our marathon gossip session, I thought of bringing up Pablo, but I froze. Although my cousins and I talked about everything else under the sun, we always avoided the topic of my adoption.

Only one time, last summer, Ruthie had mentioned it. She had been sent to stay with us for the month of August. Her therapist was on vacation, and Ruthie was out of control, Aunt Joan told Mom over the phone. Ruthie had her own version of what was going on: her family was totally dysfunctional and projecting their issues on her. Even her dad, who was the sanest, was passive-aggressive. "I wish I were you," Ruthie had said. "Then I could at least hope for a second chance with my real family."

"This *is* my real family." I felt hurt. What did she think? That I was *pretending* to be a member of our family?

Ruthie instantly took it back. "You know what I mean. Oh God, I'm sorry, Mil, oh please, Mil."

She must have apologized about a dozen times. There was no room left for me to stay hurt. And really, when I thought it over: it was my own fault. If I'd only talk about my feelings, people wouldn't be assuming whatever it was they assumed about me.

But I didn't really want to bring up Pablo tonight. More

than ever, I was feeling so much a part of Happy's family. If there were dark shadows lurking in the wings, what did I care? In my Banana Republic top, with Happy's arm in mine and my family by my side, I could handle anything.

I woke up with a start—at the very edge of my bed, which I was sharing with cousin Ruthie, the all-time bed hog. The digital clock was right in my face: 2:35, it blared, 2:36. Talk about passive-aggressive.

Just go back to sleep, I kept telling myself. But I couldn't. The question I had been avoiding for weeks popped right up: *What was I going to do about Pablo?*

I couldn't hide out forever. I had pretty much stopped going to lunch with my friends. Em and I no longer had much to talk about every night. I had to do something. Suddenly, the answer glowed like the numbers on the clock: *change schools. Of course!*

Champlain Academy was only half an hour away. I could maybe carpool with Meredith. I'd visited the school a bunch of times with Em to see Meredith, and the girls weren't at all snotty like I'd expected. The school itself was real progressive and emphasized fun, extracurricular stuff. Just this Valentine's Day, Em and I attended a performance of *The Vagina Monologues* there, which was awesome. The play, I mean. Meredith was so-so. She just was not convincing as an old lady talking about her tired uterus.

So why not transfer to Champlain? I'd still get to see Em and my Ralston High friends on weekends. The problem was the tuition, which I knew there was no way my parents could afford. Then I got another winning idea: *ask Happy!* She had talked about sending Nate to private school. Why not her granddaughter as well as her grandson?

A heavy weight was falling off my shoulders. "There will be an answer, let it shine, let it shine," as Alfie, our bus driver, liked to sing. Of course, another little tune of his was piping up in my head. Something about freedom being just another word for nothing left to lose. Sure, I'd be free of Ralston and my fears and embarrassment, but I'd also lose daily contact with my friends and my teachers.

Rather than lie there and let this little voice get any louder, I decided to head down to the kitchen for a glass of water. (Em would be proud.)

I found my way in the dark around the air mattresses and sleeping bags. On the second-floor landing, the hall lights were still on. Kate's door was closed—as was Nate's.

Downstairs, lights had been left on . . . in the hallway . . . the living room. . . . Someone was still up. Just outside the kitchen, I heard raised voices.

"I can't believe her!" Mom's voice was shrill. "How can she think we'd accept a will that doesn't treat all our kids the same? A stipend for Milly instead of a share!"

My heart stopped beating. My hands were tingling.

45

I stood there paralyzed, not wanting to hear what I was hearing.

"You know why she's doing this, don't you?" Mom went on. "Didn't I tell you she'd try to get back at you for refusing to go back to Kaufman again?"

"Well, she can hurt me all she wants, but I won't let her hurt Milly." Dad sounded the angriest I'd ever heard.

"I'll tell you one thing," Mom fumed. "I'm not accepting another penny from her. No more handouts!"

I don't know why I didn't just run upstairs and exit out of this moment in my life like I had out of so many others. My eyes were burning. My hands were burning. But somehow I knew there was no place to run away to anymore.

I pushed open the door of the kitchen. Mom and Dad jerked around toward me, their faces pale and shocked. "Sweetie," Dad began. "We were just—"

"I heard," I stopped him.

They came forward and folded their arms around me.

"It's not about you," Dad kept saying.

"We love you, honey," Mom reassured me. "We're still a family. Nothing has changed."

But everything had changed. For weeks now my life had been trying to tell me something. I *was* different. I was adopted. I was not *blood* family. Oh, I was still their daughter, Milly. But there was another me. The one who had caught Pablo's eye. The one Happy had left out of her will. The one I had kept a secret, even from myself.

3

Small Towns

Mom always says that living in a small town is good for your character. You're bitchy to the lady at the bank, and there she is at Greg's Market, rolling her cart toward you. Or her kid's on your kid's soccer team. In the city, my cousins can mouth off to some salesperson at Bloomingdale's and head uptown to their East Side apartment and no one will know. Except, I suppose, their therapists.

In a small town, you have to face the consequences.

Ditto for high school in a small town.

Hello, Pablo. How's it going, I practiced. Or should I really go all out and say it in Spanish? *Hola, Pablo. ¿Qué hay?*

47

I was standing outside the lunchroom, waiting to get brave enough to go in.

"Hey, long-lost friend!" Em came from behind me. I winced at the surprise in her voice. Had I stayed away so long it was now a shock to see me? When I turned, there was Pablo beside her!

"You coming to lunch?" Em asked, looking from me to Pablo and back. She was picking up some tension between us.

"Sure." I flashed her a smile, then tried holding it steady for Pablo.

He scowled back. Why shouldn't he hate my guts? After visiting our advanced class, he knew I could speak pretty good Spanish. I had understood him back in January. Now, two months later, I was deciding to be a nice person? *Muchas gracias*, but no thank you.

"So, are you coming?" Em prodded, as I seemed rooted to the spot.

"I've got to go to my locker first," I finally managed. "You guys go on."

I don't know what's worse: when you act stupid, or the moment after, when you're stupidly kicking yourself for acting stupid.

My stage fright with Pablo might have lasted forever. But like Mom says about small towns: everything does come around again.

One night, Dad came home with the news that he had hired a carpenter to help him with his extra jobs. "This guy can do anything with wood, I mean *anything*." He didn't speak much English, but that was no barrier for Dad. I suppose because of me, my parents kept up their Peace Corps Spanish over the years. Ever since I was a little kid, Señora Robles, whose husband taught Spanish at the nearby university, would come over for family lessons. We'd watch videos, play games, listen to tapes. Afterward, we'd all sit down to a meal where we spoke Spanish and ate tacos, enchiladas, stuff like that.

"And you'd never guess who this guy is." Dad had turned to me. Small town that we live in, I should have guessed. "Señor Bolívar, your classmate Pablo's father."

I nodded, like yeah yeah, I knew that.

"Poor family has been through hell." Dad went on to tell how Señor Bolívar's brother, a journalist, had been murdered. His oldest son had been taken away by the secret police. "They still don't know where he is. The middle son has had to go into hiding. Both sons are with this new party that's trying to get rid of that jerk we once put in control." *We* was the United States of America. We had helped some general to take over or start a civil war or something. I never can keep all the countries in the world connected with their stories. But I knew there were a lot of dictators in many Latin American countries that had been supported by our government. "Bolívar managed to get out with his wife and Pablo, don't ask me how."

I felt even worse about rejecting Pablo now that I knew what he and his family had been going through. Mom, meanwhile, was shaking her head. She sometimes talked about how hopeful she had been about the future of her host country. That's why she had gone there in the first place—to help spread the tools of freedom. The dictatorship was supposed to be temporary. But even while Mom and Dad were there, the roundups had started.

"Bolívar says they've tried to get news of their sons. They're worried sick," Dad continued. "They don't know where to turn."

That's all you have to say to Mom, Caretaker of the World, because the next words out of her mouth were "Let's have them over."

My heart did two things at the same time—it kind of soared up with relief that the stalemate with Pablo would finally end, *and* it plunged down with fear that I'd have to face him. I felt like I was having an emotional heart attack. Meanwhile, my hands began to itch.

Mom noticed me scratching them. She looked suddenly unsure. "Would that be all right with you, Mil?"

Ever since the Happy incident, Mom had been hovering all over me. I knew she was just concerned, but it made me feel like she was babysitting my feelings.

"Sure." I shrugged. A Spanish meal might actually be

fun. Last summer, the Robleses had moved back to Mexico. I was surprised how much I missed our get-togethers.

Kate, meanwhile, was jumping all over Mom's idea. "¡Por favor, invítalos!" she said, showing off. She had already taken Advanced Spanish last fall and was now doing a private tutorial with Mrs. Gillespie. "I want to keep up with mi español."

Her Spanish! Mostly, I was glad that Kate and I shared another language and country. But sometimes I felt proprietary about the one thing I had that was my very own. Kate had only been born there by accident. I was an accident.

"So's it okay if I invite the Bolívars for dinner Saturday?" Mom asked the table, but she was looking at me.

"Sí," Kate and I said together. We glanced at each other and burst out laughing. Señora Robles had told us that it was a superstition in her part of Mexico: when two people said something together, they were joined for life.

Kate held out her hand, and I slapped her five.

"Uno-dos-tres-cuatro-cinco," Nate counted, not wanting to be left out.

The minute the doorbell rang, I called out, "I'll get it!" and rushed into the mudroom. I had decided that if I waited, rehearsing what I was going to say, I'd get my usual stage fright, and the night would go by without my saying a word to Pablo.

"¡Bienvenidos!" I welcomed the surprised couple at the

door. The Bolívars were dressed like every other Vermonter in winter, in bulky parkas and clunky boots. In fact, except for their soft brown faces and the fact that they were slightly shorter than most of Mom and Dad's friends, they looked like everyone else I knew. I mean, not poor and cowering in *sarapes* and *sombreros*. I don't know what I was expecting. Movie refugees, I suppose.

Both Bolívars stepped in, full of *gracias, muchas gracias*. But Pablo was hanging back. Would he stand in the cold on the other side of the door all night until I apologized?

"Hey, Pablo." The well-rehearsed lines tumbled out of my mouth. "Funny, your dad and my dad knowing each other. Small town, all right. Everyone knows everyone else." From stage fright, I had passed on to manic motormouth. Did he even understand what I was saying? Actually, Em had told me that Meredith had told her that Pablo knew a lot more English than he let on. He had been studying it since he was a boy. But living in a dictatorship, he had learned to keep his mouth shut.

Pablo stepped inside. He was taller than his parents, but he slouched as if trying to make himself smaller and hide behind them. "Thank you for the invitation," he said, as if it had been my doing.

Mrs. Bolívar kept staring at my eyes. "*¡Qué ojos tan lindos! ¡Qué linda!*" My eyes were beautiful. I was beautiful. No one had ever said that to me just like that. *Thank you again, Banana Republic top,* I thought.

"Come on in. Everyone's waiting to meet you." I gestured with my hand in case this was more English than the older Bolívars could handle. I felt kind of shy speaking in Spanish in front of native speakers. And Mrs. Bolívar's compliments were making me feel even shyer.

Dad had appeared at the mudroom door. *"Mi casa, su casa . . ."* He went through the whole my-house-is-your-house routine. Honestly, Dad. Then he gave both Bolívars big, embarrassing American hugs.

Next was Pablo. Dad kind of threw an arm toward him just as Pablo was reaching out for a handshake. There was an awkward moment when neither one knew what to do. Finally, they did this half-and-half maneuver—hugging with one arm and shaking hands with the other, both of them laughing.

Dinner turned out to be like Mr. Barstow's World History class. Mom and Dad and the Bolívars got started talking about politics. But first, it was like Señora Robles's Spanish dinner lessons, lots of talking about the food. Mom had made rice and beans, the way she had learned to cook them back in the Peace Corps.

"They are as good as Abuelita's," Mr. Bolívar claimed.

"*Mejor*," Mrs. Bolívar protested. Even better.

Latin people, I was learning, really overdid it in the compliment department.

Talking about the food led to talking about *el paisito*. "The little country," as Mrs. Bolívar called her homeland. Every time she said it, her eyes filled with tears.

Actually, they had some good news to report. Their oldest son's name had appeared on the list of prisoners the Human Rights Commission had recently interviewed. Their middle son had come out of hiding and called to say there was a cautious but hopeful mood in the country. The United States had decided to support free elections. Former president Carter was going down in late May to be an observer. "*Tenemos esperanza*," Mr. Bolívar confessed. They were feeling hopeful.

Mrs. Bolívar's eyes had filled with tears again. She made a sign of the cross. "*Gracias a Dios*," she whispered.

Mom gave her a hopeful smile. "Things will improve, Mrs. Bolívar."

"*Angelita, por favor*," Mrs. Bolívar insisted.

During the discussion of the political situation, Pablo had joined in. But he grew quiet whenever his brothers' names came up.

"By summer, things might be settled enough to go for a *visita*," Mr. Bolívar was saying in Spanish. I could tell he was trying to brighten the mood around the table.

"I sure hope it is just a *visita*," Dad said, looking a little

54

worried. "I don't know what I'd do without my master *carpintero*."

Mr. Bolívar bowed his head at the compliment. *"Muy agradecido."* He was most grateful to his *excelente patrón*. In truth, his plan was to stay in the States until Pablo finished his schooling. To give their son *una oportunidad*.

Pablo frowned, like he didn't want the opportunity. Was he that unhappy in this country? At school? Maybe if people like me were nicer, he'd want to stay. Suddenly, I had to catch myself. Two months ago, I was hoping this guy would disappear! My emotions were like what they say about driving through small towns in Vermont, don't blink, you'll miss them.

"¿No le gusta Ralston?" Kate must have noticed him frowning, too.

Pablo's face broke into a disarming smile. "I like Ralston very much. Everyone is very nice." I sunk down further in my seat. "But I am sick for home."

"Homesick," Kate offered, eyeing Nate, who often found other people's mistakes very funny.

But Nate had his own question for Pablo. "Do you like video games?"

Pablo made the mistake of saying yes.

"Let's go play." Nate pulled at Pablo's arm, but he stopped midtug. Mom was giving him that mind-your-manners look. "May we be excused?" he pleaded. *"¿Por favor?"* Nate added, flashing his winning grin.

"¡Ay, *qué niño tan simpático!*" Mrs. Bolívar exclaimed. What a darling boy! Nate didn't know much Spanish, but he knew this lady was doting on him. *"Muchas gracias,"* he threw in, snowing her totally.

Before Nate could haul him away, Pablo turned to me. "Will you play?" He lifted his gaze to include Kate.

"They don't really know how!" Nate protested. "Come on, Pablo."

But Pablo was pulling back our chairs, as if our nods were all the knowledge we needed.

As we headed out, I heard Mrs. Bolívar complimenting Mom in Spanish. "What beautiful children you have!"

I felt a pang. Little did Mrs. Bolívar know that only two of the beautiful children were really Mom's.

From that night on, we started to see a lot of the Bolívars. Mom got Mrs. Bolívar a job next door, taking care of our neighbor, Miss Billings, who was crippled with arthritis but didn't want to move into a nursing home. Mrs. Bolívar turned out to be Miss Billings's salvation, even though neither woman understood the other's language. Days his mother worked late, Pablo was invited to come over after school. On his way driving Mr. Bolívar home, Dad would swing by and pick up Mrs. Bolívar and Pablo at our house.

I think it was especially good for Dad having the Bolívars join our family just as Happy seemed to have disowned us. Dad had told Happy that he wanted no part of her disinheriting one of his children. He could do nothing about her will, but he would no longer accept her checks. Grandma was in shock. No one had ever refused to take her money before. She responded as if *we* had disowned *her*! She had not been in touch.

Occasionally Dad would remind Nate to call his grandma. Dad would hang around, like he was half hoping that Happy would ask to talk to him. But she never did. Nate would hang up, and Dad would get real quiet and head down to his basement workshop, where he'd spend hours—doing what, I don't know. For weeks, we heard lots of hammering, but no stool or cabinet or birdhouse came out of it.

One time, I followed him down there.

Dad looked surprised to see me. Usually he was the one climbing up to the attic to "talk" to me. "What's up, honey?"

"I just . . . I mean . . . ," I began, totally tongue-tied. "Dad, I'm sorry," I finally blurted out.

"What on earth for?" Dad's head was cocked to one side, as if looking at me sideways might help him figure out what I meant.

"Grandma," I murmured. "I feel like you lost your mom on account of me—"

"No, no, no, Milly!" Dad broke in before I could finish. "Don't even think that. Your grandma wanted to hurt me. You were just the excuse this time."

"She has a point, though." I was trying hard not to cry. "Technically, I'm not a Kaufman. I don't even look like any of you guys." I went through the whole list of little things I'd been noticing lately: how everyone in the family was tall, whereas I was more *chiquita*. How Kate had Grandma's coloring. How Nate had curly hair like Great-Grandpa in the portrait above the fireplace in Happy's mansion.

Dad kept shaking his head.

"You're not listening!" I folded my arms and narrowed my eyes at him.

"You look just like your mother when you do that, you know?" Dad winked.

Great! I thought. I'd picked up all their bad traits and meanwhile missed out on the good stuff, like being tall, smart, Grandma's *real* grandchild.

One afternoon, while Pablo and Nate played video games downstairs and Kate talked on the phone, I headed for Mom and Dad's bedroom. There it sat on the tall bureau, where it had been for as long as I could remember. The Box. Dad had said there wasn't much information in it, but even a little bit might fill in a blank or two—some hint of who my parents had been, where they might have come from, why they had given me away.

My hands were itching like crazy. I felt tempted to high-tail it back to my room. But something held me there, a growing curiosity about my own story. I took it down as if it were some sacred object in a ceremony. Then I did something that totally surprised me. I brought it up to my face and touched it to my cheek.

From downstairs came Nate's excited shouts. "I won! I won!" I smiled, thinking about my own quiet victory over my fears.

"Milly?" Kate had come into the room. "What're you doing?"

I couldn't exactly say *nothing*. I'd literally been caught red-handed. "Just looking at my stuff," I said, putting The Box back. I actually wasn't sure if Kate knew what was in it. It was weird how we never talked about my adoption. And with Kate, I felt that it was her more than me who felt uncomfortable with it.

Kate let herself drop down on our parents' bed. "Come sit," she said. "You okay, Milly-pooh?" she asked, once I'd joined her.

"It's just been a weird time," I began. Kate grabbed for my hands so I'd stop scratching them. "Pablo, the Bolívars—it's all started me thinking about my . . . adoption." I tried the word. "It's like I've never really let myself feel the feelings." I could feel them welling up now, but I sensed Kate tensing beside me. "That's all," I added, as if putting a lid on both our discomfort.

In the silence that followed, I thought of a bunch of things to tell Kate. How I wished I could talk to her about stuff. How I always felt she was quick to tell me that we were no different. How I felt she just wanted me to forget the past, even more than I did. But maybe this was part of having a therapist for a mom. We let her dig stuff out of us and hadn't learned to do it for ourselves.

Finally, Kate spoke up. "Sometimes I wish I'd been the one adopted." I must have looked totally surprised, because she added, "I mean it. Then I wouldn't always feel guilty, like I got something you didn't."

So that was it! "But I got some other stuff instead," I heard myself saying. Sometimes you say something you know is true, but you don't feel it yet, like a déjà vu in your head before your heart feels it, too.

Kate looked up, hopeful. But then a cloud of doubt entered her face. "Mom told me about what happened with Grandma. I'm really sorry. Grandma can be such a bitch." Unlike our mother, my sister had no problem with her *f* and *b* words. "Anyhow, I just want you to know that you're my sister and nobody but nobody can take that away." The hug she gave me was a serious bone cruncher.

"Hey," I said smiling when we broke away. "Remember? Joined for life?"

"You said it," Kate said, giving me a firm nod. But her gaze faltered when it fell on The Box.

* * *

60

Every time Pablo came over, Nate appropriated him. For years, Nate had been asking Mom and Dad for a brother, and finally he had gotten what he asked for—or even better, an *older* brother who played video games much better than his sisters.

"Poor Pablo," Em commiserated one afternoon. She and Meredith and I were sitting at the kitchen table. From the family room came sounds of some video explosion.

"Poor us, you mean," Meredith added. Em had told me—though I was not to let on that I knew—that Meredith had a crush on Pablo. Big secret. Why else was Meredith always hanging out with us these days?

"Ay, ay, ay," Pablo cried out as if mortally wounded. He was letting Nate clobber him, we could tell. He had to be sick of spending hours playing video games with an eight-year-old. I mean, Pablo was almost seventeen. His birthday was in April. He was a Taurus. Meredith and Em had been quizzing him on his life story.

"I won, I won!" Nate shouted.

Meredith sighed for the umpteenth time. Her next comment caught me by surprise. "So is everyone from your country good-looking?"

"*This* is my country," I said, flashing Em a look. I had asked her to keep my adoption story private. Why had she told her friend?

Meredith stiffened. "I mean . . . you know what I mean."

Em was capping and uncapping her water bottle

61

nervously. The cap fell and rolled across the room—we followed it with our gaze to where Pablo was standing at the doorway. We all kind of jumped. Had he heard us talking about his native country?

"Hey, Pablo!" Em waved him over. She sounded relieved.

"So, did Donkey Kong getcha?" Meredith flirted as he sat down.

"Donkey Kong, Spider-Man, Zelda—I was defeated in every game," Pablo announced loudly. Then casting a glance over his shoulder, he lowered his voice. "I have finally won my freedom. Nate says that I play as bad as a girl!"

"Hey!" Em, Meredith, and I shouted together. It was the tension breaker we all needed. Everyone laughed.

Later that night, Em called. "I'm sorry, Mil. But Meredith's my friend and I didn't think it would matter."

"I wish you'd at least have asked first," I said, like protocol was the problem, not Em's big mouth.

"It's not like it's some awful, shameful secret. And this is a small town, you know?" Em argued.

"So does *everyone* know?" I asked. Is that what she was trying to tell me by saying Ralston was small?

"I swear I only told Meredith, and I guess I told Jake—"

"Em!" What a fool I'd been to think my secret was safe with Em! She had always been a blabbermouth, but still, I couldn't help feeling betrayed.

"I said I was sorry, okay?" Em pleaded. "Mil?"

62

"It's okay," I finally told her, wishing I meant it. "I've gotta go." I hung up before she could apologize again.

Even though I was seeing Pablo more now, we weren't ever together, just the two of us. People were always around, friends at school, my family. But then one afternoon, I found myself riding home alone on the bus with him. It was a Thursday, Mrs. Bolívar was working late; Kate had chorus; Nate, his hockey practice; and Em, well, I admit, things hadn't been the same since the afternoon with Meredith. We were still friendly with each other, but it was that hyped friendliness when what you are really feeling is uncomfortable with a person.

Up at the front of the bus, Alfie kept glancing in the rearview mirror at us.

I told myself not to get paranoid. Alfie often did his mirror check to make sure, as he said, that the natives were not acting restless. Sometimes he'd see something going on and he'd sing a few lines altered from some old song to make us behave. "What goes up, must come down, sit your little butts while the wheels spin on," when someone was standing up in the aisle before the bus had stopped. Or, "On every bus, turn, turn, turn, there are some rules, turn, turn, turn, the rule to be quiet, the rule to calm down," when we were being too rowdy. Sometimes, just for fun, he'd break into song and the whole bus would join in, "We all live in a yellow school bus, a yellow school bus, a yellow school bus," to the tune of "Yellow Submarine."

Today, I distinctly heard him humming, "Do you believe in passion in a young girl's heart . . ."

Oh please, I thought. It's true that sometimes I'd look at Pablo, drinking in everything about him. But it wasn't because I had some mega crush on him like Meredith. I'd stare, wondering, Did my birth mother have that color hair? Is that how my birth father would express himself?

At least Alfie didn't say anything obviously embarrassing as I went down the stairs. Just his usual. "Watch your step there, Milly."

Pablo was shaking his head as we walked down the road to our drive. "He says all the words wrong!"

I explained Jake and Em's theory about Alfie frying his memory cells in the sixties with drugs. "By the way, how do you know so much about the Beatles?"

"That's how I learned my English back home." Pablo strummed an imaginary guitar and sang a few bars of "I Want to Hold Your Hand," tossing his hair every which way in that Beatlemania way.

It was the first time I'd seen Pablo really let loose. I watched, laughing. Pablo had changed in the last couple of months. His jeans were fashionably faded (which could be that he'd been wearing them on and off for two and a half months!) and wrinkled (which could be Mrs. Bolívar had no time for extra ironing these days); his hair was longer, not tamped down with some hair cream. And now that he was smiling more, his dimples showed. He was looking good, but it wasn't just that. He seemed easier to talk to, a guy I wanted for a friend. Maybe it was me who had changed?

"I guess I should scream and throw myself at you," I teased. "That's what girls used to do to the Beatles, you know?"

Pablo smiled, his dimples deepening. "Why do you think I learned their songs?"

Hmm, I thought. We'd had this long discussion in Mrs. Gillespie's class about "machismo." The stereotype of the Latin guy thinking he's God's gift to women. "I thought women just automatically did that with Latin men?" I kept a straight face.

"¿Bueno?" Pablo looked at me, as if saying, Well? So? Get on with it!

"Very funny!" I folded my arms and narrowed my eyes at him. "This might come as a big surprise, Pablo. But some women prefer their men as equals."

"¡Ayyyy, una feminista!" Pablo ducked, shielding his face, as if I'd shown a crucifix to a vampire in one of those old movies. It was pretty obvious he was joking. But I didn't feel like letting him off the hook, just in case.

"Is feminist like a dirty word in your country?"

"Some men don't like strong women," he admitted. "But that just shows how weak they are, no?"

I gave him thumbs up. Good for you, I thought.

"Me, I like my women strong," Pablo went on. "That way they can take care of me." With a grin like that, he had to be joking. Still, I gave him thumbs down.

We walked up our drive, Pablo remembering some of his favorite sixties songs.

"If you love the Beatles so much, I can dig up some of Dad's old LPs," I offered. "Maybe we could reprogram Alfie."

"Reprogram?" Pablo asked, lifting a questioning hand.

I'd noticed this before with Señora Robles and in the videos we watched together. Latin people spoke with their faces and hands as well as with words. I wondered if my birth parents had been expressive. If my birth mother's hands suffered from rashes, too.

"Reprogram is, well, you erase the old stuff, then you fill someone's head with new information."

Pablo winced as if in pain. Had I said something wrong? "Reprogram," he murmured. "It is what the *guardia* do to the prisoners in my country."

"I'm sorry," I said, touching his arm before I could think to keep my hand to myself.

"I have a special favor to ask, Milly." Pablo always pronounced my name as if it had two sets of double *e*'s, Meelee. We were sitting at the kitchen table, preparing to do our homework.

66

I nodded, unsure what he was going to ask me. The thought did cross my mind that maybe Pablo was going to hit on me. And in his corny, well-mannered, foreign-student way, he'd probably ask first! Maybe he'd gotten the wrong idea from my joking about throwing myself at him?

"I want to improve my English," Pablo explained. "Ms. Morris is giving me extra lessons, but she speaks very fast." It's true, our English teacher was a speed talker. Her English sections were the only ones that always got through the yearly syllabus with time to spare. I mean, we did *Romeo and Juliet* in three days! It was like R & J are in love, then R & J are in bed, then R & J are dead—boom, boom, boom. "I wish for you to help me with my English." Pablo had lowered his voice as if he were asking for something intimate.

I was shaking my head in total disbelief. This was like my "helping" Nate with his science report two months ago!

Pablo misunderstood my reaction as meaning *no*. His face darkened with embarrassment. "I ask too much, forgive me."

"It's not that," I explained. "I'm just surprised because up to about a year ago, I was like Ms. Dodo in English. I had to take special lessons and go to a tutor every day. And here you are, asking me to be your teacher!"

"I do not understand. *You* were in need of special instruction in English?"

How much to tell him? "I had some learning problems. I'd get letters confused and write the wrong words and not make any sense. Same with reading." Actually, I still struggled sometimes. But I liked putting my failures in the past tense.

Pablo was nodding in agreement. "I have these learning problems as well. English is very difficult, Milly."

"But that's because it's not your native language. . . ." My voice kind of petered out toward the end. I mean, was English technically *my* native language? Mom and Dad hadn't brought me to the States until I was almost a year old.

"You know what?" I said, beginning to lose my nerve. "I think you'd be better off asking someone else to help you."

I was thinking of Meredith. She'd love to teach Pablo a thing or two! Though recently she'd backed off. According to Em, Pablo didn't seem interested. "Meredith says he probably has a girlfriend back home."

Now it was Pablo who was shaking his head at me. "I want your instruction, Milly. You speak in a clear way I understand. Your English is very good."

Don't ever let anyone tell you compliments don't work. "Okay," I agreed. "But you have to help me with my Spanish, too."

"One day, Spanish. One day, English," Pablo suggested. "Today, English." He opened his backpack (one of our hand-me-downs) and pulled out the ESL workbook Ms. Morris had special-ordered for him. I paged through it.

Stupid conversational skits. No wonder he wasn't making much progress. "Pablo, this is so dumb!"

"*Por supuesto,*" he agreed. "But it is the practice in pronunciation I require."

I nodded. Pablo could use help in that department, for sure. Last week in Algebra, he'd asked Jake for a sheet of paper. But instead of saying *sheet*, he had asked for a shit. The whole class had tried not to, but we couldn't help cracking up. Last period on a Friday afternoon, what can I say. We totally regress.

I opened to the first chapter: "Meeting New Friends." A man with a cap and a long robe was pictured meeting a girl. The ponytail was meant to make her look American, I suppose. Might as well start here.

"Hello, my name is Pablo Antonio Bolívar Sánchez. What is your name?" Pablo read his lines, filling in the blank with his name. Then I read out my part, asking him how he was. "I am happy to be here," Pablo replied.

"*Happy*, not '*appy*," I corrected. "In English, you pronounce *h*'s."

"Happy?" Pablo tried.

I nodded, thinking of Grandma. She had sent us a Passover card. Inside there were three checks, made out in each kid's name. On the memo line, she'd drawn a heart, even on mine. "What does she think? That she can buy love?" Mom had said, arms folded, eyes narrowed.

But Dad's face had softened. "She's trying. Happy doesn't know how to apologize. How to admit she's wrong."

"It's very simple," Mom had countered. "I. Am. Sorry." Mom said each word like it was a whole sentence.

"Where are you from?" Pablo was reading from his workbook. When I didn't respond, he looked up.

"You asked me that same question the first day I met you," I reminded him. It was high time I admitted I had understood him.

He nodded, then repeated what he had said. "¿De dónde eres?"

"I'm sorry that I pretended . . . I . . . I didn't know why you were asking me where I was from." Even now, two months later, it was still hard to talk about.

Pablo was staring at me again with that intense look of his. "I explain why I ask. Your eyes . . . they are eyes from Los Luceros."

It was a good thing I was sitting down. I felt lightheaded. My hands were tingling. "What do you mean, eyes from Los Luceros?" I managed to get out.

Moving back and forth, English to Spanish, Pablo told me about a small town high in the mountains of his country. "It is called Los Luceros, muy remoto, very remote. That is why the revolutionaries hide there. These people from Los Luceros, they all have eyes like yours."

As he spoke, my eyes filled with tears.

70

4

The Box

MY HEAD WAS SPINNING. Was I really from this small town in the mountains? Were my birth parents revolutionaries? Were they still alive? And if not, what had happened to them?

I felt like this girl, Pandora, in the Greek myths we'd studied in Ms. Morris's class. She opened up a box she'd been told not to open. Out came all the sorrows and problems in the world.

In my case, not just sorrows, but all kinds of feelings and questions and thoughts were whirling around.

Pablo touched my hand. I felt a tingling that was different from my allergies. "*¿Qué pasa, Milly?*" What was wrong?

I guess that's when I should have told him about my

71

adoption. But I was still reeling with all this new information.

"I'm fine, fine," I said, turning back to the workbook on the table before us. The next section was called "Meeting the Family": mother, father, sister, brother, grandfather, grandmother. I thought of Happy again. But for some reason, what came to mind was not her meanness but the people *she* had lost—her mother and her mother's family in the Holocaust. It had made her bitter. I didn't want to end up like that.

"My grandmother, Abuelita, still lives near the town I mention, Los Luceros," Pablo was explaining. Every summer when he was a boy, Pablo and his brothers would be sent to the mountains to stay with their grandparents. *"Extraño mi país,"* Pablo added softly. He missed his country.

"I'd like to visit it some day," I told him. I wasn't just saying it. "I'd like to see the country where my parents got married, where . . . Kate was born."

"Your sister, Kate?" Pablo was surprised. He had thought all us kids had been born in the States after my parents returned from the Peace Corps.

"No, only Nate," I explained. "Mom had Kate there. Then, a few months after Kate was born . . ." I took a deep breath. Okay, Mil, GO! I had this image of myself running down the diving board at the pool at Happy's country club, about to jump off into nothing but air. . . . "A few months later, they found me."

72

"*Found* you?" Pablo questioned, eyebrows raised.

I nodded. "S*oy adoptada.* I am adopted." I said it in English and Spanish, as if to confirm the fact in both languages.

A knowing smile spread across Pablo's face. "*Somos patriotas,*" he said proudly.

Fellow patriots? Well, that was maybe stretching it. But it was reassuring how Pablo treated the news like it was nothing to get upset about. It made me want to keep talking. So I told him the little I knew. The orphanage in the capital my parents had visited about four months after Kate was born. The sickly baby they found there. The decision to adopt. The paperwork. The final okay. The bringing me back. How I'd tried keeping it a secret so as not to feel any different from Kate, or Nate, born seven years later.

I talked on and on—the words just seemed to flow out. Pablo kept nodding, listening without interrupting, as if he knew how important it was for me to get my story out.

When I was done, it was suddenly very quiet . . . as if we were both looking down at that empty box that had once held my secret.

Pablo knowing my story definitely brought us closer. If I could tell him my deep dark secret, then I could talk to him about anything. Well, almost anything. There are some things you just can't gab to guys about—like PMS or your big butt. I did talk to Pablo about Em and how we were drifting apart.

"I want to forget that she blabbed. I really do," I explained. "I mean, I even told her that it was over and done with, but my heart just doesn't seem to want to come along with the rest of me, you know?"

Pablo nodded. He didn't immediately offer advice or respond. I liked the way he was thoughtful about what people said. Like he was really thinking about it.

"Things of the heart you cannot rush," he said quietly, as if he were speaking from personal experience. I wondered if Pablo did have a girlfriend back home, or maybe a whole slew of them. All those Beatles lyrics, I supposed. "When I was a little boy, summers with my grandparents, Abuelito and I used to plant a garden. I was so impatient for the crops to grow. I used to pull the tiny plants to see if the roots had sprouted."

I had to laugh at the thought of Pablo surrounded by mounds of plucked would-have-been onions, potatoes, carrots. "Your granddad must have loved you!"

Pablo smiled wistfully. "Abuelito would say, 'Things of the garden and things of the heart, you have to give them time, Pablito.' Poor Abuelito. He never lived to see his country free. He died when I was a boy. A natural death," Pablo added with relief. I guess in his country that was a rare thing.

This actually was the hardest thing to get used to with

Pablo. How he would suddenly switch from being just your normal teenage guy to someone brooding and absent, someone I didn't know.

"Earth to Pablo," I sometimes teased him. "Come in!"

He was perplexed the first time. I guess this spaceship routine wasn't done in his country. Sometimes Pablo would respond, shaking off whatever bad memory had overtaken him. But sometimes he was too far gone, and he would look at me from such a far distance, like he himself didn't know how to get back to me.

Those times, I really wanted to comfort him. But I couldn't yet seem to reach out and hold his hand. Things of the body. I guess you can't rush them, either.

A few days after I talked with Pablo about her, Em caught up with me on our way to Algebra. "I really feel like you're still mad at me. I mean, if you're not going to be my best friend, would you please let me know?" She looked like she was about to cry.

"Oh, Em!" I put my arm around her. It was a relief to feel the ice breaking between us.

"We never really talk anymore," Em wailed, her eyes brimming with tears. She seemed oblivious to the fact that we were standing in the hall, surrounded by wall-to-wall people hurrying to their next class. And two of them, Jake and Dylan, were heading in our direction.

"I know you're like still totally upset about me telling about your adoption."

"EM!!!" Like my New York cousins, Em thought making a scene showed a person was really being sincere.

"Hey there!" Jake and Dylan had swerved to join us. I thought for sure they would notice the high-tension wires threaded between Em and me. But they seemed totally clueless. Did Jake even remember what Em had told him about my being adopted? "What are you ladies up to this weekend?"

Em and I both shrugged. We were too into our talk to think about the weekend. Actually, mine was wide open. My parents were taking Nate to a game in Boston. On the way, Kate was being dropped off for an overnight with her best friend, who had moved to southern Vermont last summer. At first, Mom had insisted I go along with "the family," but finally she had agreed to let me stay home. The Bolívars would be around if I needed anything. In fact, I had already offered to accompany Mrs. Bolívar to the mall on Saturday to help her shop for some nice nightgowns for Miss Billings.

"We're getting together Saturday night to plan my campaign strategy," Jake was saying. This past Monday, Jake had registered to run for class president. Elections would be held in late May for officers for the following year. Jake was the world's nicest guy and every downtrodden person's Robin

Hood. But I didn't think he'd stand a chance against Taylor Ward, all-around jock and ninth-grade heartthrob. I know, it sounds like every high school sitcom—the handsome, blond hunk; the skinny, intellectual-type guy. But like Ms. Morris says, clichés get to be clichés because they ring true. The most I could hope for Jake was a happy ending to his story: skinny guy doesn't get the presidency, but he gets, I don't know, a date with Jennifer Lopez.

"Sure, I'll be there," Em was saying. I noticed, kind of sadly, that she didn't accept the invitation for both of us like she used to.

Of all things, "Auld Lang Syne" came through the loud-speakers. "You guys coming?" Dylan said. We were all in Algebra this last period.

"In a sec." I knew we were going to be late for class, but Em and I needed to plan getting together for a talk. Hopefully, we'd make it to Algebra before Mr. Oliver reached what he called his "negative numbers."

"So, when can you come over?" I asked. The hall had cleared. Even a normal voice now sounded loud.

I don't think Em heard me. She was crying again. "It's been awful lately. I've been feeling like life is just not worth it." Her parents, who were always threatening to divorce each other, were really getting a divorce this time. She had gained five pounds. Her thighs were huge. Didn't I think her thighs were huge? Meanwhile, her brother had been kicked out of his prep school, which was kind of unfair since the school was for problem kids. She was flunking Phys. Ed. Nobody flunked Yoga.

"Oh, Em," I kept saying, sometimes in comfort, sometimes in exasperation at how Em got the truly major all mixed up with the definitely minor. Why, oh why, is it so easy to spot this in someone else? But as Em talked on, I realized that a lot had been happening in her life that I didn't know about. I'd been holding on to my grudge, not seeing how much Em truly regretted what she'd done.

"I don't blame you for hating my guts," Em went on. I shook my head in protest, but Em wouldn't be convinced. "I deserve it, I know. I have the biggest mouth. But I'm really, really, really sorry!" Em squeezed her eyes shut as if to stop the tears that spurted out of the corner of her eyes.

"Em, listen, it's okay, really." This time it was my heart talking. "Truly, you are MY ONE AND ONLY best friend!" I raised my voice several decibels. Maybe if I made a scene, she would believe me.

Em blinked, as if surprised at my outburst. "Really? You mean it?"

I brought my face right up to hers, till our foreheads touched. "I mean it, girlfriend," I said emphatically, looking into her eyes.

"You sure you still love me?" Em was like a little kid sometimes. It was something else I both loved and sometimes found exasperating about my best friend.

"I never stopped," I assured her. Not that I wasn't also hurt. But that was the thing about loving somebody, you hung in there with them during the hard parts. That's what the love was for, the rest was easy.

"If I could only get mouth-reduction surgery like they do for big boobs." Em sighed as we pulled apart. I loved it when Em's sense of humor kicked in.

"So how about coming over this Saturday? My parents are going to be gone."

Em nodded. "Maybe after we talk, we can go over to Jake's—you want to?"

But I had been hatching another plan. "Actually, Em, I need your help with something."

Curiosity lit up my friend's eyes. "What?"

"I want to open The Box and I want you there, okay?"

Em's mouth dropped—she looked totally shocked. "*The Box*? Really? But I mean, are you . . . do you really think you're ready, Mil?"

I nodded, like I knew. But to be honest, I was in shock, too.

The box had been around for years before it became The Box.

It was made of this beautiful, dark wood—mahogany, Dad had said. A latch pulled down over an iron ring. One time, when we were little, curious Kate pointed to the dresser and asked Mom what was in the box. I remember Mom saying something like she kept some private papers and documents in there. That did the job. The contents sounded boring. Nothing for us to try to get into when she wasn't looking.

One summer afternoon between third and fourth grade, when we were still living on Long Island, my parents came out to the driveway. I'd been riding my new bike up and down the street—the allowable block that was visible from our house. I don't remember Kate being around, and Nate was napping. Now that I look back, my parents probably waited until the three of us could be alone together.

"Mil, honey." It was Dad. "We'd like to talk to you, Mom and I, okay?"

From their faces, I could tell I was in for something important. Several things went through my mind. I had done something wrong. But what? I always tried to be good to make up for all the trouble I was having at school.

I followed them into the house, feeling like I was going to faint. I think I actually held my breath all the way to the kitchen. Everything seemed normal, in its place. But then my eye fell on the box sitting beside the lazy Susan on the table. It was a harmless enough thing, but it was so unusual to see it there that it could have been a gun or a bloody knife the way my knees began shaking.

I sat down at my usual place, Mom and Dad on the other side facing me. They each took one of my hands, smiling this emergency-room smile like bad news was coming. I must have looked ready to cry because Mom said, "Honey, it's nothing to worry about. Remember how Dad and I have talked to you about getting you in an orphanage?"

I nodded warily. They had told me that I was adopted, but I didn't really know what that meant. I had asked if Kate and Nate were also adopted, and Mom had explained that, no, children came to families in different ways. My brother and sister had come from her belly—which sounded much more disturbing.

"Anyhow," Mom went on. "We just want to go over the whole story in case you have any questions. Okay?"

And then they told me a story I'd heard in bits and pieces before. I listened. I didn't ask any questions. Even when they asked me if I had any questions. Really and truly, the only part I worried about was when they said they weren't sure about my birth date. August 15 was just the date the orphanage had registered me. I thought they were trying to take away my birthday.

Dad was squeezing my hand. "Any more questions, honey?"

"You understand what we've told you?" Mom squeezed my other hand.

What wasn't there to understand? Once upon a time, some parents who had been in the Peace Corps decided to stay an extra year in their host country. They worked at a school teaching English. Their first daughter was born.

They called her Kate. One day, the mom visited an orphanage close to where they lived. There she met a beautiful baby who had been left at the doorstep. The mom couldn't resist; she brought the dad over; they fell in love with this baby; they knew that baby was meant for them, and so they adopted this baby. Wonderful story. But it didn't seem to have anything to do with me.

"You were just a tiny little thing." Dad held his big hands about a foot apart, smiling proudly.

Mom smiled, too, like she was really looking at that baby, not just the empty space between Dad's hands. "The sisters just adored you. Especially Sister Corita. She was the one who found the basket just outside the door. You were wrapped in a shawl with a little piece of paper pinned to your dress with your name on it. And this was also in the basket with you." Mom nudged the box toward me.

"Beautiful wood, isn't it?" Dad stroked the box. "Mahogany," he pronounced. "Shall we open it?"

I eyed the box—which had suddenly been transformed into The Box, with scary capital letters. "What's in it?"

"Nothing to worry about, honey," Mom reassured me. "It's just like a memory box, with some pictures and souvenirs and newspaper clippings. Plus, all your adoption papers and naturalization papers we put in there later. You want to look in it?"

I shook my head and pushed The Box back toward them.

82

"We don't have to open it now," Mom agreed. "Any time you'd like to look inside it or talk about it . . ."

"You okay, sweetie?" Dad was starting to worry.

"It's a lot to take in, we know," Mom added.

I knew I would start crying if I didn't get out of there soon. I looked up, and instantly their eyes were on me like they were hungry for me to say anything. *Say something,* I told myself, *make them feel better.* But all I could come up with was, "Can I go out and play now?"

My parents looked at each other helplessly. "Sure, sweetie," Dad said. "Of course you can," Mom added. But I had to tug at their hands to get them to release mine.

I stood up, pushed in my chair like this had been some kind of formal session. I remember noticing my hands. They were covered with a rash again. Maybe they were itchy, I don't know. I was too numb to feel anything.

Out in the driveway, I stared at my new bike for a while like I couldn't figure out what it was for or how to use it. I didn't know what to do with myself. Somehow it seemed like I would have to be a whole different person from now on.

Then I remembered what I'd said inside. *Can I go out and play now?* That's right. Continue as before. Put this story back in The Box and push it away.

I got on that bike and pedaled furiously around the driveway and out into the street, where I was not allowed to go. Somehow, I knew that today, I would not get in trouble for breaking the rules. Looking back now, I can see that I had kept on pedaling ever since. Until the day when Pablo leaned toward me in the lunchroom and with a simple question—*click!*—opened the lid.

Saturday afternoon, Mrs. Bolívar and I took the bus back from the mall. It dropped us off at the town center, half a block from where the Bolívars lived. I was going to walk home from there, but Mrs. Bolívar insisted that it was getting dark and a *señorita* should not be traveling by herself. So Pablo was enlisted to accompany me. It felt silly in our small town, where crime amounts to a car full of teenagers on a Saturday night bashing mailboxes or toilet-papering a girl's front yard. But I kept reminding myself that these people had been living in a dictatorship with disappearances and horrible tortures. (Mr. Barstow had just finished a whole segment on current Latin American history that was giving me nightmares.)

Not that I minded Pablo's company. Along with Nate, I had suddenly gotten an older brother and friend. More and more, I admit, there were pangs of not wanting it to stop there.

"So you're my bodyguard?" I said, once we were beyond earshot of his mother.

"A *body* guard?"

I tried thinking of the Spanish word but drew a blank.

84

"You protect me from danger," I explained. "Like if a mugger comes, or say, I were famous, you'd keep the fans away."

"Are you looking for someone for this job?"

"Yeah, right! I'm in such danger in Ralston. No, what I need is a fairy godmother to wave her magic wand. . . ." I waved my hand. And then, it was like when you shake food into an aquarium and a bunch of little fish come zooming over to those flakes. All these wishes popped into my head, things I yearned for, like Grandma's love and Kate's understanding and Em not being such a big mouth—and other wishes, too, I didn't even have words for yet, stirrings about my birth parents and Pablo and the stuff in books that's just covered by "happily ever after." But though my head was packed with them, I couldn't think of a single wish to say out loud. I guess I didn't want to sound like some whiney teenager who didn't have her life together.

"¿Bueno?" Pablo was waiting. "What would you wish for, Milly?"

I thought of saying something sappy like world peace. But instead, I shrugged. "Nada, nada." Not a thing. "But no use wasting a wish." I held out an invisible package. "Why don't you use it?"

I felt a little silly playing pretend with a grown-up guy. But Pablo didn't miss a beat. He mimed taking my package, shaking it, and listening to the contents. Then he opened it up and drew out something between his thumb and forefinger.

"What is it?" I asked. I felt a little breathless. He had me almost believing that he'd found something in our invisible wish box.

He shook his head. "We cannot name it or it disappears."

I felt like I'd opened a door that led to a place I'd never been before. I wanted him to say more. But I also wanted the magic to unfold in its own time, for the little roots to grow.

Since it was a warm spring evening, I suggested we take the long way home through the town's old cemetery. It really is a pretty spot, with clumps of birches that were just starting to get that tinge of green. Some of the tombstones have quaint inscriptions. I mean, there are people buried there from before this place was the United States. In the summer, you'll sometimes see tourists taking rubbings of them.

"Walk through *el cementerio*?" Pablo seemed hesitant.

I was about to tease Pablo about believing in ghosts when, again, I remembered Mr. Barstow's lectures—the murders, the cemeteries filling up. "Oh, forget it, let's just go through town."

"No, no, Milly," Pablo insisted. "I want to go with you."

"Are you sure?" I looked into his eyes, the way you do to see if someone's telling the truth. His eyes seemed to soften, meeting mine. A quiver of excitement went through me. I felt that pang again and looked away.

We entered through the little gate and walked down the central path, stopping now and then to read the names on interesting-looking stones.

"*¡Qué curiosa!*" Pablo noted, crouching by a tombstone.

I had seen it before and gone quickly by it. Now I knelt beside Pablo and let him guide my hand over the letters as if I were a blind person, trying to read Braille.

"It gives no name, only MOTHER," Pablo noted. "Was *la familia* afraid to put the name on the stone?"

"It's not that," I explained. "In fact, all the names are listed over on that central stone. I guess it's just that when someone you love dies, you don't lose a name, you lose a relationship."

Pablo nodded absently. I could feel him slipping away into his bad memories. "Every victim in my country is a father, a mother, a brother, an uncle. . . ." His voice faltered. Pablo had told me about his uncle, Tío Daniel, a radical journalist, who was murdered a month or so after the Bolívars had escaped to the States.

Again, I wondered about my birth parents. Had they been victims as well? I had lost them before I even had a relationship with them. No name, no stories. A blank stone.

We were quiet as we made our way down the path. It was dark by the time I got home.

* * *

87

The phone was ringing on the other side of the door. I said a quick goodbye to Pablo and raced to get it before the machine kicked in.

"Good evening. Kaufman residence." I was hamming it up, thinking my parents were calling, worried that I wasn't yet back from the mall.

There was a pause. Oh no, I thought. A pervert's on the other end and my parents are gone! There was still time to race to the door and call out for Pablo to come back.

"Who is this?" It was a woman's voice, commanding, familiar. "Hello? Sylvia, is that you?"

Happy?! Happy was calling us?! "Oh, hi, Grandma—" Or was I supposed to call her that anymore? "It's just me, Milly." I meant to make my voice go flat and uninterested, but I couldn't. Something in me still wanted this old woman to love me.

"Milly, dear. I didn't recognize your voice. You sounded so grown up. How are you, sweetie?"

Was this the Academy Awards for Hypocrisy or what? "Nate's not here," I told her right off. Just so she'd know and wouldn't waste her long-distance money talking to me. "And Mom and Kate and Dad are gone for the weekend."

"Why didn't you go?"

I shrugged. Like she was going to see me shrugging! "I just wanted to stay, I guess."

"You sound a little lonely, honey. Maybe I can send Roger up for you."

I could not believe this. My grandmother who had disinherited me was going to send her driver six hours to pick me up in Vermont?! "No, no, Grandma. Really, don't worry. Mom and Dad'll be back tomorrow. And my friend Em is coming over tonight."

"If you're sure . . ." Happy didn't sound totally convinced. She went on to ask how I was doing in school and how my classes were going. They were the same old questions she always used to ask me. But now she actually sounded interested. I mean, there were pauses between each question, like she was expecting an answer back from me.

It seemed Happy wanted to know about everyone in the family tonight, not just Nate, though we did spend a couple of minutes on this really cute card Nate had sent her, thanking her for her Passover card. (Kate and I had also signed it.) Nate had gotten the picture off the Internet. A huge gorilla holding a tiny gorilla in its hairy arms. Inside the folded paper, Nate had written "LOVE YOU, GRANDMA!!!" I remembered thinking it was perfect that this ugly, tarantula-looking gorilla was supposed to be my awful grandmother.

The doorbell started ringing spastically, no time between rings. Em was here. But I wasn't on the cordless to just walk over and open the door. And never in my life had I cut off Grandma.

"What's that sound?" Happy finally asked.

"It's just my friend Em at the door."

"I'm going to hold on while you go check, okay? Come back and tell me if it's her before I hang up." City people, I swear.

I wasn't about to tell Happy that we didn't have a surveillance camera like she did at her mansion or she'd start in on the latest crime statistics. I raced to the door, flung it open, and Em barely got out, "Where have you been—" when I cut her off.

"Talking to Happy. She's still on the phone." I didn't want my big-mouth friend shouting something like YOU MEAN YOUR GRANDMOTHER, THE BITCH?

"Grandma, it's my friend like I said."

"Good, good. I'm glad. You won't be alone, then. Anyhow, you tell your parents I called, okay? Go take care of your friend." But she didn't hang up. Instead, there was a little pause. "You know Grandma loves you, Milly."

"Love you, too, Grandma," I replied automatically, but saying it, I realized I really did mean it. I set the receiver down gently in its cradle.

"Happy?!" Em looked incredulous. When I nodded, she went on, "So was Happy happy?"

I knew Em was trying to make a joke about my mean grandmother. But I felt suddenly sad for Happy always

90

being unhappy. It struck me that Happy had called because she was feeling lonely and needed to talk to someone who wasn't paid to listen to her talk. Poor Happy. Maybe she was realizing she might lose more than the past if she kept taking out her sadness on the rest of us.

What a night it was turning out to be. The walk home with Pablo. Happy's phone call. Then Em with the latest "news." Em made quote marks in the air with her fingers. Her parents had decided they were going to stay together after all.

"They're such babies." Em sighed. "They're really not fit to be parents. I think people who want to be parents should really, like, take a test. I mean, you need a license to drive, right?"

We looked at each other in that way you can look at a close friend and not have to look away. We knew how deep down this truth went in both our lives.

"Do we even have the energy to do this?" I said, leading Em upstairs.

"It's up to you," Em said. Though I could tell she'd be disappointed if we just went over to Jake's instead.

We sat across from each other on my bed, holding hands, The Box between us. Weirdly, the moment reminded me of that day in the kitchen when my parents had told me about my adoption.

"Your hands are really broken out," Em said, turning them over. "Have you been putting Mr. Burt on?"

For Christmas, Em had given me a bag full of little tins, Burt's Bees salves, that hadn't done much of anything but make me smell like cough drops. "Nothing helps," I told her. "The doctor now says its neuro . . . something—it means it's all in my head."

Em shook hers. "That rash looks pretty real to me. Anyhow," she added, eyeing The Box as if to remind me of our task.

"I feel like I should make a wish or something," I said, trying to lighten my nervousness. Really, I felt ready to cry. I took a deep breath. "Okay, here it goes." I lifted the lid, then made myself look down.

I don't know what I was expecting. A teensy baby? Body parts? Or what? The stuff inside looked boringly normal: a bunch of envelopes, folded-up newspaper clippings. I started taking stuff out, then just dumped the contents on my bedspread.

We pored over each little thing.

"Look at this," we kept saying to each other.

Em held out a coin with a star on one side and a picture of what must be some famous person from the country's history on the other. "He looks like Pablo," she noted. Usually I don't agree with Em about who people look like, but this time she was right. This famous person had Pablo's same strong jaw and intense eyes.

Inside an envelope, we found a locket of wheat-colored hair braided together with dark black hair. My birth mother's and father's? Another envelope was full of old photos, which I hoped/dreaded would be of my birth parents or the place I'd been born. But most of them turned out to be shots of a little baby being held by a short, fat nun in a white habit with what looked like a seagull sitting on her head. There were some later shots of a young-looking Mom, holding Kate and me on her lap. Kate looked humongous compared to me. Then another of me in Dad's arms, arriving in the United States with a little American flag in my hand.

"Oh my God, you were like this gorgeous Benetton baby!" Em gushed. "You were so cute!"

"Hmm." I studied the photo. I hate it when people talk about how cute you *used* to be.

At the bottom of The Box, I discovered a tiny florist-type envelope. I pulled out a piece of paper that looked like it'd been folded and refolded often. MILAGROS, it read, written in big block letters.

Em was craning her neck, trying to make out what was written on the paper. "What does that mean?" Em's mother insisted she take French, on account of her ancestors had once been royalty over in France before they became poor French Canadians living in Vermont.

"Miracles," I said. "*Milagros* means miracles."

"Mi-la-gros," Em sounded it out. "That's so neat. It's like it's a miracle you survived."

What Em didn't know was that Milagros had been my name at the orphanage. But when my parents adopted me, they decided to make Milagros my middle name and give me Mom's mother's name, Mildred, instead. Not only would it be an easier name for my American life, but Mom wanted one of her daughters to carry my grandma-I-never-met's name. I can't say I loved Mildred—Milly's okay—but I definitely hated Milagros, and so I never used my middle name. The last thing I wanted was someone asking me, "Where did you get a name like Milagros?"

Before Em and I put everything back, I skimmed over all the official documents from the orphanage. *Mother* was listed as unknown, so was *Father*. *Place of birth* was also blank. I had hoped that maybe somewhere in all the documents I would find the name Los Luceros.

We carried the box—no longer the scary Box of capital letters—back to my parents' dresser. "Thank you, Em," I said as we turned to each other. "I couldn't have done it without you." And then, I don't know why exactly, but we both burst into tears. It felt so good to stand there, sobbing and hugging each other. Whatever distance we had felt between us had evaporated. Close and best friends. We could handle anything.

5

Elections

GIVE JAKE A BREAK. JAKE & SHAKE. Walking into Ralston High, I felt like I was in a bad rap video. Jake's posters were everywhere!

One poster showed a picture of Jake looking off into the Green Mountains: JAKE FOR THE EARTH'S SAKE. (This to win the "green" granola vote.)

Pablo made one showing Jake wearing a *sombrero* with a bandanna tied around his neck: JAKE: UN HOMBRE SINCERO. (Everyone kept asking him what it meant, so Pablo wrote the translation in tiny print below the caption: Jake: an honest man.)

Em and I did one together. We took a photo of Jake surrounded by some posters and bumper stickers of his

95

favorite causes: SAVE THE WHALES. DON'T LAUGH AT FARMERS WITH YOUR MOUTH FULL. PEACE IS NOT SOMETHING TO DIE FOR. LOVE MAKES A FAMILY. TAKE VERMONT FORWARD. Our caption read: VOTE FOR JAKE, A LOT'S AT STAKE.

Every time I glanced at one of Jake's posters, then looked over at Taylor's—Taylor in his nifty Abercrombie & Fitch T-shirt with this attitude written all over his face, like *Hey, dude, vote for me if you feel like it, no big deal*—I thought, poor Jake, trying so hard.

Actually, we were all trying too hard. The borderliners, I mean. Jake managed to talk most of his friends into running with him. Start a movement, why not? Alfie even came up with a campaign song, "You say you wanna start a Ralston-lution."

The deal at Ralston was that anyone running for an office had to get twenty-five names on a petition. Then you could register to be a candidate and put up posters and stuff. There was a three-week period to get your name in. Besides president, every class voted for a vice president, treasurer, and secretary, as well as two senators, who basically did most of the work of student government and got a trickle of the credit.

Jake got his signatures and registered right off. Then the other borderliners started jumping on his bandwagon.

Dylan, a math geek, was the natural for treasurer. Plus, his dad owns the car dealership in town, and being rich can't hurt if you're running for taking care of the money. Em kind of fell into the secretary spot, because, to be honest, none of the guys wanted to run for a position that sounded like it was for a girl. Will was going to go for VP, but then he messed up, smoking in the bathroom during one of the school dances (that's all he got *caught* for), and so he couldn't run.

Suddenly, everyone was looking at me.

"Don't even think about it," I kept saying. My friends knew I hated getting up in front of people.

But Jake was not one to give up—obviously, or he wouldn't be running against Taylor Ward. One morning, he cornered me by my locker. "Here's the deal, Mil. We really, really need you." Jake put a hand on each of my shoulders—like a handler getting a boxer revved up to go into the ring and get beat up. His blue eyes were full of conviction. I couldn't help remembering the crush I'd had on him in seventh grade. Back then, I probably would have done anything Jake Cohen asked me to do.

"You'd be super! Everyone really respects you."

This was news to me. "Why's that?"

"Oh, you know, the way you had all that tutoring, and you never complained or told us why so we wouldn't feel sorry for you."

I was trying to hear the reason for all the supposed respect people had for me in this depressing picture.

97

Finally, I caught on. "Jake, do you mean because I'm . . . adopted?"

Jake sighed with relief. "I didn't know if you knew I knew. Em told—"

I nodded. "I know. I'm just sorry I didn't tell you myself."

"I understand," Jake reassured me. "This place is so white bread." He held his arms out, meaning Ralston High, our town, Vermont—it wasn't clear. "But that's what I'm saying, Mil. You never used your adoption as an excuse for anything. I really admire that."

This was a different spin on my secrecy—bravery instead of plain and simple shame and insecurity.

"And so, my friend." Jake's voice suddenly turned parental. Oh no, I thought. Here comes the pitch after the spin. "I'm making a personal plea that you join us. Mil, we are going to change this place! More and more people are saying they're going to vote for us. We stand a real chance, we really do! But we need the best people in our class. And I know, I know—" Jake held up both hands. "VP's a lot more than you bargained for. So, how about you run for one of the senators?" The way he proposed this option, it was like Jake was giving me a real break.

"Let me think about it, Jake, okay?" I was already feeling that familiar tingling in my hands.

"Sure," Jake said, waving a hand in a no-problem gesture. But as he turned to go, he added, "I've already got your twenty-five signatures. Deadline's tomorrow. Let me know."

"I can't do it," I told Pablo that afternoon. Now that the weather was nice, we often walked home from school. Sometimes Alfie would pass us by on the bus and toot-toot some tune we'd try to make out.

Pablo had been talking about the elections coming up in his country . . . how his parents hoped the Liberation Party would win . . . how his brothers were running for local offices. I had stopped listening. Our Ralston election was all I could think of.

"Jake really doesn't get it," I told Pablo. "I just don't have it in me to get up in front of people and make speeches."

"Yes, you do," Pablo said quietly, like he knew.

"No way, José!" Only after I said it did I wonder if Pablo would think I didn't remember his name. But he seemed to know the expression and just kept smiling at me in an encouraging way.

I felt annoyed. I needed Pablo's support to stand up to all our friends. "How do you know what's in me or not?" I folded my arms, tucking in my hands to hide the irritated skin.

Pablo shrugged and held my gaze. He was probably one of the signatures on my list of twenty-five supporters.

"I mean, this is just a stupid high school election. I know Jake makes it sound like it's the beginning of changing the world . . ."

Pablo had this look in his eye like he agreed with Jake. "You are so fortunate in this country, Milly. You have always had freedom. You take it for granted."

I sighed at the lecture. "So why don't *you* run?" I confronted him.

"I am not sure I will be here next year, Milly."

I took that in. The sadness of Pablo leaving before I even knew what he meant to me—brother, friend . . . something else?

"Milly?" Pablo was trying to catch my eye. Something tender in his voice drew my gaze to him. It was the same look I'd seen in the graveyard. This time, when I tried to look away, I couldn't. "You have my vote," he said. Then, giving me a little bow, he added, "And I would like to offer my services as your guardbody."

"Bodyguard," I corrected. I could feel myself caving in.

"Bodyguard at your service." He spread his arms as if to shield me from adoring crowds.

I couldn't help but smile. "Okay, okay." I sighed. "I give up. I'll run. I'll change the world. I'll save the whales. I won't laugh at farmers with my mouth full."

Pablo let his arms drop. He looked puzzled. "Milly, all you are doing is running for senator, no?"

"Oh? Is that *all*?"

Pablo nodded sincerely. I guess sarcasm isn't always easy to get in another language.

Just then, as we were coming out the north side of the cemetery, Alfie went by on the bus. *Toot, toot, toot-toot-toot, toot toot,* he honked when he saw us. I swear I heard our campaign song, "You say you wanna start a Ralston-lution," in those honks.

The night of their country's national elections, we went over to the Bolívars. They had hooked up the old TV we had given them to the cable network so they could get the Spanish-language channels and keep up with news from their part of the world. Dad said that Mr. Bolívar had been a nervous wreck all day, hanging a door wrong side in, picking up a panel before the paint was dry. The future safety of his two sons as well as of his country was riding on the triumph of the Liberation Party. How could the poor guy think 'remodeled pantry' at a time like this?

Until tonight, I had put their elections out of my mind. Like everyone else at Ralston, I was caught up in our own elections. Incredible as it seemed at first, it now looked like the borderliners might stand a chance. Jake's enthusiasm was infectious. In a desperate move, Taylor and his pals were throwing a big dance with a DJ at his parents' lake house the Saturday before school elections. Everybody—except us—was invited.

The Bolívars' apartment was above the hardware store near the town green. Mom and Dad and Kate and I marched up the stairs with sodas, a bottle of wine, and a flan Mom had made using Señora Robles's foolproof recipe. Nate, who whined that he didn't understand the Bolívars' fast Spanish, had been dropped off for an overnight at a friend's house. A worried but gracious Mr. Bolívar met us at the door. We could hear the hyped-up voice of the Spanish newscaster behind him.

Mrs. Bolívar and Pablo were getting up from the couch as we walked in. The small living room seemed even smaller with so many of us trying to find a place to sit. Except for our hand-me-downs, the Bolívars hardly had any furniture. A small wooden crucifix hung on the wall at an odd level, probably where there had already been a nail. The whole scene was making me sad, the bare walls, the sparse furnishings, the Bolívars so apologetic and helpless. It reminded me of those TV specials about poverty in the Third World: some scrawny mother and her kids crouched in front of a tiny hut, looking frightened. I'd start thinking about my own birth family. Maybe they were starving, too? Maybe they were sleeping on a dirt floor with nothing but rags to wear? Soon I'd be feeling guilty, like I had deserted them instead of the other way around!

While the Bolívars talked with Mom and Dad in front of the TV, Kate and I sat with Pablo on cushions on the other side of the living room, which was kind of like his room.

"So what's going to happen if the Liberation Party doesn't win?" Kate asked.

Pablo sunk his head in his hands. I had never seen anyone our age do that.

Kate flashed me a panicked look. I could tell she felt really bad. "I mean, I'm sure everything will be all right."

Pablo shook his head, ignoring Kate's reassurances. "If the Partido de Liberación does not win, it will be *un baño de sangre*. What do you call it, a bath of blood?"

"Bloodbath," Kate offered in a small voice.

Mr. Bolívar had been cruising through the channels for any news of the elections. Suddenly, he hit on an English-speaking channel that was highlighting the country's elections. *"Vengan, vengan,"* he called us over to watch.

The anchorman was giving an overview of the history of the country. Stuff Mr. Barstow had gone over, but in a long-winded, textbookish way, hard to follow. But this was history in sound bites, easy to digest. The anchorman explained how the dictatorship had been put in place by the military, supported by CIA operatives and funds. Whatever that meant.

But about seventeen years ago, the people's movement had gotten started in the mountains, the anchor guy continued. The dictator tried to eliminate them. A state of terror reigned. There was some old, blurry footage of helicopters shooting into a village; a church in flames; bound men being shoved into trucks. My hands felt on fire. My heart raced. Maybe one of those guys was my birth father. But how would I even know it was him?

Finally, the movement got the attention and support of some U.S. senators. Their faces flashed on the screen behind the anchor guy. Let's hear it for senators! I thought. A bill was passed cutting off any further aid. Under pressure, the dictator agreed to hold free elections. The rebels came out of hiding to campaign. Support for their Liberation Party was overwhelming.

I swear I almost jumped up and cheered. I had gotten so caught up in the story of this struggle.

The anchorman now turned to a screen beside him for a live report. A leathery-looking reporter with a phony-sounding British accent was interviewing an official at election headquarters. The guy looked very uncomfortable.

"There seems to have been a huge turnout in support of the Liberation Party," the reporter observed. It wasn't really a question, but he stuck the microphone in front of the official.

"*Actualmente*, both parties have received many votes. We are showing the world that we have a *democracia* here."

"When shall we expect news of the winners?" the reporter wanted to know.

The official looked over his shoulder nervously. The camera took in a flank of generals in dark glasses standing behind him. "We, at headquarters . . . some returns have been lost . . . we must have a recount . . . a delay of several weeks."

Mrs. Bolívar lunged toward the television. "¡Criminal! ¡Mentiroso!" she screamed. She seemed to have forgotten she was sitting in an apartment in a small town in Vermont, not standing at the polling center in front of this official. But then, if she had been there, she probably would not have dared call him a lying criminal.

"Ya, ya, Angelita, cálmate," Mr. Bolívar was saying. But he didn't look all that calm himself.

The camera was now panning the tanks crawling down the streets of the capital. "We shall see if this nation is indeed ready for democracy," the reporter signed off.

Mom had put her arm around Mrs. Bolívar, who was crying quietly now. Mr. Bolívar had turned off the TV and was pacing up and down the room. Poor Dad was staring down at his work boots like they might tell him what to say.

"We must have faith," Mr. Bolívar finally spoke up. "For the sake of our sons, for the sake of our country. El paisito will liberate itself!"

Mrs. Bolívar glanced over at her husband, her face like that of a little girl just aching to believe some story she'd been told. But tears kept falling down her cheeks.

"Sí, Mamá," Pablo agreed, his voice barely a whisper. "Like Tía Dulce says, '*Milagros ocurren.*'"

I didn't know who Tía Dulce was, but maybe because Milagros was my original name, I felt like Pablo was talking directly to me. Miracles do happen, I told myself. All I had to do was look around me. I'd found a friend in the person I thought would ruin my life. After years of secrecy, I was opening up about my adoption. My impossible grandmother seemed to sort of in her own way be trying to apologize, and I was sort of in my own way trying to forget about her rejection. Pablo and his Tía Dulce were right. Miracles do happen. But sometimes, like that old needle in a haystack, you just had to find them.

The weekend before school elections, we drove down to Long Island on Happy's invitation. For the first time ever, we were going to be staying in her mansion—even though renovations were not finished.

All the way down, Dad kept bursting into song, "Over the river and through the woods, to Grandmother's house we go." You couldn't blame Dad for being in such a good mood. Grandma had apologized—something she'd never done in her life that Dad could remember. She'd told Dad and Mom, each on an extension, that all of us were her grandchildren. She loved every one of us the same. She had been wrongheaded and she was sorry. I guess Dad tried to blame it on Mr. Strong's bad advice, but Grandma took full blame. "Not at all, Davey. Eli Strong told me I was being a fool, and I should have listened to him."

I guess I should have felt good, too. But now, with everyone being so cheery, like we were some big ole happy family after all, my old feelings returned. I couldn't seem to forget that Happy's unconditional acceptance had been on second thought. All the ride down, I stared out the window at the sunny spring day outside. Mile by mile, the trees kept getting fuller and greener, the air warmer, the sky bluer. But gray, wintery clouds hung over my heart. I scratched and scratched at my hands.

I think Mom and Dad sensed I was still brooding, and that's why they started in on their Peace Corps stories. The happy beginnings of our family. *Your* family, I thought, your *blood* family. Any time now, we'd hear all about the orphanage, the baby in the basket, the memory box, Sister Corita with the seagull hat. Please, I thought. Somehow, today, I didn't want *them* talking about *my* adoption.

"It was love at first sight!" Dad was recalling the first time he met Mom. "I get there and this very foxy lady at the Aereopuerto Internacional is holding up this sign that reads CUERPO DE PAZ, and boy, did she have a *cuerpo* on her!"

"What's a *cuerpo?*" Nate wanted to know.

Mom and Dad and Kate burst out laughing.

"SOMEBODY TELL ME WHAT A *CUERPO* IS!"

Nate hollered, his bottom lip quivering. He hated to be left out.

Mom was in too good a mood to scold Nate for yelling in the car. "Honey, *cuerpo* means body. In Spanish, the Peace Corps is called Cuerpo de Paz, Body of Peace."

"But her *cuerpo* did not bring me any peace, no sir," Dad continued. "Day and night, that's all I could think about—"

"The Peace Corps might be going back soon," Mom cut in, her prim Mormon genes taking the upper hand. Right before we had left, the Bolívars had called. The generals had tried to stop the vote count, but the commission of international observers had threatened sanctions. Crowds were turning up everywhere in support of continuing the count. It looked like the Liberation Party would win by a landslide.

"Bolívar already told me that they'll probably be going down in August for several weeks," Dad explained. "Maybe I should take some of that time off, too. How about we all go up to Maine and see the ocean. What do you say, kids?"

"I want to go to Disney World," Nate pleaded. For his birthday last year, he'd gone with Happy, and he still talked about that trip in excruciating detail.

"Well, we'll have to take a vote," Dad said diplomatically. "Kate? Mil?"

Kate shrugged. "Whatever." She never got what she asked for anyway: a week of shopping in New York City with the cousins.

I usually went along with the group plan, so I don't know why I even said what I did. It's not like I had thought a whole lot about it. "I want to go with the Bolívars when they go down."

There was a sudden quietness in the car. Mom and Dad exchanged a glance, and then Mom turned around in her seat. "Honey, I can understand that you'd like to visit. But things are so unsettled there right now—" She stopped herself, her therapist training kicking in. "Maybe next summer we can all go for a visit?"

"That's a terrific idea!" Dad looked in the rearview mirror to check on my reaction.

I sat there like some naughty four-year-old, arms crossed, shaking my head no. "I want to go now. And I don't want to go with you guys. I want to go by myself."

"But why?" Dad's voice sounded hurt. "Honey, you're too young to travel by yourself to a foreign country."

"It's not a *foreign* country. It's my *native* country." I felt like a horrible, ungrateful daughter, but I couldn't stop myself. Until election night at the Bolívars' apartment, I hadn't ever thought a whole lot about the country. But now its struggle to be free seemed somehow personal to me. "And I wouldn't be going by myself," I persisted. "I'd be with the Bolívars. Mrs. Bolívar invited me." Months back, during one of our shopping trips, Mrs. Bolívar had mentioned that someday she would like to take me to the *mercados* in her native country. This hardly amounted to a real

109

invitation. But for some reason, right now it seemed like enough of one to me.

Kate, who'd been staring out her window throughout this discussion, suddenly turned to me, her face red and angry. "It's my native country, too, you know?"

I was about to get into it with her—a tug of war over whose native country it really was. But Kate's face was crumpling up. Horrible sobs were coming out of her mouth. I felt awful, like I'd thrown a rock at an apple on a tree and suddenly heard the crash of glass. What had I done to make my sister cry like this?

"I . . . I . . ." Kate could hardly talk. "I feel like you're giving us up as a family."

It was like hearing an echo from my own heart: Kate was afraid of abandonment, too! Before I knew it, I was crying, and then everyone in that car was sobbing, and here we were pulling into Happy's driveway, and Happy herself was coming down her front steps toward us, waving and smiling happily.

We put on a pretty good show of the happy family arriving at Grandma's. Later, Mom and Dad came into the bedroom Kate and I were sharing, and we all collapsed into a big, tearful family hug. "We understand, we understand," they kept saying, and I kept apologizing, "I'msorryI'msorryI'msorry," though I didn't really know for what. I still felt what I felt, only now I was determined not to show it.

At dinner, Happy sat me next to her as if to prove that I was no different from any of her other grandchildren. Except for Della, Grandma's housekeeper, serving us, the whole night could have been a repeat of Happy's birthday dinner. Aunt Joan, Uncle Stanley, and the cousins drove out from the city. Mr. Eli Strong was back. Knowing how he had stood up for me made me want to hug him. But shy as we both were, it would have been doubly embarrassing to do so. Instead, I complimented his cuff links, small, gold happy faces like those smiley yellow ones people stick on envelopes. Even that made him blush and stammer thanks.

That night, Kate joined the cousins next door for their usual marathon gossip session. Grandma had put us in three adjoining bedrooms, and Nate had his own pullout couch in the pool room—the place *is* a mansion. Anyhow, I bowed out. "I'm real beat, guys," I explained. Glances went around the room.

I lay in bed, unable to sleep, hearing the occasional laughter or dramatic rise and fall of voices through the wall. A while later, Kate came into our room. She sat on the edge of her bed in the dark, like she wanted to say something.

"What?" I asked.

"Nothing."

Brilliant, I thought. At least I had an excuse for not

being good at heart-to-heart stuff. I wasn't the *real* child of a therapist. "Kate," I said, sitting up in my bed. "Do you want to talk about it?"

I could see her faintly shaking her head. Then, after some more tense silence, she spoke up. "I just want to say one thing, Mil. We don't have a perfect family, okay? But it's not the worst, okay? So, please, please, please, think about what you're doing before you go and . . ."

"And what?" I challenged. "What is it you think I'm going to do, Kate?"

"I don't want to talk about it!" Kate sounded fierce and scared, both. "I don't know about you, but I would like to get some sleep tonight."

"Kate, I swear, nothing is going to come between us—"

"I said I didn't want to talk about it!" Her voice was so loud. A second later, there was a knock at our door. The cousins. "Everything okay in there?"

"We're fine," Kate called out. I'm sure the cousins were not convinced. But very unlike them, they didn't barge in. Maybe Kate had talked to them. Great, I thought. That made me feel even less like I belonged in this family.

I lay there, helpless and also angry. I wanted to tell Kate that she was the one creating the separation between us by refusing to even let me talk. But it's like what Pablo had told me his grandfather had said. Things of the heart, you couldn't rush them. Kate would come around when she was ready. I just hoped I would be ready then, too.

112

We tossed and turned. I don't think either of us slept a whole lot that night.

Sunday morning, while everyone lounged in the sunken living room, recuperating from one of Della's huge breakfasts, I slipped into the library to be by myself. I reached up for *To Kill a Mockingbird*—we had read it last fall in English class—and a whole panel of painted books popped out. I was snapping it back in place when I heard steps behind me.

"I've been wondering where you went to!" Happy was wearing a colorful robe she called a caftan. It made her look dressed up even though it was basically a long nightgown. She sat down in her red velvet Queen Something chair and patted for me to take the love seat in front of her.

I sat there, feeling awkward, not knowing where to look. When I finally did glance up, Grandma's eyes were looking straight at me.

"You have the most beautiful eyes. You know that, Milly? They don't hide anything. They show me how sad you are."

Don't you dare cry! I ordered those eyes. *Or I'll be really pissed at you!* "I'm okay, Grandma, really," I managed.

Happy let out a weary sigh. "No one in this damn family ever tells me the truth. But I'm going to tell you the truth, Milly. Your grandma can be a real bitch."

The shock of hearing her say so stopped whatever tears had been congregating at the corners of my eyes. Grandma! I almost laughed right out.

"I've made a lot of stupid mistakes," Grandma went on. "Just ask your father. He'll tell you." She paused as if looking back over a lifetime of mistakes. "You might not believe this, Milly, but we have a lot in common. I didn't really have parents. Poor Mother, losing all her family. She couldn't let herself feel, no less be somebody's mother. Father was always too busy. I had parents but I didn't have them. And everyone wondered why I never smiled!" She smiled now, a wise, sad smile. Then leaning forward, she took my hands in hers and whispered fiercely, "You're one of my babies, and that's all there is to it!"

I couldn't help it. Tears began running down my face.

Grandma dabbed at hers, then handed me her handkerchief. I didn't want to blow my snot into something with a monogram on it, so I just kept balling it up in my hand and sniffling. Happy went on to say that if I ever needed something, I was to call on her. Did I promise that I would?

I nodded, just so she'd know I'd forgiven her.

"Now go ahead and use that hanky, dear. You can't go out and face the world with a runny nose. Remember you're a Kaufman. No matter what comes our way, we meet it with style."

As we were leaving the room, Grandma pointed to the

114

shelves. "Daddy patented those, you know. Book panels. So much easier to keep clean."

The drive home late Sunday seemed twice as long as the drive down. None of us had gotten much sleep the night before. Kate and Nate dozed on and off. But I couldn't seem to nap. I kept thinking about Happy. Could it be that she really felt a lot like me?

I was also thinking about election day tomorrow at Ralston. All candidates had to give a speech at a class assembly first thing. Just a few words summing up why everyone should vote for us. Not only did I hate public speaking, but the only thing I could think of to say was *Pleasepleaseplease, don't vote for me.*

Not that anyone was going to vote for me. Despite what Jake had said, I couldn't believe that all those years of special tutoring wouldn't work against me. And though I really didn't want to win and be in student government— a whole year of public speaking, ugh!—still, the thought of losing in front of the whole school was too awful to think about.

Up front, Mom and Dad were reminiscing about the weekend. Could you believe Aunt Joan going on and on about Uncle Stanley's vasectomy? What about Happy giving Eli those cuff links with *happy* faces! Hmm. Maybe old Eli's been softening up Happy's hard edges! Back and forth,

Mom and Dad sifted the visit, looking for I don't know what.

Every once in a while, Mom would turn around and, seeing me awake, reach her hand out for me to take. Dad kept looking in the rearview mirror. His way of making sure I was okay, I guess.

The truth was, I was feeling better. About Grandma, anyhow. And Kate and I had sort of made up with a sleepy bear hug this morning. But it's funny how a heavy mood will lift, but because of it, you know something you didn't know before, like something the tide left behind. I really *did* want to go back to the country where I was born. To see if it would feel like the place where I belonged.

Mom switched on NPR for the evening news. A report on the elections was in progress. "We've won!" Mom cried out, turning up the volume. Kate stirred awake. Nate yelped that she had kicked him.

"Another big step for democracy," the newscaster was concluding. The dictator had left the country with his generals. The people were all out on the streets, celebrating. We could hear shouts and music in the background.

Mom, Dad, Kate, even grumpy Nate broke out cheering.

I slumped in the backseat, feeling a welter of relief and, surprisingly, sadness. Would *they* be celebrating—my birth parents? Now that they were free, would they be sorry that they had given up their baby? Or did being free include being free of *me*?

* * *

Black Monday. I couldn't remember what Mr. Barstow had said about it—some Monday in history when someone had gotten beheaded or an important battle had been lost. All I knew was that it was my Black Monday: voting day at Ralston High.

"You each get five minutes," Mr. Arnold, our principal, coached us. He held up five fingers like we were kindergarteners.

The ninth graders began filing into the auditorium. Our class seemed smaller today. I'd heard Mr. Arnold say something about an unprecedented number of absences. Maybe some kids had gotten caught bashing in mailboxes or tipping over cows this weekend.

When everyone was seated, Mr. Arnold gave a brief welcome, which lasted more than five minutes, then the candidates marched on stage to wait for our turn to talk.

I wish I could repeat what everyone said, but I was truly in a state of terror. I do remember Taylor and his pals looking a little hungover. Probably they'd gotten wasted at his party this past weekend. Maybe that's why there were so many empty seats out there. I remember Jake sounding like if you voted for him, he was going to save the planet, not just Ralston. A little while later, I remember Em going on and on and on, Mr. Arnold stage-whispering that her time was up, Em finally hearing him, getting all flustered, then spending another minute apologizing to our class before sitting back down.

Then it was my turn. I was in such a sweat that the backs of my legs were stuck to the seat of my chair. Great, I thought. Now I'll make a fart sound when I get up.

But there was no sound. In fact, I made it to the podium without fainting or tripping. I even managed to unfold my short speech, which was not much longer than two sentences if I took out all the thank-yous. But when I looked down, the words began swimming around that piece of paper. In a panic, I glanced up and my eyes found Pablo. He was beaming me his intense look as if he was drawing out some native courage I didn't quite believe I had. The NPR bulletin flashed in my head. His country was free! I had not had a chance yet to congratulate him.

"This is a special day for a member of our class," I began, my voice all trembly but audible. I told about the victory of democracy that very weekend in Pablo's country. The assembly broke out in cheers.

"It's also a very special day for my family," I continued when the clapping had died down. "You see, we have a close connection to Pablo's country. My parents met there in the Peace Corps. My sister, Kate, who some of you know, was born there. And I . . . I was . . . adopted there."

Em later told me that looking out at the audience was like seeing a choir singing on TV with the sound on mute. A sea of mouths dropped opened in an *oh!* of surprise. I wouldn't know. All I could see was Pablo looking back at me. I plowed on, my burning hands clutching the podium.

"I'm not telling you guys this to get your sympathy vote. I'm saying it because I feel lucky. Real lucky. It's no joke. A lot of people in the world don't ever get the chance to vote. I know, it's just a high school election. I've told myself that, too. But really we're practicing being free. So vote—even if it's not for me. We all win when we have a democracy."

Finally, my courage gave out. I felt like one of those cartoon characters running out past the cliff, looking down, and yikes, there's no ground beneath her! I turned, wondering how I'd ever navigate my way back to my seat. I remember finding my chair, Em putting her arm around me, Jake giving me his solidarity hand clasp. I remember the audience clapping. A while later, we came off stage and filed down the aisles as kids called out the names of their favorite candidates. Maybe my name was among them, I couldn't say. I was feeling numb, like I was tumbling down some rapids, carried by the current of whatever was going to happen next. It was an effort to keep my head above water.

Until I heard Pablo's voice. He was standing up in his row, waving and calling, "Milly, Milly." All around him my friends were taking up the chant. And suddenly, my Black Monday turned—like that song Alfie always sang to us—"a brighter shade of pale."

* * *

A kind of nervous excitement carried me through the rest of that day. But the following morning, I hid my head under my pillow. Oh my God! What had I done? Today I'd have to face the consequences of my big mouth.

One good thing about having blabbed my secret was that I was no longer worried about the elections. I'd been dreading the announcement of the winners over the public address system this morning. But now I had something else to worry about. Was I really ready to have everyone know I was adopted?

I was wondering which excuse might work for not going to school today—PMS or instant flu?—when I heard the phone ringing downstairs. Moments later, Mom brought up the cordless. "It's for you."

"*Hola, Milly.*" It was Pablo. Could I meet him at the entrance before school today?

I sat up in bed. "Something wrong?"

"Wrong? No, no, Milly," Pablo reassured me. "For me, it is very good. I hope for you, too."

"Give me a hint, please, Pablo," I pleaded. Take pity on me today, I thought.

"My parents are here with me, Milly. They say hello."

I caught on. Pablo couldn't talk freely. But what on earth did he have to say to me that was so urgent and couldn't be mentioned in front of the Bolívars? He had assured me it was good. And it was his promise and my curiosity that finally propelled me out of bed and into my Banana Republic top and best faded jeans. I put on a little lipstick, a little mascara, all the time pep-talking myself, *Go, Milly, go! Win or lose, you do it with style, girl!*

Pablo was waiting at the front door of the school, pacing back and forth, just like his father had the night of their national election. His face brightened when he saw me. He nodded toward the picnic table directly in sight of the front office. It was almost always unoccupied.

"I never congratulate you properly," Pablo began. It was true. Yesterday, I'd been swamped with well-wishers. Em kept saying, "You should have run for VP, Mil. You would have won."

"Your speech was beautiful, Milly," Pablo went on. "I told Mamá and Papá. They are so proud that you are from our country." He said loads of people had come up to him afterward. Mr. Arnold had even mentioned organizing a group from Ralston to go down next year on a service trip. "This is all because of you, Milly," Pablo added.

It wasn't that I minded hearing praise, but the national anthem was going to play soon. "Did you have something urgent to talk to me about, Pablo?"

Pablo nodded. "Your mother, she called my mother last night about the invitation."

"Invitation?"

"To accompany us this summer for our trip home."

I had totally forgotten that I'd invited myself on their trip! I hid my face in my hands, too mortified to worry about the ugly rash spreading on my skin.

"No, no, Milly, don't be that way," Pablo protested, pulling my hands away. "I told you it is good. My mother, she asked me if I asked you. I told my mother, yes, of course, I invited you."

I looked up at Pablo's face in shock. He was grinning, but when I kept sitting there with my mouth open, his smile faded. "I hope you accept my invitation? You will come, no? Mamá and Papá say you are very welcome."

"Hey, Pablo, Milly, get in here, you two!" It was Mr. Arnold hollering out the window. "The anthem played five minutes ago. You don't want a late pass your first day as class senator, do you?"

I felt like those newborns on TV when they get slapped on the butt. Right before they burst out bawling, they always look so shocked, kind of surprised at the air rushing into their lungs. Well, I was shocked by all this unexpected news. I was truly surprised my legs could carry me across the lawn to the front doors. And sure, I wanted to bawl. But I didn't have a tissue, and I was wearing mascara, and I didn't want to end up with raccoon eyes and a snotty nose in front of my class. I kept remembering what Grandma had said about the Kaufmans, "Whatever comes our way, we meet it with style." Especially winning, I thought.

Part Two

6

El Paisito

"THERE IT IS!" Pablo was pointing down.

I leaned over to look out his window. The clouds had parted. Below lay mountains upon mountains of green jungle—just like Mom and Dad had described. But I kept searching for something *more*. I don't know what I was expecting—a tiny mom and dad outside a little *casita* waving up at me?

You'd think the Bolívars had just sighted Treasure Island. "*¡El paisito, el paisito!*" they started crying.

Mr. Bolívar motioned toward the ground. "*¿Qué piensas, Milly?*" What did I think? "Beautiful country, no?"

I nodded and smiled.

I was already feeling homesick.

125

*   *   *

Not that the home I had left behind that morning was a warm, inviting nest to think about. Everyone had been so upset with me—except Mom. She had wanted to come to the airport, but the car was going to be too crowded with Dad, me, the Bolívars, and all the luggage. Mom offered to drive on her own if I wanted her along, but I knew it'd just make it harder when the time came to say goodbye in front of everybody.

After her initial shock, Mom had been super supportive. "I think you should go," she kept encouraging me. "It's obviously the right time. I just thought it would happen when you were a little older. And that maybe I could hold your hand through it."

"Oh, Mom!" I wailed. "It's not like I'm going to get tortured!" It did cross my mind that not too long ago, people were getting tortured there.

"I know, I know," Mom said, hugging me. It seemed like every chance she got these days, Mom was throwing her arms around me. "However you have to do it, honey. I trust your judgment." The one thing she insisted on was that we tell the Bolívars about my adoption. It was too big a secret to keep from them.

"Mom, they already know." I explained about my speech at school, how Pablo had reported it to his parents. How just this last Saturday when I'd gone to the mall with Mrs.

126

Bolívar to help her buy gifts to take to her family back home, she had said how proud she was that I was from her country. What I didn't tell Mom was what Mrs. Bolívar had said about my eyes. How they were like the eyes of her sister-in-law, whose name I'd heard before, Dulce, the widow of Mr. Bolívar's murdered brother, Daniel. Dulce came from Los Luceros, the place Pablo had also mentioned. Hearing all this, Mom might think that I was trying to track down my birth family. And really and truly, I thought of this trip as a chance to get acquainted with the country where I accidentally happened to be born. That was all. Anything more than that would have been scary to think about.

By the time I had finished telling Mom about my speech, she was shaking her head. "The truth is, you've been doing a lot of growing up, Milly. I'm really proud of you." She hugged me then, too.

Not everyone in the family was so understanding. At first, Dad wouldn't even hear about my going on this trip. He was worried about my safety, he said. Every few weeks, he'd call the State Department to find out if it was okay to travel to a country that had only recently been liberated. They kept reassuring him that the U.S. embassy was open for business, that the new government had won in a clean sweep, that its human rights record in the last three months was impeccable. In fact, the new administration's Truth Commission was holding trials to investigate and punish all past abuses.

Once he had to admit safety would not be a problem, Dad started in on the cost of the ticket. We couldn't afford it, he argued. We had to be saving for college tuitions.

"What if I pay for the ticket myself?" I challenged, folding my arms in front of me.

"Where are you going to get seven hundred dollars?" Dad challenged back, folding his arms. Sometimes, at least with our gestures, we did all act like family.

"I have people I can ask," I said vaguely. "So will you let me go if I pay for it?"

Dad was in a bind. "I guess . . . well . . . your mother might not . . ." He glanced over at Mom, a desperate look in his eyes.

Mom stood by me, arms folded, waiting for Dad to complete his sentence.

Dad threw his hands in the air. He turned and headed down to his basement workroom, too upset to think up another pretext. I almost ran after him, ready to give up on my trip. It wasn't worth this much grief. But Mom held me back. "Dad'll be all right," she reassured me. "Remember, he had to disappoint Happy in order to grow up, too. He'll understand."

Days went by and Dad did not seem any closer to understanding my choice. Finally, Mom had a talk with him— one of those talks where they shut the bedroom door—and first it's like an overloaded washing machine in there, thundery, off-balance sounds. Then soft, persuasive sounds (rinse cycle), and finally, kissing sounds like a light breeze blowing on the laundry!

Not that Dad came right out and said yes, Milly, you can go on this trip with my blessing. He just suddenly shifted into talking about the best kind of backpacks for traveling. How I needed a money belt for walking around in the capital. What medicines I should take in case I got dysentery, malaria, typhoid fever . . . What about AIDS, Dad? I almost asked. But I knew that would totally freak him out.

Then there was Nate. For weeks, my little brother followed me around the house, pulling at me to please stay, not to go away. Kate, meanwhile, just would not talk about my trip. The morning of my departure, she refused to come out of her room to say goodbye. Okay, it was six in the morning, but still. Later, I did find a note tucked inside my bag: "YOU BETTER COME BACK OR I'LL KILL YOU!!!" Kate signed off with a smiley face—well, the smile was more like a straight line, and instead of her name, she'd written "YOUR BIG SISTER FOR LIFE."

At the airport, Dad chatted with the Bolívars, but when it came time for us to say goodbye, he clammed up. Great, I thought, a parent with stage fright during a major scene in my life.

As I went through security beyond the point where Dad could go, I felt a pang. Maybe my family would never take me back again? I turned, ready to run and ask to return home, but when I looked to see where he was, Dad was gone.

We had about two and a half hours in the waiting area. Mrs. Bolívar had insisted on being at the airport way ahead of time. Like we were going on a safari to hunt an airplane, not just board it. "It is the custom in our country," she explained.

"The custom of nervous people in our country," Pablo teased.

We sat around, Mrs. Bolívar digging stuff out of her purse, worried that I had not eaten breakfast. *"¿Un choco-latico? ¿Una mentica?"* A little chocolate? A little mint?

"No gracias," I kept refusing. My stomach was having a nervous breakdown. I hadn't skipped breakfast for nothing.

"Ya, ya, Mamá." Pablo came to my rescue. "Milly is going to change her mind about coming with us." Pablo knew how exasperating his mother could be. But I had to admire how patient he always seemed to be with her.

"Remember we won't be eating until we get to *el paisito,*" his mother reminded him.

El paisito. I had been reading up on it in the Lonely Planet travel book Dad had bought me for the trip. In the full-page map in front, *el paisito* had a sprawling amoeba shape, as if it were breaking out of the ruler-straight borders drawn by some king in Europe. And really, the "little country" didn't look all that little. But then, it wasn't just *el paisito* that Mrs. Bolívar called "little." Lots of things were little: a little trip, a little meal. Señora Robles had once explained that people added this ending to words in Spanish to show affection.

"*¡Tus manos!*" Mrs. Bolívar exclaimed. She had caught sight of my hands. For months, I had tried to hide them from Pablo. Now he, too, was staring down at them. "*¡Pobrecitas!*" Poor little things.

"It's just an allergy," I managed, my face as red as my hands.

The truth is they looked pretty bad. With all the commotion of the last few weeks, my rash had gotten worse. Mom had taken me to a new dermatologist in town where I had to fill out a medical form. Was there any history of skin diseases or allergies in my family? I passed the clipboard over to Mom, who read it, sighed, and put her arm around me. She understood.

"I get the same malady in this country," Mrs. Bolívar explained in Spanish, showing me her chapped hands. She dug around in her purse and pulled out a tin. I half expected it to be Burt's Bees hand salve that Em had converted me to using. But no, this was a greenish ointment, the last of some potion she had brought with her from home. "This *yerbabuena* will take away the itch. Shall we put some on?" The lid was off and her fingers delving inside before I could say yes or no.

"Mamá," Pablo reminded his mother.

"It's okay," I assured him.

As Mrs. Bolívar worked on my hands, I couldn't help thinking of Dad and his calamine lotion. *Dad . . . Mom . . . Kate . . . Nate. . . .* I felt homesick all over again. One last call home in case the plane crashes, I promised myself.

A little later when I tried, our line kept being busy. I couldn't call Em, as she was away at a special leadership camp sponsored by the governor for members of student governments. I'd actually been invited, too, but I had already planned this trip. I had promised Em that I'd send tons of postcards and bring her back some live contraband: a gorgeous Latin hunk in my suitcase, provided I could get him through security!

The only other person I could think of to call was Happy. (555-Hi Happy, easy to remember, Nate's trick.) Surprisingly, early as it was, Grandma answered. "Milly, darling! I've been thinking about you. Isn't it today you leave?"

"I'm at the airport. I made it through security."

"Good for you!" she congratulated me, like I had cause to worry.

"Grandma, thanks so much for paying for me to do this." When Dad had tried using the price of the ticket as a reason for me not to go with the Bolívars, I had called Grandma with that favor she'd said I could ask her.

"Don't you mention it. You feeling a little nervous, honey?"

"Nah," I bluffed, then remembering how Grandma said nobody in our family ever told her the truth, I added, "Just that Kate wouldn't even say goodbye. And Nate had a tantrum at the door."

"Don't you worry about them. They'll be just fine. I've invited Kate to come down and go shopping with me in the city. Roger's picking up Nate when Scout camp ends on Friday, and we'll all go to a Yankees game."

Suddenly, being with Happy on Long Island sounded like a lot more fun than being some place where people were still recovering from a dictatorship.

But this had all been my choice. Grandma had even offered to buy tickets for everyone in the family to go with me. But I hadn't been sure I wanted them along. Mom had suggested that I play it by ear, see how I felt, and once I was there, if I decided, just call and the family would join me. Grandma's offer was still open. "And I've cleared the decks. I'm free all August, and Dad was going to take two weeks off anyway."

Standing there at that pay phone, I was so tempted to tell Happy to go ahead and buy their tickets now. But I knew if they came down, the whole thing would turn into a family trip. Mom would hover. Dad would be a safety freak. Nate would whine that he didn't understand people's fast

Spanish. And Kate would be competing over *our* native country. No, I really didn't want them along. I wanted this to be my journey, my country, my story—before they became ours.

After the excitement of sighting land had died down, Pablo noticed my silence.

"Are you preoccupied, Milly?" Pablo wanted to know.

I nodded. "Not because of what I'll find there," I went on to explain. Well, maybe some of it was that. "But what I left behind. Some members of my family, I guess they're having a hard time with my going on this trip." I hadn't wanted Pablo or his parents to feel bad, so I hadn't mentioned anything, until now. "It's like they're afraid the truth is going to break up our family."

"The truth, *la verdad*." Pablo repeated the word slowly, as if he were trying to understand its meaning in English, and then failing that, in Spanish. "In *el paisito*, we have now the Truth Commission to bring to justice the guilty ones who helped the dictatorship. Some say let us forget the past and build the future. Others say we cannot build the future if we do not know the past." It was strange that now that we were on this trip where I was supposedly going to practice my Spanish full-time, Pablo was always speaking in English. "*Para no olvidarlo*," he had explained. So as not to forget it.

"I think the truth is the most important of all," I said, jumping right in.

Pablo looked thoughtful. "I believe in the truth, too, Milly. But I had an uncle. I loved my uncle. I was a very good uncle. But he was also a general. Maybe he was not so good a person when he was a general. I would never want to punish the good uncle. But what to do about the cruel general?"

I felt totally confused. Maybe the truth was more than I wanted to know, too? What if my birth father turned out to be some horrible general like the military guys I had seen on TV in their dark glasses? Maybe I'd inherited his genes and that's why I was hurting my family out of my own selfishness? "So, what about your uncle?"

Pablo glanced out the window at the cloud bank we were entering. The cabin darkened. "My uncle is dead," he murmured. "He punished the bad general himself. He shot himself a few weeks after the dictator left."

"Oh, Pablo, I'm sorry. I didn't know." I had never heard the Bolívars mention this relative. Maybe they were ashamed of him? The one they often talked about was Mr. Bolívar's brother, Daniel, the journalist who had worked for a newspaper that published articles against the dictatorship. One night, about a month after the Bolívars had left the country, Daniel disappeared. Days later, his body was found in a ditch with those of other journalists from the same paper. Daniel's widow, Dulce, and daughter, Esperanza, were now living in the Bolívars' house with Camilo and Enriquillo, Pablo's brothers. Suddenly, it struck me that this was probably a bad time to be visiting a family grieving so many deaths.

"It is a happy time as well as a sad time in our history," Pablo reassured me, as if reading my thoughts. "Our nation is a cradle and a grave."

Our nation, he called it. It didn't feel like mine. My country was the U.S. I felt a wave of homesickness. Dad and Mom had tried to spare me. I pictured them sitting in our kitchen in Vermont, holding hands, wondering if I would be okay. Looking down at my own hands, I realized that they had not itched since Mrs. Bolívar had put her potion on them. But they were still red.

The minute we entered the terminal, we were swallowed in a crowd. This was the first time that I'd ever been around so many people from my birth country. I could not stop staring.

The guidebook was right: this sure was a country of mixtures—brown people with straight brown hair, white people with jet-black hair and high cheekbones, black people with Asian eyes. A white woman carrying a brown baby stood by a black man who was holding the hand of a pale boy with kinky hair. Talk about melded families! I wondered about my own family. What did they all look like? I kept glancing around, hoping to find someone who looked like me.

My head was spinning. A couple of times, I got separated from the Bolívars in the crowd pressing toward the open booths in the Immigration area. People here didn't seem to be able to make lines.

One thing that spooked me was all the soldiers hanging around in camouflage with machine guns. Maybe because there'd been a dictatorship here, I kept thinking that a revolution was going to break out. But Pablo explained that the soldiers were here to monitor passengers who might be on the Truth Commission list and trying to sneak into the country.

"I don't get it. Wouldn't they be trying to sneak out?"

"That, too. But many times they come back to start trouble."

Finally, it was our turn at the Immigration booth. The young official was eager to try out his little English. "Where did you receive those beautiful eyes? You look like a girl from Los Luceros." Pablo and I exchanged a glance. "That is where the most beautiful women come from," the guy added, winking at me.

"You have to be careful," Pablo coached me when we had gone through the line. "Men from this country will always flirt with a pretty girl."

So Pablo thought I was pretty! I had never noticed *him* being flirtatious with me. Back at Ralston, he hadn't seemed interested in anything as frivolous as flirting. Every once in a while, there'd be that look, or he'd cut loose but then pull back, as if jolted by some memory.

We had to wait forever for our luggage—actually, I waited by the carousel while the Bolívars stood by the exit, peeking out whenever the doors swung open. Suddenly, they began waving wildly. They had spotted their family in the lobby.

An officer approached them. I thought he was going to tell them to move away from the doors. But it looked like he had recognized the Bolívars. They threw their arms around each other, embracing. Then the officer went out the exit doors and came back with his arms around two guys. Mrs. Bolívar rushed toward them. "Camilo! Riqui! ¡Mis hijos! ¡Mis hijos!" she called out. Her sons! Her sons! People turned around to watch. Soon, all the Bolívars were hugging and crying.

The suitcases started arriving. The Bolívars' bags were easy to tell apart, huge and overpacked and tied with red ribbons—the color of the Liberation Party. This was so they wouldn't get confused with somebody else's, Mrs. Bolívar had explained. As I reached to lift them off the belt, a bunch of guys rushed forward to help. Wow! If Em could see me now!

Mrs. Bolívar must have spotted all these guys around me. She hurried over, the rest of her family behind her. The introductions began. It was just like the families I'd seen inside the Immigration area. The officer, who turned out to be a cousin, was dark-skinned with slanted eyes. He had been in the Movement with the Bolívar brothers and was now a supervisor in Customs. Then there was the middle brother, Camilo, tall and thin with pale brown skin like Pablo's but instead of Pablo's straight hair, Camilo had a kinky Afro. Riqui, short for Enriquillo, the oldest brother, was very dark and short like Mr. Bolívar, with straight black hair and dimples like Pablo's, though his showed more in his chubby cheeks every time he smiled—and boy, did he ever do that a lot!

It surprised me: how tubby and jokey he was. I guess for months I'd had this torture-prison image of him as all skin and bones with ugly scars that made you wince just thinking about how he had gotten them. But Riqui kept making jokes, teasing Mrs. Bolívar on how *buenamoza* she looked in her American pantsuit. So good-looking! Papá better watch out or those gringos would steal her away!

"Milly, *¡qué placer!*" he said, throwing his arms around me like a long-lost brother. "What a pleasure! Thank you for being a family to my *familia.*" I felt embarrassed, thinking about how I had rejected Pablo at first.

Once our bags were piled on several carts, the cousin led us to the exit marked NOTHING TO DECLARE. No inspection was necessary for the family of two Liberation heroes!

"What about me?" I asked Pablo. I didn't want to get in trouble because I hadn't done what I was supposed to do as an American.

"You are our family," Pablo said, putting his arm around me. I told myself he was just imitating his older brother, but I could feel myself blushing. Since we'd landed, Pablo seemed so much more relaxed and happy.

"But if you want to declare something, Milly?" Pablo teased, pointing toward the long lines under a big sign that read, ALGO QUE DECLARAR: SOMETHING TO DECLARE.

"What does a beautiful girl like her have to declare? We are the ones who have to declare to her." Riqui put his hand over his heart and sighed like some corny, old-time actor. I could see that I was in for some teasing in the next two weeks.

"My brother lost the little knowledge he had about women in prison," Camilo noted dryly. His face was so long and serious that at first I couldn't tell he was joking. "All women have secrets, Riqui," he lectured his older brother.

Pablo looked at me pointedly as if he knew my secret— that this was mi paisito, my little country, as well.

But that was not the secret packed away in my heart. I was determined not to declare it, even to myself. Enough things going on already on this trip! The secret of Pablo. Friend, brother, or . . . something else?

* * *

Outside in the lobby, even more relatives were waiting to greet the Bolívars. Aunts and uncles and cousins, as well as Pablo's *tía-madrina* and Mrs. Bolívar's *comadre*—relatives we don't really have names for in English. Only Dulce had stayed home, preparing the food, everybody explained.

Seeing them all together, I felt that familiar pang of not belonging. I stood apart, with the bags on the curb, wishing I could crawl inside one of them. But Pablo spotted me and hurried over. "Ven, ven, Milly," he insisted, pulling me into the circle of his *familia*.

People kept taking my face in their hands. My eyes were so much like Dulce's!

"*¿De dónde viene tu familia?*" they wanted to know. Where did my family come from?

What to say? Thank God, everyone was talking at once so my not answering went unnoticed. It was just like a Kaufman get-together!

A girl about my age approached Pablo. She was pale and looked so sad, dressed all in black. The minute he saw her, Pablo put his arms around her, closing his eyes as if with deep feeling. She clung to him, her head buried in his chest. It was like a *Romeo and Juliet* scene, I swear. I felt a pang of jealousy. I remembered what Meredith had told Em about Pablo probably having a girlfriend back home. True, he had never mentioned one to me. And knowing what awful stuff was happening to his brothers and family, I had never asked him a whole lot of questions about the life he'd left behind.

141

Finally, Pablo and this girl came apart. That's when she turned to me, and I noticed her eyes. They looked just like mine: light yellow with brown flecks! No wonder Pablo had been so mesmerized by mine. They had reminded him of his girlfriend's eyes.

Pablo introduced the girl. Aunt Dulce's daughter.

His cousin who had suffered so much! "Hi," I managed, my voice as small as I felt.

"*Bienvenida,*" she welcomed me. "My name is Esperanza," she added in English as if she wasn't sure I could understand Spanish. "It means hope."

"*Soy* Milly," I introduced myself. For a moment, I wondered how it might feel to say, "I'm Milagros. It means miracles."

Esperanza looked surprised to hear me speaking in Spanish. "*¿Hablas español?*"

"*Un poquito.*" Just the little bit between the two fingers I was holding up.

Pablo was shaking his head. "Milly speaks very good Spanish." I couldn't help thinking about our first meeting in February. At least now I was admitting to speaking some Spanish.

The reunion at the airport might have gone on for another hour, but Dulce was waiting at home with our welcome dinner. She was cooking *puerco asado*, Esperanza told me, the roast pork people always made for special celebrations in this country. My mostly vegetarian diet was going to have a hard time in the next two weeks. Mom had already warned me. "Don't ever refuse a dish. People take it as a personal insult. Unless you say you're allergic to something, you better eat it and ask for seconds."

Maybe I could be allergic to meat for the next two weeks? Thinking about allergies, I looked down at my hands. They had really calmed down! Mrs. Bolívar was right. My body knew it was back in the little country it had come from.

But the rest of me was still in a daze.

Driving in from the airport, I had this sense of being suspended in the air. Like I hadn't yet landed on the ground anywhere.

So much was happening at once, so many new people, names, and relationships to take in; so many conversations going on, most of them in a fast-moving Spanish that— I had to agree with Nate—wasn't always easy to follow. Everything was so different: the light, the heat, the sounds, the earthy smells wafting in through the open windows, like being near the compost bin in the garden in Vermont in the middle of the summer. Again I felt a wave of missing home.

As we drove to their house, the Bolívar brothers were giving me a crash tour of the capital. Esperanza, Pablo, and I were in back—I was at one of the windows so I could see the sights. We, the young people, had been purposely put together by the older Bolívars, who had gone directly home in another car.

We passed the main plaza with the statue of the father of the country, Somebody Estrella. I recognized his face— the man on the coin that was in my box! Over there, Riqui pointed out, was the national cathedral, right beside the fort where the colonists had fought for their freedom from Spain. Could I see the eternal flame to liberty just inside the entryway?

"Eternal since yesterday," Camilo commented dryly.

The National Theater, the Palace of Justice, the Congress . . . (I don't know why people think monuments are the best way to show you their country.) Riqui even drove out of our way so I could see the Presidential Palace, which I guess had once been white and was now a creepy blood-red.

"The people, they went crazy with joy when the dictator left," Riqui explained. "They wanted *el palacio* to be the color of the Liberation Party. The people don't say they painted it; they say they liberated it."

I felt I had to say something, so I said, "Well, you can't miss it."

What crowds! Not just cars but mules and carts, bicycles and motorcycles and people jammed the narrow streets. The sidewalks were blocked with chairs and stands and small tables with big boom boxes blaring salsa and American

144

rock music. People were hanging out like this was a block party, except it went on, block after block after block. "Before the liberation, people were afraid to gather together," Riqui explained. "It was against the law. Now they have their freedom."

"Freedom from one tyranny," Camilo added. He seemed a lot less gushy in his enthusiasm. "The tyranny of poverty is still with us."

I could see what he meant. Poor people were everywhere. I mean, it wasn't like we didn't have poverty in the States, but here it was right in your face. At red lights, beggars crowded around the car. Little kids in rags threw wet sponges at the windshields, hoping to earn some money wiping them clean. Every time they did so, Riqui yelled at them for messing up his car.

I guess revolutionaries have tempers, too, I thought.

A man with no arms was wheeled up to my back window by a young boy. The man wore a Yankees baseball cap and a ragged T-shirt with the sleeves sewn up. His face was all scarred, like maybe he'd been burned or something. I rummaged through my backpack, but I hadn't changed any money, and the smallest I had was a twenty. "Here," Camilo said, handing me a large, colorful bill that didn't look like real money. "I'll pay you back," I said stupidly. I didn't even know how much money it was.

As I was rolling down my window, I panicked. The man didn't have arms. How was I supposed to hand him the money? Before I could think what to do, the boy had put the bill of the man's baseball cap in his mouth. As soon as I dropped the money in, the man wiggled his lips in a way that flipped the cap back on his head, like he was a monkey performing a trick. He grinned, then showered me with blessings, *"Dios la bendiga."*

God bless *you*, I thought, rolling up my window slowly, hoping to give the moisture in my eyes a chance to dry. It wasn't exactly tears. Just that burning you get when you see some wrong you can't put right.

Pablo spoke up beside me. "It is the sad reality of our little *paisito*, Milly." The look on his face said he, too, felt pained by the poverty around us.

"It's just that I'm not used to it," I explained.

From the front seat, Camilo sighed. "Don't ever get used to it, Milly. Or the dream dies."

We were quiet the rest of the ride.

"Where have you been?" Mrs. Bolívar scolded as we walked into the house. "Dulce has been waiting to serve." Everyone had been sitting at the table in the open courtyard for the last half hour.

"So nice to see you being your old self, Mamá!" Riqui humored her. "We were just showing Milly our beautiful capital."

That stopped Mrs. Bolívar's scolding. How could she be

upset with her sons when they were just being polite to her guest?

A woman came rushing from the kitchen. She gave out a cry of joy when she spotted Pablo. "Tía Dulce—" Pablo managed to get out before she had him in a killer hug. She was an older version of Esperanza, pale and slender, with *our* same eyes, as I now thought of them. Like her daughter, she was dressed completely in black, but somehow the black seemed blacker on her, maybe because of the contrast with her white apron. A silver cross hung around her neck. I remembered Pablo saying that Tía Dulce was very religious.

"Pablito, Pablito!" she sobbed, holding him at arm's length to make sure it was him. She could not seem to stop.

"*Ya, ya, Tía Dulce,*" Riqui said, patting his stomach. "We're dying of hunger. Where's that wonderful *puerco asado* we were promised?"

Hungry people! That did it! Tía Dulce turned on her heels and disappeared to the kitchen to get *la comidita*, the little meal, on the table.

Little meal?! It was a feast! I couldn't wait to tell Mom about all the different dishes—some were ones Mom herself cooked from her Peace Corps days—or at least talked about, bemoaning the fact that she couldn't get ingredients like plantains in Vermont. I piled my plate so high, I didn't think anyone noticed that I hadn't served myself pork. "Save room for dessert," Dulce kept warning us, but she was the first to urge seconds and thirds the minute a plate was half full.

The platters kept making their rounds back to me. Everyone seemed especially concerned that I not starve while I was in their country.

"¡Ya! Dejen a la pobre Milly tranquila." Pablo was trying to protect me from the full onslaught of his family's hospitality. Let poor Milly be. But it was impossible to stop them.

When the dinner dishes had been cleared away, Esperanza brought out the dessert: a cake with an odd, lopsided shape, like a little kid had put it together. I was wondering whose birthday it was when everyone burst out singing the national anthem. That was when I realized the cake was a replica of the country. We were celebrating its liberation. One lone candle blazed in the center.

Even after the singing stopped, no one seemed to want to step forward and blow it out. We watched it burn almost down to the frosting. Finally, Mr. Bolívar reached over and pinched it out between his thumb and forefinger. Everyone hugged and cried, remembering the absent ones.

I felt sad, especially for Dulce. At one point, she slipped out to the kitchen—to get a knife to cut the cake, she said. When she came back a little while later, her hair was wet at the hairline, like she had washed her face after having a good cry all by herself.

Servings of cake went round and round and round the table. Everyone was too stuffed to eat another bite.

148

Mrs. Bolívar was full of apologies for the bad eaters. After Dulce had gone to so much trouble!

"It will not go to waste, don't worry," Dulce reassured her. "I will send it to *las monjitas* for the children. Maybe later the boys can drive it over."

Las monjitas . . . The little nuns, the children . . . It was summer, so it couldn't be a school. An orphanage? I glanced at Pablo, who nodded as if to confirm what I was thinking.

I looked around the open courtyard like someone just waking up in a strange place, trying to figure out where on earth she is. A vine of bright red flowers tumbled down from a trellis, the blossoms as big as my dinner plate. Teensy iridescent hummingbirds plunged their bills inside the petals. A lone parrot sat on its perch, shifting from foot to foot, watching us. His beak opened as if he were about to say something, but then closed like he thought better of it. Brown and white faces surrounded me, some strange, some familiar. The daze I'd been in since leaving home finally lifted. I was really here!

It was hours since the Bolívars had arrived at their *paisito*. But it was only now that I landed in my little country, too.

7

A Cradle and a Grave

WE ACTUALLY DIDN'T MAKE it to the orphanage that same day. The visitors hung around into the evening, when appetites started waking up again. Dinner was a serving of Dulce's cake and a sweet tea made from *yerbabuena* leaves.

"This will help you sleep your first night, Milly," Mrs. Bolívar recommended.

"Isn't *yerbabuena* what you put on my hands at the airport?"

"Why do you think it is called 'the good grass'?" Mrs. Bolívar boasted. "When we go back, I will take as much as I can carry."

Dulce, who had just finished wrapping the leftover

150

cake, sat down heavily in her chair. "You are going *back*, Angelita?"

Mrs. Bolívar looked uncomfortable. She stared down into her steaming cup as if it might tell her what to say. "Antonio thinks it's best for Pablo's education," she murmured. I knew the stay in the States was the hardest on Mrs. Bolívar. Though she loved working for her little *viejita* Miss Billings, Mrs. Bolívar was often homesick. She complained of the cold. Her skin was always irritated. But *sacrificio* had always been her lot in life, she had told me. Unlike Mr. Bolívar, whose family had lived comfortably on their own land in the mountains, Mrs. Bolívar's family had been poor. *"Pobre, pobre,"* Mrs. Bolívar said, repeating the word as if to double the strength of its meaning. "This is just for a few years, Dulce," Mrs. Bolívar added, "until Pablito is graduated."

"So many absences." Dulce sighed, wiping her eyes with a corner of her apron. "Perhaps then . . . if you are not returning, I will move back to Los Luceros with Esperanza."

"Ay, no, *Mamá*," Esperanza wailed.

"We will see." Dulce made the sign of the cross and then kissed the crucifix around her neck. "Nothing has to be decided tonight."

Later, as I was getting ready for bed in the room I was sharing with Dulce and Esperanza, Dulce prayed out loud. "Our Lord, enlighten us so that we may see and accept Your divine will, amen." She sunk her head in her hands.

Esperanza was kneeling opposite her mother, facing me. I didn't know if, as a good guest, I was supposed to join them, too, but it seemed hypocritical since I wasn't in the habit of praying on my knees. When her mom asked the Lord to guide her, Esperanza looked over at me and rolled her eyes heavenward.

I bowed my head, struggling to suppress the giggles I knew would burst out if Esperanza and I looked at each other again.

The next morning, Dulce shooed me out of the kitchen. No way she was going to let me help with breakfast. "*¡Esta es tu casa!*" she scolded sweetly. I hated to tell her, but back at my house I was expected to help with meals!

I wandered into the courtyard where we'd gathered for dinner yesterday. At the far end, I caught sight of Pablo, his back to me. He was barefoot, dressed in jeans and a rumpled T-shirt that looked like he'd slept in it. He was gazing around slowly, taking it all in. I stood still, not wanting to intrude upon this private moment of homecoming.

He must have sensed my presence, because he turned abruptly. His face broke into a smile when he saw me.

"Must be nice to be home," I said, joining him.

"We have lived in this house since I was born," he explained. "Everything brings a memory—that stump from the old mango tree, the big ceiba over there. This bush was

152

planted the day my parents married." He snapped off a stem and offered it to me to smell. Two teensy red flowers grew from the same stem.

"And you, Milly?" Pablo wondered. "When you see things here, do they seem at all . . . familiar?"

I shook my head. How could I expect to remember things from when I was a baby? But *not* remembering felt like a kind of failure. "That orphanage your aunt mentioned yesterday. You think we could go see it?" I hesitated even as I said it. Our discussion on the plane had made me wary of the truth.

"I myself will remind Tía Dulce," Pablo promised. His eyes lingered on my face. "I hope you are liking it here, Milly?"

I wasn't sure yet what I was feeling. One moment I felt totally at home. Another, I felt totally out of it. In some ways, nothing much had changed!

"I really like your family," I offered. "Your brothers are so funny."

Pablo laughed, as if recalling the scene I'd overheard last night. His brothers had been teasing him about the *novia* he had brought back from the States. *Novia,* I remembered from Señora Robles, meant both girlfriend and bride in Spanish. "I have nothing to declare!" Pablo had shot back, laughing.

"They like *you* very much, Milly," Pablo was saying now. "Everybody does."

Everybody? Suddenly, I couldn't look him in the eye. He would know, he would know. I glanced down at the tiny double flower Pablo had offered me. He had said it was called *tu-y-yo*. You-and-me. A new memory.

As we were finishing breakfast, Pablo reminded his aunt about the cake delivery at the orphanage.

"Perhaps we should forget it," Dulce debated, looking at the remains of the cake. "There is not much left and so many children there."

"We'll buy some fruit at the *mercado* on the way," Pablo offered.

"What an *angelito* my nephew is!" Dulce threw her arms around Pablo and showered him with kisses. Pablo ducked in mock resistance, but I could tell he was loving the attention from his favorite aunt. Later, in the car, Esperanza teased Pablo about what an angel he was. "Maybe you can talk Mamá out of moving back to Los Luceros. It would be so . . . depressing," she added, her voice breaking.

Since Los Luceros had been a big hideout for the rebels, the army had carried out the worst massacres there. "The town is a graveyard," Esperanza explained. She and her mother had not been back since the liberation. "Mamá said it would be too hard. Now she wants to go live there!" Dulce's sisters and her mother, all widows, were rebuilding the family business, a little store called El Encanto that had been destroyed when the military came through.

I felt so bad for Esperanza, not only losing her father but lots of family on her mom's side, it sounded like. "Maybe you can come visit sometime in the States, you think?"

Esperanza looked up, hopeful, but then shook her head. "Mamá would never let me." She turned away, hiding her tears.

I glanced helplessly at Pablo, hoping he would know what to say. Only with Em had I tried mental telepathy before.

"Ay, *primita*, don't be *pesimista*," Pablo comforted her. "Like your mamá always says, miracles happen. We just have to find one that will work on her."

We came up with all kinds of miracles, including the classic voice from heaven: *My Esperanza must go to Vermont and spread the True Faith to all those Protestants!* Soon we were all laughing. It felt good to see Esperanza happy for a change.

At the *mercado* we loaded the trunk with fruit—sacks of pineapples, oranges, small pinkish mangoes. The vendors all insisted we taste their wares, which was kind of a hook because once we ate free samples, we felt obligated to buy at least a dozen. It really was a meal to go shopping.

At every stand, Pablo and Esperanza kept reminiscing— these mangoes reminded them of the delicious mangoes from the tree that was cut down in the backyard; those oranges, of the sweetest oranges Abuelito used to grow. . . .

I found myself wishing Em were with me, so I'd have someone to share the surprises of being back in a native land I couldn't remember. At the last stall, I bought her a souvenir, a necklace of red and black seeds. The old man selling them said it would bring good health and a long life. Better than eight glasses of water, I thought.

"What about love?" Esperanza wanted to know. "Will it attract a husband?" she prodded.

"As many husbands as you want," the old man obliged.

Pablo scowled. "Won't one husband do?"

"If he brings good health and a long life." The old man smiled, revealing a mouth of missing teeth.

We laughed and ended up buying four: the two I got, one for Em and one for Kate (I figured if these beads could bring husbands, health, and long lives, they could probably chill out my uptight big-sister-for-life); and two more Pablo bought, one for Esperanza and one for me. His eyes met mine as he slipped my necklace over my head. "Feliz viaje," he wished me. A happy trip. My hand kept wandering up to my neck, touching the tiny seeds.

The orphanage was a long, depressing building painted a military green, with bars at the windows like a prison. CENTRO DE REHABILITACIÓN INFANTIL read the sign above the door—Center for the Rehabilitation of Children. Even the name was depressing. Before leaving Vermont, I had copied all the information from my adoption papers. The name of my orphanage had been La Cuna de la Madre Dolorosa. The Cradle of the Sorrowful Mother. Pretty depressing, too. (Who names these places? I wondered.) Pablo and I had tried looking it up in the phone book this morning, but there was no listing. Dulce had told us that all Catholic orphanages and hospitals had been closed when the dictator nationalized church properties. But since CRI was state owned, it had remained open. After the liberation, the new government had enlisted some nuns to run it.

The woman who answered the bell started hugging us before we were even in the door. She was tall with short, silvery white hair that looked like a halo around her head. She introduced herself as Sor Arabia, though in her navy skirt and white blouse she looked more like a flight attendant. Dulce had mentioned that most nuns no longer wore habits, a protective move during the dictatorship that had now become a habit!

"Dulce called and said you were on your way," Sor Arabia explained. "Oh my goodness, look at all the fruit! God bless you! Sor Teresita, come see."

The problem with calling Sor Teresita was that she came with a kite's tail of little kids, all wanting not just to see, but to eat what we had brought. They ranged in age from little kids to boys and girls about nine or ten—though their

157

age was hard to determine; they all looked kind of scrawny and undersized. Their hair was cut super short, boys and girls. (Seemed like the only difference was that the girls got bangs with their buzz cuts.) In their identical aqua blue uniforms, they looked like little prisoners. Their faces, though, were lively and full of mischief. They snatched at the fruit, which the roly-poly Sor Teresita kept trying to stuff back into the sacks. They seemed, well, if not happy, like they were having an okay life—I mean, not like some of those horror stories I've seen on 60 Minutes.

"Who gave you *permiso* to come in here? Out! Out!" Sor Arabia stamped her foot like she was scatting kittens. The children ran off with their booty, giggling. Obviously, they knew Sor Arabia's temper was not to be taken seriously.

Esperanza went off with Sor Teresita to serve the children the leftover cake. It turned out she came here often with her mother. Mostly, she helped out with the older children, keeping them busy with games: cards, Bingo, checkers. Jacks was real popular with the girls, pebbles intermingled with the metal jacks, which were always getting lost.

Sor Arabia offered to give Pablo and me a tour of the Centro. We were about to start out when a young guy appeared at the door of the office. Begging our pardon, he bowed to me and Pablo, but he had a *problemita* to report.

Sor Arabia flashed him an impatient look. "I will be only a minute," she excused herself, walking over to hear what the little problem was.

Sor Arabia came back, sighing. The toilet in the nursery wing had been running all night. The young man had tried fixing it, but the whole bathroom had flooded. "Hipólito is one of our boys," Sor Arabia confided, lowering her voice. "He has a big heart. Ay, God forgive me, but his head can't hold a thought." I guessed everything Hipólito repaired broke down worse than before. But what could be done? Trained handymen were so expensive. The plumber she'd called last time had charged like an American, by the hour.

"Let me take a look at it," Pablo offered. He had picked up some plumbing experience from helping out his father and mine on construction jobs.

Sor Arabia shook her head. She could not allow such a thing! Pablo was a visitor! He would dirty his nice clothes! She went on with her refusals for a full minute. But I knew from Señora Robles's Spanish lessons that this was the way a nice lady responded to a favor she was embarrassed to accept right away. I guess it applied even to nuns.

"It would be an honor," Pablo insisted. Sor Arabia sighed, relenting at last. As she turned to Hipólito to lead the way, Pablo's eyes met mine. Phew! I thought. He *is* exaggerating. Sometimes, listening to the way people talked here, with all this extra apologizing and complimenting, I felt like a rude visitor from another planet with my one-word *sorrys* and *awesomes* as the epitome of praise.

We walked down the hall to a set of double doors decorated with stickers of little chicks and bunny rabbits. Sor

Arabia turned to us, a finger to her lips. We'd have to go through the nursery to get to the toilet. The little ones were taking their morning nap.

The nursery was a long, dark room lined with cribs, those high iron ones, painted white—the kind you always see in orphanages and hospitals in old movies. The shades had been drawn, but through tears in the fabric, bright gashes of light fell across the wood floor. The air smelled of talcum powder and of a strong cleanser trying to mask the odor of poop and urine—a combination that reminded me of when Nate was a baby. From all around us came the soft breathing sounds of the little sleepers and, once in a while, a wail or babble, the rustling of sheets.

As we walked by, I couldn't help peeking. Some of the babies looked so tiny, others like they'd soon be walking around, stealing mangoes, wanting to play jacks. I peered closely at their faces. I don't really know what I was looking for. A little version of myself whom I could reassure? *Don't worry, you'll soon get a mom and dad, promise.* Esperanza had said the younger the babies, the better chance they stood of being placed. It became harder for the older ones. Some stayed here until they were sixteen. Some even became the Centro's handyman.

Crib after crib after crib, so many babies! I must have lagged behind, because when I next looked up, Sor Arabia and Hipólito and Pablo had disappeared. I was alone in the room. Ahead, a toddler had just raised himself up on two legs and was looking over the end of his crib at me. His eyes—at least I think it was a he—were those big, sad eyes you see on poster kids you can sponsor in Third World countries. His pouty mouth was turned down.

"It's okay, little guy," I whispered, approaching. I meant to plant a kiss on his sweet face.

That baby saw me coming close and let out a shriek. It was like hitting an alarm. All over the room, babies started bawling. I looked around, panicked. Which way to go? Where to hide to stop this avalanche of crying?

Sor Arabia came hurrying in from a door at the back of the room. "¡Ya, ya!" she said, clapping her hands. Instantly, the sound of crying decreased. She scooped up the unconsolable instigator and patted his little bottom. "What a baby you are, crying like that!"

"Do not worry," Sor Arabia reassured me. "It is almost their wake-up time. Mariana, Socorro," she called. A couple of girls about my age appeared, each carrying a basket full of baby bottles, which they began to distribute to the ones who could hold them. The tinier babies would have to be fed individually.

"Can I help?" I offered. I felt awful about messing up the babies' nap time.

"Since they do not know you, perhaps it is better if we continue our tour," Sor Arabia suggested, slipping her arm in mine and leading me out of the nursery. She explained that Pablo had discovered what was wrong with the toilet, and he and Hipólito were trying to fix it. What an angel that young man was! This was the second time today that Pablo had been praised as God's gift to the world. I wondered if some of the macho stuff you hear about didn't come from guys getting not just praised, but worshipped. Thank goodness Pablo didn't seem to let all this gushing go to his head.

We walked down a long, echoing hallway into a side wing, peeking into bedrooms lined with cots instead of cribs. The older children slept here, Sor Arabia explained. Beyond lay the sisters' quarters, tiny cell-like rooms much smaller than Happy's walk-in closet. The walls were bare but for a crucifix and a peg with another blue skirt, another white blouse on a wire hanger. There seemed to be five nuns in all. Some older girls who had been residents stayed on as helpers. "We cannot pay them very much." Sor Arabia sighed. "But we give them their food and clothes and a home." What a life, I thought.

It wasn't that the place was a dump or anything. Everything was clean, just old and run-down. The stucco walls were crumbling. In the backyard stood a rusty jungle gym and a basketball pole with no net on the hoop. The swing set had been patched up with pieces of rubber tires for the seats. I thought of all the stuff we'd see at the recycling center where we took our plastic and bottles once a month that could have equipped this place royally.

We were heading back toward the front of the building when I finally got the courage to ask. "Sor Arabia, have you ever heard of an orphanage that used to be in the capital, called La Cuna de la Madre Dolorosa?"

Sor Arabia stopped in her tracks. "Of course I know La Cuna. I myself worked there many years."

"I've been trying to find the address . . ."

Sor Arabia shook her head sadly. "The building was burned to the ground by those *criminales*, God forgive them."

I'd been hoping the building still existed, that I could at least walk the halls of the first place that had been home. "Was it at all like this place?" I wondered aloud.

"No, no, no." Sor Arabia shook her head. "This is nothing to be compared. La Cuna was connected to our mother house, so it was like having the children in our own home. We had gardens with fruit trees and flowers and *vegetales*. Sor Corita had a green—how do you say, green hands?"

"Thumb," I barely managed to get out. "Sister Corita, you said?"

"Sor Corita, yes, our mother superior. She died over ten years ago, God rest her soul."

My face fell. Sor Corita was dead! The orphanage burned to the ground! The little I had of a past here was gone! I felt like Gretel in the forest, looking back only to find that her trail of crumbs has disappeared.

Sor Arabia was watching me closely now. "How do you know of La Cuna and Sor Corita?"

I looked at her, wondering where to begin, and I think that's the first time she noticed my eyes. She did a little double take, as if it was dawning on her who I was, as if she already knew what I was starting to tell her. How I'd been adopted from La Cuna almost sixteen years ago by an American couple who had been in the country with the Peace Corps.

"¡Ay, Dios santo!" Sor Arabia said, raising her hands in wonder and praise. "Milagros!"

Was she remembering my name or was she saying it was a miracle that we had found each other? Either way, it seemed the same to me right then.

In the dining hall next to the kitchen, the children were just finishing up their cake. They sat at long tables on benches, the older ones next to the younger ones, probably to help them cut what needed to be cut. Sor Arabia was full of news for Sor Teresita. This americana girl was one of their babies from La Cuna!

It struck me how differently people here dealt with the issue of privacy. Sor Arabia hadn't even asked if I minded her announcing my story to the room. I mean, I hadn't even told Esperanza.

I glanced toward her, and the way she looked away, I could tell she already knew about my adoption. Probably Mrs. Bolívar had told Dulce, who had told Esperanza. I doubted that Pablo had said anything. He knew how private I was about my story.

"Sit down, sit down," Sor Teresita insisted. I had to have a piece of cake. And a "good" fork with no missing tines to eat it with. Both sisters were making such a fuss over me, like I was some returning hometown hero. The kids looked on. Maybe they were wondering which one among them would someday get to be as lucky as me. One little guy who'd been sitting several spaces down somehow wormed his way next to me. I thought he wanted to be close to my success story, until I saw him pinching off little bits of the cake I was ignoring.

"He's eating the señorita's cake!" several voices cried out. One of the helping girls rushed toward him with a lifted hand.

"No, no," I intervened. "I asked him to help me." I thought of how Pablo had recently saved my hide by taking the rap for my inviting myself on this trip.

"Ay, *Dios mío*," Sor Arabia said, suddenly remembering. "Pablo!" The little guy who'd eaten my cake volunteered to go fetch him. Perhaps he wanted to get back in the good graces of the sisters? Or perhaps he just wanted a chance to sit beside this other visitor and avail himself of another bit of cake?

Pablo came back with some not-so-good news for Sor Arabia. "Please," Sor Arabia stopped him. "First you sit down and have your *bizcochito*." Your little cake.

But Pablo insisted on reporting his findings first. I thought of how Nate always had to tell us his practice triumphs the minute he walked in the door. The running toilet was temporarily fixed but it needed . . . Pablo rattled off a bunch of different parts that had worn out.

As he spoke, Sor Arabia kept shaking her head at the expense that lay ahead—or so I thought. But when Pablo was done with his inventory, she sighed. The truth was that Pablo was *un genio*!

A genius?! I glanced over at Pablo, trying hard not to laugh. He smiled back, one eyebrow raised. Well? Didn't I agree?

Finally, he laughed, letting me off the hook. "I'll pick up the parts and come back later to fix it," he told Sor Arabia.

"No, no, no!" She could not accept that. "It would be my pleasure," Pablo insisted. Back and forth, for two rounds.

"This has been a day of *milagritos*," Sor Arabia concluded. So many little miracles. "God sends us visitors to resolve our problems, and one of our children from La Cuna returns."

Pablo glanced over at me like he wasn't sure it was okay to be discussing this subject openly.

"I asked Sor Arabia about La Cuna," I explained. "She was actually working at La Cuna when I was there."

"I remember the day Sor Corita found you," Sor Arabia said, smiling at the distant memory. The children had fallen silent, as if listening to a fairy tale. "I remember because it was the Feast of the Assumption, Sor Corita's saint's day—Corita Asunción was her full name. She had gotten up early to prepare the altar of the *capilla* for early mass—we had our own beautiful little chapel. When she heard a knock at the door, she was afraid to open. Imagine, with all the disappearances and raids going on. But the knocking grew desperate. I remember it woke us all up. We were ready to evacuate the children the back way, but then we heard a baby crying, and we knew there was a new orphan in the world. The minute Sor Corita opened the door, a car drove away. Someone had been waiting to see that the child would be saved."

I felt a rush of sadness—for those parents, whoever they were, at that anguished moment; for that poor, clueless baby just beginning to sense their absence. But I couldn't exactly cry in front of these kids and upset them. After all, they shared the same sad story . . . without my lucky ending—as of yet anyhow.

"That baby was so debilitated," Sor Arabia continued. "We guessed the little creature had been living under some rough conditions. Maybe hidden, maybe abandoned to strangers, *¿quién sabe?* We didn't know who her parents were, where she was from—*nada*. But though that child had no history, she came with a name, Milagros. Every day she got a little stronger."

"What about the box that came with me?" The coin,

the two strands of hair braided together. I wanted to know whatever little thing Sor Arabia could tell me.

"Ay, ay," Sor Arabia lamented. "My memory does not hold that much."

"Maybe you remember how old I was? I mean, approximately?" The adoption papers gave August 15, the day I'd been found on the doorstep, as my birthday.

"You were so tiny"—Sor Arabia's hands spread about a foot apart—"and so very weak. I want to say about four months. But I cannot be sure."

The little guy, who was now squeezed in beside Pablo, looked at the space between Sor Arabia's hands and then at me. "¡El diache!" he said. I hadn't a clue what the word meant, but I knew he was impressed.

If I'd really been about four months old in August, that would put my birthday in April. I'd be Kate's same age, or older. (But still a grade behind her. Great!) April was also Pablo's birthday—a Taurus, I remembered from Meredith and Em's gossip sessions. Did Tauruses get along with Tauruses? Em would know. Needless to say, Em was into that stuff and had me half believing in it, too.

"And then one day a norteamericana came with a donation of clothes," Sor Arabia went on with her history. "This americana had a little one who had outgrown them. That señora fell in love with all the children, but especially with Milagritos. She started coming every day and bringing her own baby along. The *americana* lady even brought her husband a few times. Then one day, it was decided. They would adopt Milagritos. It took three more months, so many *documentos* to draw up, as we had no papers for you. The day you finally left La Cuna for good, Sor Corita cried and cried. She was very upset with herself. She knew better than to get so attached to one child. But she had a special feeling for you. She had found you on her saint's day. She died, as I told you, over ten years ago. May she rest in peace."

"*Qué descanse en paz,*" Sor Teresita echoed, crossing herself.

The phrase must have been the equivalent of saying *The End*. The children began to stir and make noise. Several little girls tugged at Esperanza's arm to come play with them.

"I have to attend to my guests," Esperanza explained. Besides, five games of jacks was enough for one day!

"But you can't go yet." Sor Teresita pointed to Pablo's plate. "You have to let Pablito finish his snack."

Pablo looked down at the piece of cake that had been set before him. "I think I will have to pass, Sor Teresita," he excused himself. At the *mercado*, he had filled up on fruits he had not been able to enjoy for eight months. "But I am sure it will not go to waste here." He made the mistake of looking around for a taker. It caused a minor riot. The children tumbled across the table or lunged from the side. Before it was over, cake was smeared on a dozen hands.

"No manners! We will never have cake again," Sor Teresita announced crossly, lining them up and marching them out of the room. They followed sheepishly, their little heads bowed. Sor Teresita was probably not a scolder by nature, and seeing her upset was, well, upsetting to them.

"If you would like to know anything else," Sor Arabia was saying, "I am at your orders."

There were dozens of things I could have asked. But right then, my heart felt full enough. I shook my head.

Sor Arabia bent down and traced a small cross on my forehead. "God continue his miracles."

"Hi, honey!" Mom was on one extension. "Milly, how's it going?" Dad on the other. An international stereo phone call. Great! The line also had an echo. And it didn't help that the only phone at the Bolívars' was in the parlor, where the TV was kept on all the time with the trials of the Truth Commission. Riqui was sitting in front of it now. Out of courtesy, he had turned the volume down.

"Did you get my message?" I asked. I had called last night to let them know I'd gotten in safely, but their machine had kicked on. With Nate away at camp and Kate down with

Grandma, my parents were probably getting some time out from being parents. I was glad for them, but it had worried me that they hadn't called back. Were they already starting to forget about me?

"We did get your message, honey. We were out seeing that new film—oh dear, I've already forgotten the name. Honey, what was it called? Anyhow, it was late when we got back so we were afraid to call. We tried you this morning, but Dulce said you'd already gone out. Really keeping you busy, eh?"

(At least this is what I think Mom said—what with Dad remembering the movie's name, and then mentioning something about calling the airline to see if my plane had gotten in safely, and all the static, I'm not 100 percent sure I caught everything Mom was saying.)

"Dulce said something about getting ready for a memorial. We'd love to send some flowers. Could you buy some in our name? We'll wire you some more money if you need it." Mom was always thinking of everything.

I'd heard about the memorial being planned for Tío Daniel. The family had been waiting for the Bolívars to come back from the United States so the whole family could be present. The trial of the murderers had been going on for months, and finally the officers involved had confessed and been sentenced. It was time to move on. The Bolívars had set out this morning to take care of last-minute details associated with the ceremony. They wanted to spare poor

Dulce the painful preparations. The plaque to be unveiled by a delegation from the government had to be reviewed, the flowers for the memorial mass at the cathedral to be ordered. It was depressing to think that a funeral required as much attention to details as a wedding, and no happy ending to keep you going.

"I'll get some flowers," I promised. "Too bad I didn't know earlier. We were at the market this morning, picking up fruit for this orphanage we visited." My news was met with total silence. "Mom? Dad?" I could hear my echo: *Mom? Dad?*

"What orphanage?" Dad finally spoke up. "Milly, our understanding was—"

"A search is a big emotional step—" Mom interrupted.

"To undertake by yourself—" Dad continued through Mom's interruption.

"We would want to be there with you—" Mom's voice was a softer version of Dad's.

"You guys!" I cried. Riqui, who'd been absorbed in watching two colonels' testimony on TV, shot a glance in my direction and turned the volume even further down. I pulled the phone cord as far as it would go into a narrow hallway. As calmly as I could, I explained that the orphanage in question was one where Dulce volunteered. I had gone with Pablo and Esperanza to deliver some leftovers. "I'm not on some search! Give me a break." My voice broke. I felt defensive. They were accusing me of something I hadn't planned. But

172

they were partly right. I *had* started looking around in this graveyard of a country for the cradle of my birth—only to discover that every trace of me was gone.

"We overreacted," Dad admitted. But he sounded relieved.

"It's because we love you," Mom added.

"Love you, too," I said, and heard my echo repeat, *Love you, too.*

On the television, the judge was bringing down his gavel on two more of the accused.

After the call with my parents, I wanted to be alone, a concept that would not fly here, I soon discovered. Just mentioning taking a walk by myself caused a minor uproar.

"A girl can't be out on the streets alone," Mrs. Bolívar reminded me. She made taking a walk sound like a prostitute soliciting.

"It's just a walk," I defended myself.

Mrs. Bolívar shook her head. "Ay, no. One of the boys must accompany you, Milly."

"Camilo went out," Esperanza reminded her. We all knew Pablo was over at the orphanage on his angel mission. "I'll go with Milly," Esperanza offered, her face brightening at the possibility.

Dulce shot her daughter one of those looks you have to be family to know what it means.

"I myself will go," Mrs. Bolívar volunteered, getting up from her chair. "I need the *ejercicio*."

"Exercise? You need the rest!" Dulce reminded her. "All those months *allá*." Over *there*. She pointed with her chin in the air. She made it sound like just *living* in the U.S. was exhausting.

It seemed my walk was not going to happen after all.

"Riqui can take her. Riqui!" Mrs. Bolívar called, but there was no answer from the patio. Riqui was giving the parrot remedial lessons, I guess you could call them. Pepito had stopped talking when Riqui was taken prisoner. Even after his master was released, Pepito refused to utter a word. Mrs. Bolívar and Dulce had actually expressed relief, as most of what Riqui had taught Pepito were swear words.

Just then, Pablo surprised us by walking into the kitchen. "*¿Ya?*" His aunt clapped her hands together. "You have fixed the problem already?"

Pablo shook his head. "It turned out the toilet was not the problem after all. The orphanage needs a whole new plumbing system. But Sor Arabia says there is no money for that."

"God Himself will send an angel in due time," his aunt reassured him.

I didn't know about toilets, but God had sent me what I needed right now. "Want to go for a walk?" I asked Pablo before some new plan could come up.

"*¡Qué buena idea!*" Mrs. Bolívar accepted for him. Not

174

that Pablo needed any encouragement, judging from the grin on his face.

"But the poor boy is tired," Tía Dulce worried. "A *refresco* first?" She opened the refrigerator and pulled out a bottle of what looked like beer. Pablo shook his head.

"Tired? Ha!" Mrs. Bolívar disagreed. "You should see the way that boy works *allá* with his father and *el señor* Kaufman." Mrs. Bolívar began her account of her son's daily schedule in Ralston.

Pablo flashed me a look I didn't have to be family to know what it meant. *Let's get out of here!*

"It is difficult for girls here," Pablo commiserated as we headed toward the central square. I had told him about the bad phone call with my parents, about my vetoed attempts to go on a walk afterward. "And girls have an even harder time in the countryside. Why do you think Esperanza does not want to move to Los Luceros?"

"We should have asked her along," I said, feeling guilty. It had crossed my mind, but the truth was that I wanted to be alone with Pablo.

"Do not worry," he assured me. "Her mother would never let Esperanza go on the streets like this. Only to church or the orphanage. I was not joking when I said it would take a miracle to change my aunt. I love Tía Dulce, but she is too strict. And as you can see, Mamá would

175

be just as bad if she had daughters." Pablo lifted his eyebrows. I already knew the brothers called their mother La Inquisición.

"You'd think people who've gone through years of being imprisoned in a dictatorship . . ." I trailed off. I didn't want to be ragging on his family. "I mean, it's understandable. They've been through so much." Murders, disappearances, suicides. Suddenly, I felt spoiled, getting all upset about my parents. "My stuff is so stupid, compared."

Pablo stopped midstride. "It is not stupid, Milly. Nothing is small if your heart feels it." His gaze lingered on my face. He seemed to want to say something else but thought better of it.

As we neared the central square, the sidewalks grew even more crowded and noisy. Merchants hawked their wares from wheeled stands. Radios blared. It seemed like the whole country was still on a holiday. Pablo and I had to walk single file to get through the press of people.

He touched my shoulder and leaned forward so I could hear. "I have a special place by the ocean. Shall we go there?" I nodded, relieved.

We walked several blocks, climbed over a low sea wall, and there it was—the ocean! I took off my shoes and broke into a run. It always has that effect on me. I'm with Dad and his yearly push for going to the Maine coast. Nothing compares with the sea. For me, it's better than a church or a temple. Gulls calling and sails belling out on windy days and that wonderful sound of the surf splashing on the sand. God saying over and over again, *here I am, here I am.*

Pablo caught up with me, laughing. We walked down the beach, the little waves breaking over our feet and washing away our footprints. The crowds of bathers got smaller. Where the beach ended, we put our shoes back on and climbed up a rocky cliff. On the other side lay a breathlessly beautiful beach, the kind you see on postcards and posters at travel agencies, with palm trees and a romantic couple walking hand in hand. That would be us, I thought. The secret in my heart rose up into my thoughts, then withdrew, like a wave.

On the opposite cliff at the far end of the cove, we could make out a stone marker, its metal plaque flashing in the sun. "It was not there when I was last here," Pablo noted.

Once on the beach, we could not resist. Warm, tempting waves were splashing against our legs. Suddenly, we were both running into the ocean, clothes and all. Oh boy! If Mrs. Bolívar and Dulce could see us now! We swam until we were tired out, then lay down to dry ourselves in the late afternoon sun.

In the ocean, my clingy T-shirt and skirt had been hidden. But now I felt self-conscious lying on the warm sand beside Pablo. As we'd come out of the water, I'd caught his eyes taking all of me in. I started to wonder if maybe Pablo had secret feelings for me as well. But I told myself to be still. I had enough things on my mind right now.

We lay for a while, silently watching clouds form and dissolve, feeling the breeze picking up, the palm trees waving. Mom, Dad, the phone call . . . everything was melting into that big blue sky. Over and over, the waves broke on the beach, washing first our toes, but as time went on, our ankles, our calves. Slowly, my heart stretched out into that huge mystery of where we all came from. How silly to worry about my teensy part of it!

Nothing is small if your heart feels it, Pablo had said.

"I think we better start going back," Pablo finally said, sitting up. In the evening the tide came in and most of the cove went underwater. "But first, I want to see what that stone says."

It's funny how I had wanted to do the same thing before we left.

We slipped into our shoes and headed for the marker. The climb was easy. Steps had been carved into the side of the cliff all the way up to the monument. At the top, we stood a moment, catching our breath, looking out at the ocean, a palette of turquoise, aquamarine, navy—every blue you could think of. Above the water, the palette changed to reds—scarlet, orange, crimson-gold—as the sun descended toward the horizon.

"On this spot"—Pablo read the plaque out loud in

Spanish—*the noble martyrs fell and with their blood gave birth to a new nation.*" Eight names were listed. They had been shot personally by the dictator before he boarded his yacht with most of the country's money packed in a specially installed vault.

How tranquil and happy we'd been, not knowing what had happened in this place only months before. I felt my head spin in that way it always does when I take in too much and don't know where to put it. Some things, I thought, might be too big for the heart to feel all at once.

Or for the heart to feel all by itself. Suddenly, I was so glad Pablo was here beside me. I turned to thank him, and I was surprised to see *his* secret surfacing in his eyes. *Now?* my eyes asked. *Yes!* his said. Weird as it sounds to say this about a grave, it was the perfect place for what happened next—his lips touched my lips, and we fell into an embrace.

8

Los Luceros

UN MILAGRITO, A LITTLE MIRACLE, had happened! I was in love with someone who was in love with me!

I couldn't wait until I got back to tell Em! I bought one of those corny postcards of a couple strolling down a tropical beach and scribbled a note on it: "Little Miracles Do Happen." I signed it "Milagros."

Em would figure it out. After all, she was always saying it was going to take a miracle to make me fall in love. For one thing, I was older than most of the guys in my class—a stumbling block for them if not for me. Oh, I'd had crushes here and there—a big one on Jake in seventh grade; last fall, Dylan and I had sort of hung out together. But I'd never been in true love before. As Em herself said, it was hard to

180

get serious with guys you'd grown up with, been through their voices changing, their braces, their zits. Of course, it never crossed our minds that they might feel the same way about *us*!

But now I was in love in love in love. Half the time, I felt like I was in a musical and wanted to break out in some hokey song. The other half, I worried I'd get in too deep and no one would be around to fish me out. I mean, what if what if what if. Somehow, I'd inherited Dad's worry genes, no doubt about it.

Among my worries was that the Bolívars would find out and get as strict with me as Tía Dulce was with Esperanza. But everyone was too caught up in the preparations for Daniel's upcoming memorial to notice.

Almost daily, Pablo and I found a way to slip away to our cove. We'd go out for an errand or Mrs. Bolívar would suggest Pablo show me this or that site in the capital. We'd rush through our mission, whatever it was, then go for a dip in the sea. I was making good use of my backpack and bathing suit and becoming adept at changing behind the sea-grape tree with a towel wrapped around me. Em would have teased me for not skinny-dipping, but I'm self-conscious enough in a one-piece. Mom's Mormon influence, I suppose.

When we got back, our street clothes were always presentably dry, but honestly, didn't anybody notice our tangled hair? Actually, Esperanza did. One time, in my backpack, I found a brush and comb I knew I hadn't packed. That day, I brought her back a seashell still dusted with sand.

Esperanza let her mouth drop in mock surprise. "So, now they are selling these historic shells at the national museum!"

It wasn't just that I wanted to be alone with Pablo. I needed to get away from the testimonies on the TV. I'd listen for a while. All the men in a village tied together, made to lie facedown, and shot. Women raped in front of their families. Little kids stuck with bayonets. I'd have to leave the room. My nightmares started coming back, awful dreams like the ones I had when Mr. Barstow did the segment on recent Latin American history.

I don't see how the Bolívars could sit there, hour after hour, listening to this horrible stuff. But it was like they needed to do it. As a way of bearing witness, that was what Pablo called it. He himself would sit up late with his brothers. One time, I walked in on them, heads bowed, their arms around each other. It was the night that Tío Daniel's murderers got their sentence reduced. They had just been following orders, I think was their excuse.

The next day, Pablo was quiet as we walked on the beach. We weren't going for a swim, as the day was overcast. Instead, we climbed up to the marker and looked out. "If I didn't have you . . . ," Pablo began, but he couldn't finish his sentence. Tears welled in his eyes. I felt so helpless. Except for Dad's voice breaking or Nate bawling, I really hadn't seen guys crying. So I just did what felt right—I put my arms around him and held on tight.

As the day of the memorial approached, more and more visitors began dropping by to express their condolences. They hugged me right along with the others and told me that this too shall pass, that they would remember me in their prayers. No one questioned whether I was part of the family. They looked at my eyes and thought, Ah yes, one of Dulce's people from Los Luceros.

And every time they mentioned it, I'd feel a strong desire to visit the place.

It seemed like the house was crowded day and night with visitors. Poor Dulce was being run ragged, attending to everyone.

"This is too much on your shoulders!" Mrs. Bolívar worried. "The truth is, these people have no manners!"

"Ay, Angelita! It is a sign of their love for Daniel," Dulce reminded her sister-in-law. "And I have more helpers than tasks." She motioned toward where Esperanza and I were setting up a table with the snacks she had made early that morning. Pablo was carrying the parrot inside for fear it would steal the little cakes. "God always sends an angel when a soul is in need," Dulce exclaimed, looking up with heartfelt gratitude.

"They are the only angels you're going to see around here!" Mrs. Bolívar grumbled.

I had to agree with Mrs. Bolívar. Dulce was looking more and more worn out. At night, between my bad dreams and her own, she wasn't getting much sleep. I'm sure Mom would have recommended antidepressants and therapy.

As for me, I had my therapy: Pablo to talk to and be with. And I was drinking tons of *yerbabuena* tea.

The opportunity to go to Los Luceros came in the form of being a good guest.

It turned out that Daniel's memorial ceremony would be in two parts: a public ceremony on Friday, in the capital, which included the unveiling of a plaque at the park near where he had been murdered, followed by a High Mass at the cathedral; then Saturday, Daniel's remains would be taken for private burial in the cemetery near the old family farm, where his mother still lived, next to the village of Los Luceros.

At first, Mrs. Bolívar would not hear of taking her guest on such a sad, tiring trip. "This is not turning out to be a vacation for you, Milly." She had made arrangements for me to stay the weekend with some friends who lived near the beach. I must have looked super disappointed, because she added, "Of course, if you would like to accompany the family, Milly, you are very welcome."

"It would be an honor," I told her. I was starting to sound like a native.

It was a slow, sad caravan up the winding mountain road behind the hearse. When we passed people on foot, the men took off their *sombreros*, women fell on their knees and made the sign of the cross. This had been happening frequently, I guessed: the dead being brought back for their final rest to the place where they'd been born.

I didn't want to ask a whole lot about it—but from what I understood, when his body was found, Daniel had been given a quick, secret burial. The family had been afraid. The dictator often used funerals of his enemies to round up people who might be against him. So it was only now, months after Daniel's death, that the double ceremony was taking place. This drive up to his mountain home was the final part of Daniel's journey.

I never in my life thought that I'd be part of anything this sad. But I didn't want to be an overprotected American wimp about it. Especially when I thought about what Dad had said, how our government had partly caused some of this tragedy. Besides, I really wanted to go to the mountains. Maybe my body needed to go back to the spot where it had come from, too.

I rode in the car with Mr. and Mrs. Bolívar and Pablo. Riqui and Camilo were up ahead in the rented vans with officials from the Liberation Party who had known Daniel. Whenever the Bolívars got distracted, involved in their reminiscences or pointing out some landmark on the road, Pablo's hand reached across the backseat and met my own reaching toward his.

We didn't arrive until late afternoon. The light was falling. The village was deserted. An official riding in one of the vans had a cell phone to call the mayor. Everyone was already at the cemetery, we were told.

Our first stop was the old farm house where Abuelita was waiting for us. She had a bad, bad heart, Mrs. Bolívar had explained to me, which is why the family had thought it best not to drag her down to the capital for the first part of the ceremony. "If anything were to happen to her . . ." Mrs. Bolívar could not continue. Her eyes filled with tears. She seemed to have a special place in her heart for *viejitas*.

Abuelita came out to meet the cars, a thin, birdlike woman about Nate's size, I swear. In her old, lined face, I could make out the dark, beautiful eyes I kept getting lost in when I looked at Pablo. The minute she saw Mr. Bolívar, she threw her arms around him and wept. "Ay, *Antonio . . . el único que me queda.*" The only one left to me. Suddenly, it struck me. It wasn't just Daniel she had lost. That general who killed himself was also her child.

Pablo came forward. He kissed her hand, then bowed his head, asking for her blessing: "*La bendición, Abuelita.*" Pablo had told me this was the old country way of saying hello and goodbye to your elders.

"Pablito, how you have grown!" She had to crane her neck to look up at her tall grandson. The pleasure of gazing upon the young man she recalled as a boy put a momentary smile on her tragic face. She hooked her arm in his and said, "*Ya*, it is time. Let us go bury my Daniel."

A crowd of mostly relatives was waiting at the village graveyard. Blood family—I could really see what that term meant here. Grandsons and nephews, granddaughters and nieces to continue the story. I wondered if, in a nearby village, a grandmother was grieving a daughter or son without the consolation of a granddaughter to carry on.

That night, by gas lamp, we ate the feast that Abuelita and several of the women in the village had prepared. We hadn't eaten all day, so we were starved.

"*Cuéntenme, cuéntenme*," Abuelita kept saying. Tell me, tell me. She was torn between wanting to know right away all about the Bolívars' life *allá*, over there in the United States, and wanting them to have seconds and thirds.

While we finished eating, Abuelita started in on her own stories. Fondly she recalled the days when Abuelito was alive. Plantains, sweet potatoes bigger than the ones we were eating tonight, oranges, coffee, you name it. Everything Abuelito planted turned a profit. She laughed, twisting the gold band on her finger as if to be in touch with him. In the old face, I could see she was still in love with the man she had lost over a decade ago. What a pity that none of her sons had taken up farming! Daniel, her youngest, always so clever, went off to the university; Antonio, the hardworking oldest, became a builder; *el pobre* Max, poor Max, with his bad temper, joined the military. A strange silence followed the mention of this name.

Late that night, the visitors began saying farewells. I was so drained from the long trip and the sad burial ceremony that I could have fallen asleep right where I was sitting. But somewhere on the list of dos and don'ts for guests—even though Mom had not mentioned it—I knew there had to be a rule about not going to sleep while your hostess is still talking.

One thing I wondered was *where* we were all going to sleep. The house looked tiny. Maybe in the Bolívars' car . . . Pablo and I in the backseat . . . our fingers intertwined . . . heads together . . .

Mrs. Bolívar must have seen my eyelids drooping. "We have to get everyone situated, Abuelita. Where are you going to put us?"

Abuelita stood up, taking charge. "I have it all arranged!" Riqui, Camilo, and Pablito were sleeping in her sons' old room. The dignitaries were being housed by the mayor. Mr. and Mrs. Bolívar here in the front room, on a mattress she kept stored in the back. She, on that cot. Esperanza and Dulce and I could take the big bed in her room.

"No, no!" Dulce protested. How could that be! Take away her bed? "Don't even think it." Especially when Los Luceros was just a short distance away, and her family would be upset if we didn't stay there.

"I'll drive them over," Pablo was quick to volunteer. My heart started beating so loud I was sure everyone could hear it.

"*¿Tú estás loco?*" Mrs. Bolívar scolded. Was he crazy? "You are not accustomed to driving in this country, no less on mountain roads!"

A discussion followed about whether or not Pablo should be the one to drive us in one of the rented vans. I thought about how everyone had opposed my taking a walk down crowded, daytime city streets. Years of fear, Pablo had mentioned, made everyone's worst-case-scenario imagination work overtime.

Riqui finally cast the decisive vote. Good old Riqui, who had supposedly lost his knowledge of women in prison, seemed to have picked up on the *milagrito* everyone else had missed.

"Let this boy become a man!" he pronounced, holding up the keys to one of the vans. "He's the safest to drive, Mamá, believe me. The rest of us have had our *tragos* tonight." I had seen the rum bottle making its rounds. Pablo, I knew, did not have a taste for the liquor, which along with overly sweet sodas, *cafecitos*, and *yerbabuena* tea seemed to be the favorite beverages in this country.

"*Bueno*," Mrs. Bolívar finally conceded. Okay. Pablo could drive us over, but she did not want him driving back alone tonight. "You stay there and bring everyone back in the morning."

Pablo and I glanced at each other, both of us trying hard not to smile at this added opportunity to be together. When I looked away, I noticed Riqui winking at his brother.

And so at that late hour, with the headlights of the van and a star-studded sky and half moon to guide us, we drove the short distance to the neighboring village of Los Luceros. If I had been sleepy before, I was wide awake now. Every little house we passed, I held my breath, hoping for a voice or a silhouette in a dark doorway that would trigger some memory of my original family.

"That must be the old coffee estate." Dulce was pointing out the window.

Two tall posts held the twisted remains of a gate; many of the bars were missing. Overhead, the iron grillwork spelled a name I couldn't make out. The driveway led up toward what looked like the ruins of an old house.

I was about to ask about it, but just then Esperanza called out, "Look!" Hundreds, no thousands, of stars filled the night sky. There were so many, I couldn't really say there was a "first" to wish by. I wondered if people here wished on stars the way we did in the States.

190

"They say each one is a soul," Dulce observed in a dreamy voice. "No wonder so many can be seen above Los Luceros! Our dead are watching us."

Looking up, I couldn't help thinking of the long list of names that had been read out at the burial this afternoon. So many had been lost in these mountains. Suddenly, there was only one thing I could think to wish for: peace on earth.

We drove into Los Luceros in silence, watched by those stars.

That night, I ended up in a room with Esperanza and her girl cousins at her aunt's house. Dulce slept next door at her mother's, where Pablo was also invited to stay. But he insisted on bedding down in the back of the van. Later, Pablo told me that the room offered to him had been that of Dulce's brother, who had been killed in one of the massacres. He didn't have to explain to me why he wouldn't want to sleep among ghosts.

I myself didn't sleep a wink, thinking of mine. What had happened to my birth parents? Why had they given me up? All night, vague faces kept approaching—my birth parents, looking sometimes like Dulce, sometimes like Mr. and Mrs. Bolívar or Mom and Dad. I would sit up to take a closer look, but the faces dissolved before my eyes. It was like one of those sketch pads I used to love as a kid where you'd lift the plastic sheet to erase your doodles. Sometimes I'd draw a face I'd think of as my birth mother's. Then I'd lift the sheet and watch her slowly disappear.

Finally, light began seeping in through the cracks in the wall. I couldn't bear another minute of lying there. I slipped out of bed, dressed quickly, and found my way through the quiet house to the front door. My plan was to sit on the porch until Pablo came by. Maybe we'd get a chance to take a walk through town before the others woke up.

The front door was a creaker. Poor Esperanza if she moved here, I thought. This was a perfect alarm system to alert parents if you got in after curfew. Then I remembered where I was. Esperanza wasn't allowed out in the capital, forget here. And even if the old rules started changing with the new democracy, there weren't any guys around to date. On the drive over, Dulce had said that hardly any males over ten and under sixty were left in Los Luceros.

From the porch, I could see the small central square straight ahead. A tall, shady tree spread out over most of it, making a second night underneath its branches. There was no sign of the van on the narrow streets. Pablo had probably parked in the back alleyway so as not to block traffic. Not that there were any cars around. Pablo had told me how in the mountain villages people mostly rode donkeys or motorbikes or used "God's wheels," their own two feet.

Small wooden houses lined the square—side by side

as if huddling together for protection. Some were missing pieces of tin from their roofs, slats from their windows. Some seemed abandoned, all boarded up. Most of them could have used a fresh coat of paint. At the corner, the family store was undergoing repairs. The sign had been taken down and the paint scraped off, but you could still make out the shadow letters, EL ENCANTO. Dulce had mentioned that the family wanted to change the name. They hadn't yet decided to what.

On the far side of the square stood a small adobe church, postcard pretty except for a creepy detail. It had been guillotined—no kidding, that was what it looked like. The bell tower ended abruptly in a charred crater, as if the church had been bombed or shot at from the air. Next to the church was a graveyard with a newly painted white picket fence over which hung bunches of yellow roses. It looked like the most tended spot in the whole village. I decided to go over and explore.

The little cemetery was as crowded as the nursery at the orphanage. The light was still dim, so I had to get up close to see the names written on the stones. Almost all the deaths were recent, within my lifetime anyway. And so many of the dead were young! It was almost a relief to find a real old-timer—I mean what would be considered an old-timer here, sixty or over. Some markers seemed crude rush jobs: two pieces of wood bound with twine, the name roughly sketched with a knife. A few had elaborately carved crosses. There were flowers everywhere. The air smelled like a florist shop.

"Are you looking for someone, Milly?" It was Dulce, kneeling beside one of the stones. She looked like she'd been crying.

I must have jumped as if I'd seen a ghost. "Pardon me for startling you," Dulce said. "Come over here." She patted a space beside her.

I walked over and sat on the other side of the stone that she introduced as "my brother." EFRAÍN SANTOS VARGAS.

Embedded in the stone was a plastic bubble with a photo inside. Condensation had clouded the plastic and the face was a blur. But I sensed those telltale Los Luceros eyes looking out at me.

"Angelita tells me your American parents adopted you from our country?"

I nodded. "From the capital."

Dulce shook her head. "You might have been adopted from *la capital*, but your eyes tell me you are from here."

"Everyone keeps saying that." Absently, I had started picking at the stray leaves and few weeds around me. There wasn't much to groom. This cemetery, like the one yesterday at Abuelita's village, was obviously well tended.

Dulce was studying me, like she was trying to remember someone in the village I might look like. After about a minute, she gave up.

"I left this place many years ago," she explained. "My father had some friends in the capital, an older couple, who were childless. They needed someone to help them. Times were hard, and Papá had girls to spare. We were six daughters, and the one son. Our Efraín," she added, caressing the grass in front of his stone. "I don't know how it was decided that I should go. The couple were very kind and treated me like a daughter. They insisted I attend the university. That's where I met Daniel. He was my professor. I am much younger," she added, as if she could tell I was doing the math in my head.

"So, you see, I have not lived in Los Luceros for many years," she went on. "I was not here during the worst massacres sixteen years ago. Angelita tells me that is your age?"

"More or less," I explained. "Sor Arabia, she worked at my orphanage, La Cuna. You've heard of it?" Dulce nodded. "According to Sor Arabia, I looked about four months old when I was left there in August. But she couldn't be sure. There was no birth certificate, nothing."

"Those eyes *are* your birth certificate," Dulce said fiercely. "And this is your *pueblo*." She struck the ground with the palm of her hand. She seemed proud to claim me.

Suddenly, I wanted to tell her everything I knew. "There was a box left with me. My dad, my adopted dad, I mean, he's my real dad, anyhow, he's a carpenter, so he knows his woods. He said that the box was made of mahogany. In this travel book I'm reading, it says that mahogany is native to this country."

"*Caoba*." Dulce pointed to a beautifully carved cross several plots away from her brother's. Then, turning, she indicated the tall, shade tree in the square.

"Inside the box, there was a coin." I described the two sides.

"That is the old *peso* with a likeness of our national founder, Salvador Estrella, who was born in Los Luceros." Dulce was shaking her head at the wonder of it all. "The truth will come to light."

I tried to remember what other things had been in the box. "There were two locks of hair, black hair and brown hair, very light like yours, intertwined. . . . And really, that's it. Except for a little paper pinned to my gown that said Milagros."

"Was that your name?"

"It's what they called me at the orphanage. It got . . . changed in the States." I felt ashamed to admit how I used to hate my middle name. "My parents named me Mildred, Milly, after my mom's mom. My adopted mom, I mean, my real mom." Here we go again, I thought.

"Milagros," Dulce pronounced it slowly. "Milagros. Is it okay if I call you that?"

I nodded. And I wasn't B.S.-ing her. It felt like that should be my name in this place. "Do you think . . ." I hesitated, not sure exactly what I wanted to ask. "Maybe someone here might know about my birth parents?"

She looked thoughtful. "Only one person in this town knows all the stories. Doña Gloria. She must be very old now." Dulce pointed to a side street across the square that climbed out of the little village. "If my memory is not wrong, she lives up that road."

I rose quickly to my feet. "Can we go?"

Dulce pulled herself up to stand facing me. She pushed my hair back gently from my face. "We will need transportation."

Just then, we both heard the car door. Beyond Dulce's shoulder in the growing light of day, I made out the van parked under the huge shade tree. Pablo had just stepped out of the back. Dulce turned, following my gaze.

"God always sends an angel when a soul is in need," she murmured. Again, I had to agree with her.

"We must leave the vehicle here," Dulce explained to Pablo.

We had reached the end of the dirt road. Up ahead, the mountain dropped away sharply into the valley below. A few doll-size houses were visible through the mist rising up from the river. It was like the view from an airplane.

Dulce pointed up the steep mountainside. "It is at the end of that path."

I had to crane my neck to see the stony outcrop at the top. "How do we get there?"

"God's wheels," Pablo and Dulce said at the same time, laughing. (I should have known!) "It is not far," Dulce reassured me.

We began climbing. Here and there, goats grazed on the rocky pasture, their curled horns snug against their heads. They looked like they were wearing protective helmets in case they slipped and fell down the slopes. "What I want to know," I gasped, "is how an old woman can make it up this steep path?"

"People come to her." Dulce had stopped to catch her breath. "She has our history in her head. Thank God she was spared, or we would have lost so much of our past. Those *criminales* stopped at nothing. Look at what they did to God's own house. Lord have mercy on them."

We resumed our climb in silence, too out of breath to talk. Finally, under a tall pine, I made out a small stone house built right up against the mountainside. Its walls were made of what looked like boulders from this very spot, so it blended right in with the stony outcrop. No wonder it had escaped sighting by the military helicopters and so been spared the fate of the church steeple. "I can see why the rebels hid up here," Pablo noted, surveying the rocky, desolate place.

At the top of the path, a young girl appeared. Like Dulce and almost everyone else I had met since we'd arrived, she

198

was dressed in black. She stood still as a statue, watching us. Even after Dulce called up, introducing herself, the girl said nothing. When we were almost level with the house, she turned on her heels and slipped inside.

"That must be Doña Gloria's great-granddaughter," Dulce guessed. "What a shy little bumpkin!"

At the door, Dulce again announced herself, calling into the dark interior. She gave what seemed like a whole family tree of local relations. She had come, Dulce explained, to give her greetings to Doña Gloria. She had brought her nephew and a special visitor. Would Doña Gloria receive us?

Up to this point, we had not seen or heard a peep from Doña Gloria. But after a moment, an old, croaky voice answered. "*¡Pasen, pasen!*" Come in, come in.

Inside the dark hut, my eyes took a moment to adjust. At the center, in a rocking chair, sat the oldest old woman I'd ever seen. Her bony arms reached out in the direction of our voices.

"Come, come," she quarreled with our slowness. "Come closer." When we did, she grabbed us, saying hello by feeling our hands and faces.

It was then that it hit me, Doña Gloria was blind! If she could not see my face, how could she guess who I might resemble? Again, I felt that lost-Gretel feeling of the trail disappearing behind me.

"*La bendición*, Doña Gloria," Dulce began. Pablo and I echoed the greeting.

"Sit, sit," Doña Gloria commanded.

The girl had brought over three chairs. *"Gracias,"* I said smiling, then asked for her name. The girl hid her face in her hands, as if ashamed.

"La muda," her grandmother answered. The Mute was her name!

I was shocked by what seemed a common practice here: people named after some handicap or sensitive detail you'd never mention in the States. At the orphanage, a fat little girl had been called *la gordita. El cojo* was the boy with the club foot. As for the very dark boy who loved to steal cake, he was *el negrito!*

"Muda?" Even Dulce was looking surprised. She didn't know Doña Gloria's great-granddaughter was mute?

Doña Gloria gave a curt nod as if to cut off any further questions. Perhaps this was too painful a subject to discuss, especially with her great-granddaughter standing right in front of us.

For a while, Dulce and Doña Gloria chatted about the village. It turned out Doña Gloria already knew about Daniel, the memorial Mass at the national cathedral, yesterday's service at the graveside. How had this news traveled so fast up to this remote spot? The burial had happened only yesterday, and late in the day at that!

"People come by all the time," Doña Gloria explained. "They want to tell me things. They know I will remember. But I am getting old. You see the blindness has set in."

Of course we had noticed. But I wondered if anyone in Los Luceros would dare call Doña Gloria *la ciega*, the blind one.

"I am tired, the body can resist no more." Doña Gloria sighed wearily. "But how can I die, tell me? Who will remember then?" Her voice was filled with a sadness I'd never heard before. It was sadness for all the suffering down the generations. I wondered how she could bear that heavy load.

"I was raising this one's mother to remember the stories," Doña Gloria went on, rocking back and forth, the rocker keeping rhythm with her voice. "That was after I lost my daughter to the bombing in Los Luceros. My granddaughter had become my hope and my future memory. But that was not to be. That Friday . . ."

Doña Gloria gripped the armrests of her rocker as if bracing herself for the pain of the story she was about to tell. "That Friday, I went to market alone. My granddaughter was expecting a second child and was far gone, so she stayed. This one—" Doña Gloria motioned in the air to her left, where the girl stood sentinel, her hand clutching one post of the rocker. "This one was only a little thing but already babbling stories." Doña Gloria began rocking wildly. Dulce reached out and touched the arm of the chair as if to calm her.

"The *guardia* came, and they did their business with my granddaughter, and then they cut her throat. This child was there when it happened, she saw what they did.

They were merciful. They did not kill her. They cut off her tongue. So she knows the stories, but she cannot tell them."

One hand flew to my mouth in horror, the other reached for Pablo, who had doubled over as if he'd been punched in the stomach.

The girl meanwhile had turned her face to the shadows. She was making a low, moaning sound like a wounded animal. "Ya, ya," her great-grandmother soothed her, reaching blindly for her arm.

Dulce was on her knees in front of her chair, sobbing, her arms folded in prayer. "Ay, Doña Gloria, ay! Only God can forgive this."

"Not even God, I think." Doña Gloria's laugh had no laughter in it. "This was many sorrows ago now," she noted. "I am surprised you had not heard."

"I have not been back for a while," Dulce admitted. "And even those with tongues have been afraid to speak."

Doña Gloria turned her head as if to let the breeze blowing in the door soothe her weary face. Every inch of it was lined. It looked like one of those scrap papers you can't write on anymore.

"I, too, have to tell my story from time to time, you see." Doña Gloria began rocking herself again, gently back and forth, like moms do when their babies get fussy. "But you did not come to hear of my sorrows." She paused, waiting for us to tell her what we had come for.

How could anyone follow up her story with a request? I couldn't even find my voice right now.

"Everyone comes here wanting to know something," Doña Gloria prodded. "They have the beginning of a story, but not the ending. They have a valuable part, but they don't know where to put it. I would say, Dulce, both your visitors here have questions. I don't know that I can answer either of them."

Any other time, I might have felt disappointed. But right this moment, all I wanted was for the past to be over, period.

Dulce, who was still on her knees, sat back down in her chair. She looked over curiously at Pablo. "You have a question, too, Pablito?"

Pablo shook his head. Like me, he was probably still in shock over the story Doña Gloria had just told us. "Not really, Tía," he finally replied when he had control of his voice.

Doña Gloria laughed as if she knew better. "*Bueno, bueno,*" was all she had to say about that. Well, well. "And the young lady?" She turned her face in my general direction.

When I didn't say anything, Dulce spoke up. "The young lady is a special case. Let me explain her situation."

Dulce went on to tell Doña Gloria my story, the little we knew. As she talked, Doña Gloria began rocking herself. Each rock seemed like a nod, as if she were saying, *Yes, yes, I remember!*

"So the question would be who might have given birth the spring of that year," Dulce concluded. "I wouldn't know, Doña Gloria. You see, I had already been gone from Los Luceros a year."

Dulce fell silent. The only sound now was the clack of the rocker, backward and forward, backward and forward.

Finally, on one of the forward swings, Doña Gloria planted both feet on the floor and stopped herself. She lifted her face toward me. Her eyes were clouded with a white film, but they were the same gold eyes with brown flecks as Dulce's and mine. They seemed to be looking right at me.

"What did you say your name was?"

I didn't have to think about it. "Milagros," I told her.

9

Dar a Luz: Give to the Light

DOÑA GLORIA LAID HER old hands on my face. They were rough and callused. But her touch was gentle.

"Sixteen years ago . . . after the fields were burned, the drought came. Many went hungry. It was then that your father sent you away to the capital, Dulce. He could not feed that many mouths. The couple that took you in were old friends who were childless." Doña Gloria knew the whole story!

"The next year, the rains came," she went on—one finger, then another lightly tapping my face. "A second flood to punish the wicked! But then, the waters stopped. Everything turned green again. The earth teaches us to be

205

forgiving." Doña Gloria was shuttling back and forth in time, weaving her story.

"Sixteen years ago," she repeated, her fingers outlining the features on my face. "In the spring of that year, *¿quién dio a luz?*" Who gave birth then? Some things I like better the way they're said in Spanish, and this was one of them. Giving birth, *dar a luz,* to give to the light.

"Margarita's girl came later that year. Ricardo Antonio's *mujer,* that woman gave birth in December. And hers was a boy." Doña Gloria was running stories through her fingers. They tapped busily on my face as she went on, murmuring names, humming details, dates. She was a river of memories, flowing.

Finally, her hands dropped to her lap. In her old, croaky voice, she began bringing to light what her fingers had found on my face.

"Those years, there were not many births. Some women stopped bleeding altogether. The body knows when it is not a good time to give to the light." Doña Gloria paused as if to gather her strength for the stories that lay ahead.

"If a woman did have a child, she hid the fact, out of fear that it might be taken away from her. To make her speak what many times she did not even know."

The light in the room was dim. The wooden shutters

were closed. Guests had come before the morning's chores could be done. But just inside the opened door, sunlight fell in a shaft on the floor. It swarmed with tiny dust particles like that picture in our biology textbook of thousands of sperm trying to find an egg to fertilize.

"In the spring of that year . . . in all of this area we call Los Luceros, I can remember two newborn girls. How happy we were in those times to hear of the birth of girls. They stood a chance for a better life than boys."

The young girl made her low, moaning sound again. She was standing beside Doña Gloria, swaying with the rhythm of the rocker, as if she were helping her grandmother remember.

Doña Gloria's hands flew up to my face again, lightly touching my cheeks, my lips. She sighed and let them drop again.

"I cannot say if you were one of those two births. Perhaps you were a third or a fourth birth I never heard about. Not all the stories reached me in those years. As Dulce says, even the people with tongues lost them for a while. Everyone was afraid to speak."

Suddenly, I felt afraid. I remembered Pablo's words on the plane about The Truth I argued was important to know. Did I even want to hear about those two births? What if Doña Gloria told me a story as horrible as the one that had happened to her family?

"About the two baby girls, Doña Gloria?" Dulce reminded her. Maybe because this was her hometown, Dulce, at least, was eager to learn its secrets.

"The first was the child born to Rosa Luna. You remember Rosa?"

"*Rosa, la buenamoza.*" Dulce was nodding as if Doña Gloria could see that nod. Rosa, the good-looking one. It was a nicer quality to single out than her weight or a handicap.

Doña Gloria's rocker was picking up speed. Her great-granddaughter had taken hold of one of the back posts. She seemed to be directing the pace of the rocking. "Rosa had our gold eyes and that bright hair from her mother's family."

I thought of the two locks of hair, light braided with dark.

"By the time Rosa had seen twenty years, she had four children, all from different fathers. You could not blame her. The men were constantly disappearing: it was wiser not to get attached to just one. Los Luceros has always been a cradle of freedom." Doña Gloria turned her face in my direction, as if she wanted to be sure I understood this point of pride. I had not been raised in this country. I might not know these important things.

"But sometimes in this cradle, the freedom an individual wants . . . *bueno*, well, it's for private consumption." I could not tell if the cackle had come from Doña Gloria or from her rocker as it moved forward, backward.

"The *guardia* were always patrolling this *zona*, checking on the cradle that has always given this country its liberators. Once in a great while, the commanders would drop in to inspect the operations. This one colonel saw Rosa at the square—and that man fell like a ripe mango. He visited often, even when his own militia was moved to another area of the country. He was a great friend of Don Max's." Doña Gloria turned in the direction of Dulce. "They would come up for the weekends together, the colonel telling his wife he was on a secret mission. Soon enough, that mission was not so secret. Rosa's belly began to show."

My heart fell. My birth mother might have been a prostitute and my birth father a torturer who cheated on his wife! Pablo touched my hand as if to remind me he was there.

"That colonel bought a piece of land up here and built a love nest for himself and Rosa. But then, right after the new year began, the colonel insisted on moving Rosa to a house he had set up for her in the capital. That is how the townspeople knew the raids were coming. We evacuated to the mountains into caves and shelters we constructed out of whatever we could find. This house was built back then."

The young girl clutched the post as if to still her grandmother's rocker. Doña Gloria must have sensed this reining in, because she started tying up the ends of her story.

"There is not much else to tell. Rosa left her children with her mother and took off to the capital. The baby must have been born there. We never again heard from her. Some say she fled the country with the colonel when El Jefe and all his people left. Others say she became one of those women who earn their living on their backs, neglecting that poor baby until it was close to death. *¿Quién sabe?* Who knows? People criticize her, *las malas lenguas,* the bad tongues. But I remind them, had it not been for Rosa and the advance warning of her move, the whole town would have been wiped out. We were saved by Rosa's indiscretion."

"You are right, Doña Gloria." Dulce's hands were clutched on her lap as if she were forcing them to pray. "It is not for us to judge God's creatures. Ay, but when I think of those *criminales,* Doña Gloria! You heard their sentences were reduced to three years? My Efraín, my Daniel lost their lives and those monsters get three years! I do not want to be vengeful, God forgive me, but where is the justice here?"

Doña Gloria was silent. Even she could not answer such a question. She was rocking more slowly now. Soon, it seemed, the rocker would stop. I had something I wanted to ask before she was totally finished with this story.

"What did the colonel look like?"

Pablo glanced in my direction. I could see it dawning on him why I was curious. I had told him about the two locks of hair.

"I never saw the man," Doña Gloria admitted. "But

they called him Pelo Negro because his hair was black as night."

You can't base a whole life story on that, I reminded myself. Of course not. But not too far back, I had based it on a lot less: a past I never thought about, secret feelings kept from everybody, even those I loved.

Doña Gloria seemed to have dozed off; her chin was almost to her chest, her body bent over. But then the girl gave the rocker a sudden jerk, and Doña Gloria startled awake.

"What story was I telling?" she wanted to know. "I have forgotten. See how my mind is going."

"You said there were two births in the spring of that year," Pablo reminded her. "Rosa's child, and then another?"

"Ay, *sí, sí.* The second birth, the second one." Doña Gloria hummed, remembering. The girl began to rock her, gently, as if to get her going. "You must have heard of Don Gustavo Moregón? He owned the big coffee plantation on the road between here and the Bolívars' farm?"

"We saw the ruins on the way," Pablo told her.

"Ruins now, but that place used to be a mansion. I remember when they built it on the side of the mountain. Everything had to be carried up by workmen and mules. They say there is a small cemetery at the foot of that mountain. On the roof, Don Gustavo painted GOD BLESS EL JEFE in huge letters. He was a sly one, all right. They didn't call him *el sabio* for nothing. Imagine! That roof was not only a show of loyalty, but it protected his house when the planes came up here on their bombing missions. After the liberation, that place was overrun. The people carried off everything. I don't know where the roof tiles ended up, but just the other day, someone was telling me that he saw the gold-framed mirror with the naked *angelitos* in the barber shop. Elegant lamps and platters painted by the poor of some faraway country. The señora's gowns and shoes disappeared. As for the house, the people took it apart, board by board. But no one wanted that unlucky wood to rebuild their houses. It was sold to some merchants from the capital for good money."

Last night, at her mother's house, Dulce had served me a *guanábana* tea in a dainty porcelain cup. When I turned it over so the drops could drain—Dulce's mother could read the future from the stains, so she claimed—the bottom said HECHO EN FRANCIA, made in France.

"Don Gustavo had several sons, but his weakness was his only daughter, *la señorita* Alicia. During the year, *la señorita* was away at a fancy boarding school in England to learn her English. But the summers, Don Gustavo would send her and her *mami* up here, away from the heat and fevers of the capital. They would arrive with their many suitcases and *maletas* of clothes. Weekends, the sons and Don Gustavo drove up with their military friends to relax and have parties. I remember the summer *la señorita* turned fifteen. Her father threw her a big *quinceañera* party. People arrived from the capital in their big cars. El Jefe made an appearance, flying in on his helicopter. Señorita Alicia invited the whole countryside to come eat cake. We all went in our Sunday clothes, but the *guardia* turned us away."

As Doña Gloria talked, the movie Ms. Morris had shown our class kept running through my head. *The Great Gatsby.* Music in the big mansion. Lots of sad people with tons of money looking for happiness they would never find there, Ms. Morris had said. Back then, it sounded like one of Happy's house parties.

"The summer would have been just another round of parties and outings. But Don Gustavo had hired a groom for his horses, a young man from Los Luceros. Last name of Bravo. That young man had a way with animals. And a way with women. Tall, with dark hair and our light eyes, the back straight, he looked like a flamenco dancer. He was only seventeen, but the women in town were already wild about him."

"Manuel Bravo!" Dulce cried out. "Ay, Doña Gloria, I remember him! I was one of those girls. His father was the master *carpintero.* That man understood wood. Like your father, Pablito." Dulce nodded at her nephew. "People with money would come up from the city to buy the beautiful things he made, hope chests for brides and cradles for babies and keepsake boxes for important papers. There was a time everyone in Los Luceros had one of those boxes. You see, now you have reminded me of this story."

Doña Gloria sighed as if a weight had been lifted from her shoulders. "You finish it, Dulce. Go on, you know the story."

"There is not much more to tell." Dulce picked up the thread where Doña Gloria had left off. "Alicia, the lonely *princesita*, and Manuel, the young groom. It's like a *telenovela*. Everyone can guess what happened."

Doña Gloria closed her eyes and smiled as she rocked. She seemed to enjoy hearing someone else tell the story.

"Soon *la señorita* was spending a lot of time in the stables," Dulce continued. "In no time, she learned to ride bareback, and Manuel, he mastered the English saddle right away."

Doña Gloria and Dulce giggled like two schoolgirls. I glanced over at Pablo, who was shaking his head at these corny old-timers. Of course, I understood enough Spanish to know Dulce had made some off-color joke. But I've never been good at dirty jokes even in English. Back at Ralston, Em always had to explain them to me. It took the dirtiness out of them, she always complained.

"Ay, Lord forgive me." Dulce was already feeling guilty about her naughtiness. "We must respect their memory because what came to pass was not funny at all. Don Gustavo had spies all around, but that summer they failed him. By the time he caught wind of what was going on in his stables, it was too late. His *princesita* was pregnant, and the *señora* was very Catholic, so there was no question of the solution rich families often take. Alicia was hurried to the capital. I was already living there with the old couple. The city was full of rumors."

Alicia would have been my age that summer! Once in a while girls in Ralston got pregnant, but almost all of them had abortions. I always felt so bad for them. I didn't know what I would have done. One thing I knew: I was too young to be anyone's mother and too old to stop a life because of my bad judgment.

Dulce raced ahead like she wanted to be done with this sad story. "At the end of that summer, Alicia did not go back to her school in *Inglaterra*. The family said she was ill—some condition that required bed rest. Then one night about five months later, a doctor and a midwife were seen entering the Moregón house in the capital. They took away a little bundle with them, who knows where it went? The couple I lived with heard from a friend of the cook in the house that the baby was premature, that it could not live for very long, that the midwife kept it for a time. But only Our Señor knows the truth of what happened. The next season, Alicia was attending parties again. But in her pictures in the papers, she looked haunted. They couldn't fix her up enough. She was not a beautiful girl, but she'd had a fresh, young face that was now a mask with a frozen smile. Her long *cabellera* of hair was all cut off in a modern cut. They say it was her way of mourning Manuel."

"What exactly happened to him?" I almost didn't want to find out. The story was already too much like *Romeo and Juliet* to have a happy ending.

"Who knows," Dulce said, shrugging. "Do you know, Doña Gloria?"

Doña Gloria shook her head. "God only knows. But if you go to the cemetery, you will see where his family put up a cross, a beautiful one his father made of mahogany."

Pablo had been kicking at the ground as the story unfolded. Maybe he identified with Manuel, who had been his age when he disappeared. I was thinking about the boxes Manuel's father used to make. Perhaps Manuel had given one to Alicia to keep her jewelry?

Bright sunshine was now pouring in the doorway. Dulce's family would be wondering what was taking us so long. On our way out of town, Dulce had told *el viejo del centro*, the old man on the square, where we were going. According to Dulce, *el viejo* was like the town crier. He would spread the word. But by now, her family would be expecting us back. Pablo, Dulce, and I looked at each other—time to go.

"I don't know that either story belongs to you," Doña Gloria concluded, nodding in my general direction. "But these are the only two girls born in the spring of that year."

Suddenly, her great-granddaughter began violently shaking the back of the rocker. She made pained sounds, like she was trying to say something she had just remembered.

Doña Gloria reached out and seized the girl's hand. "*¿Qué? ¿Qué?*" What is it? "Get the stick!" Doña Gloria ordered. "Write it for these people."

The girl ran and grabbed a long stick propped up in the corner by the entrance. Its end had been sharpened, as if just for this purpose. She brushed off the dirt floor in front of her with a bare foot and painfully began to draw some letters. Each twisted shape took great effort—exactly how I used to write before all my tutoring lessons!

We waited as she scratched out the name.

"Dolores Alba," we read out loud when she had finished.

"*¡Ay, Dios santo!*" Doña Gloria exclaimed. "This girl remembers more than I do. There was a third girl born that spring. Dolores Alba had her baby some months before they captured her."

"Dolores," Doña Gloria said as she rocked forward. "Alba." She rocked backward. "Dolores Alba. How could I forget the pride of Los Luceros!"

Dolores Alba, Dolores Alba, the clacks of the rocker now seemed to repeat, over and over, forward, backward.

My hands had been totally calm since I'd landed in this

country. Now—it wasn't exactly that they itched, they were tingling with excitement.

"Dolores Alba was the first woman to join the rebels," Dulce explained to Pablo and me. "Isn't that so, Doña Gloria?"

Doña Gloria rocked forward as if nodding yes. "Dolores came from a long line of freedom fighters. On both sides, she was related to Estrella, the founder of our nation." Doña Gloria nodded a reminder in my direction. "That was why the family had the custom to carry a *peso* with their ancestor's picture on it—you've seen those old coins?"

My coin! It must have come from Dolores! Of course, the mahogany box could have come from Manuel and Alicia, the locks of hair braided together from Rosa and Pelo Negro. But Dolores was brave and her family were freedom fighters. I wanted her for my birth mother.

"Like all of the Estrellas, Dolores had a fire burning inside her," Doña Gloria went on. "I don't know how to explain it. They all seemed to be born with an itch they couldn't get to. Thank the Lord that our Estrellas here in Los Luceros have always used that passion for the good. But there were scattered Estrellas who joined the military, and that same fire was used in the service of you know who."

I wondered if, as a scattered member of the family, I would misuse that fire, too? Did I even have it in me? Maybe it had gone out when I was adopted and moved to another country? Maybe it had been reduced to the burning of a skin rash?

"This Dolores, *pobrecita*, by the time of her first bleeding, she was already an orphan. Her father had been taken away for organizing the coffee pickers. Two brothers were shot by the *guardia* during one of their massacres. The third was smuggled out of the country but then returned and was captured. After torturing him, they dumped him from one of their helicopters. Dolores's mother could not bear up under all this grief. One morning—who knows if it was an accident—her body was found at the bottom of a cliff, *muertecita*."

A little dead? Even in Spanish, you couldn't make some things sound less horrible than they were.

"But what the mother couldn't resist, the daughter learned to bear. She had been well named, Dolores. Sorrows. But her *apellido*, her last name, was Alba, the dawn, the sun coming up after the dark night. In this way, too, nature teaches us to hope."

"*Dios no nos abandona*," Dulce agreed. God does not abandon us. Just hearing about Dolores seemed to be making Dulce more hopeful.

"The men who had not been killed joined up with the guerrilla and went away to their hidden camps in the mountains. Dolores's cousin, Javier Estrella, among them. I don't know how that boy lived to be a man. Since he was a little thing"—Doña Gloria motioned with her hand just above the floor—"that boy was fighting the dictatorship. One time the *guardia* came through Los Luceros, and from the roof of the feed store, Javier shot off the colonel's cap with a slingshot!"

"Ay, *Dios santo*, I remember that day!" Dulce exclaimed. "¡Ay, *qué susto!* What a fright we had! The men were lined up in the square. We thought they would all be shot. But as they stood in plain sight, a second shot came and tore off a medal from the colonel's chest. There was the proof! The culprit could not be one of our men. *Gracias a Dios*, thanks be to God, they were all spared! Meanwhile, the *guardia* combed the town, but nada. Nothing. I don't know how that little monkey got away!"

Doña Gloria kept nodding as Dulce recounted the incident. "*Ése mismo*, that same Javier, became a revolutionary *comandante* with the guerrilla. Young as he was, he had the love and trust of the people. Many in Los Luceros joined up. Dolores tried. She made several petitions, but the *comandante* turned her down. Back then, the guerrilla was not taking women. But the different cells needed a safe drop-off house for the whole area, so Dolores offered hers. Of course, the whole town knew. *El viejo del centro*—that old man repeats everything! His ears are connected to his mouth."

"I hope *el viejo* told Mamá about our visit this morning," Dulce worried out loud. The shaft of sunlight now cut deeper into the room, slicing the interior into brighter and darker portions. "Everyone now thinks the worst if one is late."

"This will not take much longer," Doña Gloria assured her. "*Lamentablemente,* such tragic lives make brief stories. A lamentable thing. The next time the *guardia* came through Los Luceros with their tortures, the weaker ones crumbled under the rod and revolver, and they talked. The name that kept coming up was Dolores Alba. Of course, the *guardia* raided her house. But it was not her *destino* to die that day. As it happens, she was down in the valley buying supplies, delivering messages. Someone got word to her there, and she knew not to come back to the village. There was nothing for it, Dolores was obligated to go underground. The guerrilla had to accept the first woman among them."

"What a life for her!" Dulce was shaking her head. "A woman alone in a rebel camp with all that bombing and fighting."

"But even in times of war, love reserves some arrows for the heart," Doña Gloria reminded her. "Dolores and her cousin Javier fell in love. Fire joining with fire. They were going to save the world together."

"Third cousins." Dulce had worked it out. "They would not need a dispensation for marriage."

"Marriage? Ha!" Doña Gloria gave a decisive shake of the head. "You didn't know those two! They would come and stay with me from time to time. A night stolen from

221

the revolution. After I fed them, we would go out and sit under the stars, and those two would start in on their theories and ideas. One time I mentioned marriage, *ay, Dios mío*, why was that? Marriage was an oppressive, capitalist institution, an extension of the mentality of ownership. *¡Qué sé yo!* What do I know? It gave me a headache to hear them talk. I told them, how can you win a revolution with ideas that we simple people can't understand? 'You know more than all of us put together!' they laughed back."

"Marriage is a holy sacrament," Dulce said, as if Javier and Dolores were there to be improved by her lecture. "Ay, Doña Gloria. You hear that kind of talk now all the time from the young people." Dulce glanced over at Pablo, trying to look cross, but smiling in spite of herself.

"Marriage or no marriage, Dolores was soon with child," Doña Gloria went on. "I remember one night she appeared here by herself and said to me, 'Compañera Gloria'—oh yes, that was what she called me; she said *doña* was a title that promoted the capitalist class system—'Compañera Gloria, a child is a luxury I cannot afford right now. I need to get rid of it.'"

My heart had been soaring with pride for my chosen, freedom-fighting birth parents. Now it plummeted with the realization that the one mother I would have wanted hadn't wanted me to even be born!

"I gave that girl a scolding like you would not believe." Doña Gloria scowled, as if remembering that scene. "You see, that was the reason I didn't remember this third birth right away. For a time, I assumed Dolores had found a way to abort that *criatura*. But then I heard from some of her *compañeros* that Dolores was fighting alongside them, wearing a man's shirt to hide her growing belly. Sometime that spring, Dolores gave light to her little girl. When Javier went down to the capital to organize the urban guerrilla, Dolores went with him. That's where they were captured."

"Do you think she really didn't want me?" I blurted out before I even realized what I was saying. "I mean, didn't want her child?"

Pablo reached for my hand again. For the first time, Dulce seemed to notice another pair of young lovers right before her eyes. She blinked in surprise.

Doña Gloria squinted into the distance like she could see something that the rest of us could not make out. "If Dolores were alive today, she would thank me for the advice I gave her. Without our children, we lose the future. We lose our stories. Our dreams die!"

"I am sure that Dolores was very glad to be a mother in the end," Dulce threw in. "Many times God spares us from making mistakes we will later regret." I knew she was trying to make me feel better. But sometimes I wished she wouldn't put her God spin on everything.

"What finally happened to Javier and Dolores?" Pablo asked. It was as if by holding my hand, he had absorbed the question which I both dreaded but needed to ask.

"Javier and Dolores were captured one night in the capital, delivering arms in a borrowed car. No one knows if the child was with them. But all three vanished without a trace. So many, so many"—Doña Gloria motioned with her hands in the air—"every story one tells these days marks a grave."

By now, the room was bright with sunlight. It shone on Doña Gloria's old face. I wanted to put my hands on it and soak in her stories. Dolores and Javier, Alicia and Manuel, Rosa and her colonel, any of them could have been my birth parents. Maybe I could claim a part of each one, just as there was a little detail from each story that fit into the puzzle of my past.

"Thank you for these stories, Doña Gloria," Pablo spoke up for all of us. "We will not forget them," he promised.

"You must do more than that!" Doña Gloria scolded, wagging her finger blindly at the air in front of her. "You are all we have left. You must bring about the harvest of what we have planted!"

Just hearing her say that made me feel trembly all over. Not only my hands were tingling now. It was as if Doña Gloria were lighting that Estrella flame inside me.

Doña Gloria had stopped her chair. She reached out, flailing her arms in the air until she found what she was looking for, her great-granddaughter's arm. Slowly, she lifted herself to her feet and walked us to the door. We stood basking in the sunlight, enjoying the warm brightness shining down on us. It felt like a blessing after the dark stories in the dark house.

Dulce stepped up first, bowing her head for a blessing. "*La bendición,* Doña Gloria."

"Your blessing, Doña Gloria," Pablo echoed.

It was my turn to say goodbye, but I couldn't get the words out. Suddenly, I could not help myself. I threw my arms around Doña Gloria, as if she were the birth mother I'd been searching for. I could feel her taking me in with her whole being. Doña Gloria had saved my life—not only by preventing my abortion, if Dolores and Javier were indeed my birth parents, but right now by telling me stories that made me feel lucky just to be alive.

"*Gracias,* Doña Gloria." I was sobbing. I couldn't seem to let go.

"Milagritos," Doña Gloria was whispering in my ear, as if to put little miracles inside me, as if to give me back my name. When I had calmed down, Doña Gloria released me. I felt ready to go.

"*La bendición,*" I asked, bowing my head.

Doña Gloria lifted her hand in blessing. Her blind eyes looked off toward the path, the van waiting below, the horizon, the whole world out there waiting for us. "I'm counting on you," she said. It was like she was sending us out on a mission or something.

"To do what?" Pablo wanted to know.

"To bring more light," Doña Gloria replied.

10

Finding Miracles

WHEN I SAW THE glint of silver in the distance, I started waving like crazy. We were waiting for Mom and Dad's plane on the observation deck of the Aeropuerto Internacional de la Liberación del Pueblo. Liberated names seemed to go on and on. I often wondered what would happen if I ever had to say something fast in this country.

On the way, Pablo and I had stopped first at "our" cove for a quick dip and then a climb to the memorial stone. It was a weirdness I couldn't get used to: how really fun stuff was all mixed up with really tragic stuff. Or maybe I was just noticing it more now?

At the airport bathroom, I looked in the mirror and wondered if my parents would even recognize me. My hair

226

was wild and flyaway, my skin so deeply tanned that people came up to me and automatically started speaking Spanish.

"If you are not careful, you will forget all your English," Pablo teased. "You will have to stay here forever." He cocked his head, waiting for my reaction.

"No way, José!" I was not joking. I loved this country. But I missed home. I was looking forward to going back to Ralston. First, though, I wanted to share this place, where I had found a *familia* of friends, with my family. "That has to be their plane!" I insisted. The glint was now a tiny jet, getting bigger as it drew closer.

Pablo checked his watch. "I have never known the airlines to be early. But miracles happen—"

"As Tía Dulce always tells us," I chimed in. Now that I had adopted her as my aunt, I could tease her all I wanted. If only she would stop trying to convert me. She had actually called Sor Arabia and found out that all babies at La Cuna had been baptized. According to Tía Dulce, I was already Catholic. Wait till my Jewish grandmother got a load of that!

Meanwhile, everyone, even Pablo, was calling me by my new nickname, Milagritos. Little miracles.

Only a few people were out on the observation deck with us. One woman held a parasol to keep the sun from darkening her skin. I mean, what's the point of being on an observation deck, then obstructing your view under an umbrella?! But it was midday and it was hot. Most

227

people preferred the air-conditioned lounge downstairs in the terminal. But I was so excited. I didn't want a thick sheet of glass between me and my first glimpse of Mom and Dad!

I had called them the minute we got back from the mountains on Sunday night. They were so happy—actually, relieved was more like it. They had been worried, three whole days without hearing from me, no answer at the house. Dad had flipped out and bought a ticket to come down in search of me.

"You what?" I couldn't believe it. "But I told you guys we were leaving for the weekend!"

"Why would we have worried if you'd told us?" Dad countered. "I called the State Department hotline, so I knew about the demonstrations."

"What demonstrations?" I looked over at Pablo, who shook his head. He didn't know of any demonstrations, either. "Dad, everything's super peaceful here. You must have punched in the wrong extension and gotten a report for another country."

"What do you think, I wouldn't have noticed? I called more than once, you know."

"I bet you did."

Mom had been quiet at her end, listening to Dad and me bicker back and forth about whose fault it was that he was worrying. Finally, she got a word in. "We're just glad to hear from you, honey. How are you doing?"

The gentleness in her voice did it. I burst into tears, right there in the Bolívars' living room in the middle of all the unpacking. Everyone started tiptoeing out of the room. Except for Pablo, who came and put his arm around me and let me cry while he explained to my parents that I was fine. It had just been a hard weekend: the official ceremony in the capital, the trip up the mountains, the actual burial near his grandparents' farm. Thank God, Pablo did not mention Los Luceros and Doña Gloria's stories, given Dad's present state of mind.

When I had calmed down, Pablo handed the phone back to me. "I'm sorry I worried you," I said. "So much has been going on. Maybe I did forget to tell you."

"I'm the one who's sorry. I guess your old dad is turning into a real tyrant."

Tyrant? That was not a word I could use lightly anymore. And Dad was hardly a tyrant. Just a worrywart, overprotective, pain-in-the-butt parent I was suddenly missing like crazy. "So you've already bought a ticket, Dad?"

"Don't worry, it's refundable. I was just going to come down if I couldn't get ahold of you."

"But I want you guys to come."

"Oh, honey, really?" Mom didn't wait for me to have second thoughts. "We'll have to see when we can get a flight down," she told Dad on his extension.

Dad cleared his throat. "I, ah, I . . . I actually bought tickets for everyone . . . in case we all had to come down." He sounded a little embarrassed about it. From her end, Mom said, "You did?"—like this was news to her. "I just thought . . . ," Dad tried explaining.

"We'll have to rebook Milly's return so she can come back with us." Mom was already thinking of everything.

Tía Dulce peeked in the doorway to make sure I was okay. I motioned for her and everybody to come back. It was raining outside. This was the only place to sit all together and have a bite before we crashed after the long drive.

"I'll ask Pablo's family about hotels around here." I practically had to shout into the receiver above the voices of everyone returning to the living room.

Mrs. Bolívar overheard me as she brought in a tray of tea. "Tell them they have to stay here." Everyone in the room started chanting, "*Sí, sí, que vengan aquí.*"

"You hear that?" I asked.

"Where are you?" Dad wanted to know. "It sounds like a bar."

"Dad! I'm in the Bolívars' living room." Actually, the house was quieter than usual. The TV was off. And instead of the crowds we'd had before, now it was just *la familia*, eight human beings, and one jabbering parrot brought in off the rainy patio. After a long bout of silence, Pepito was now screeching all the swear words Riqui had taught him during the dictatorship.

Dad had to repeat their flight information several times. I could hardly hear. "Love you, guys," I said before hanging up. We always said that for goodbye. It struck me it was our way of asking for *la bendición*.

On the way to the airport, Pablo and I had picked up the van Dad had reserved with his credit card. It seemed huge. But it was the only size left, and Dad had wanted something where we could all fit with our luggage. Before I even got a chance to ask, Mom had mentioned inviting Pablo to come along with us.

The plan was to spend a few days in the city followed by a couple of days traveling through the interior, then back to a beach resort near the capital for fun and relaxation. Dad was going to get his wish after all. Not the rocky coast of Maine, but palm trees and white sand and a lot warmer waves.

Part of my plan when we traveled inland was to take my family up to Los Luceros to meet Doña Gloria. Her voice still sounded in my head. *I'm counting on you*, she had said. But how was I, Milagros—I was taking my name back!— supposed to bring more light to my corner of the world? In a little over two weeks, my corner would be Ralston High.

How would I even explain Doña Gloria to Em and our friends?

Pablo's hands were on my shoulders. "*¿Qué pasa?*" I guess I did look like I was about to fall over from sunstroke.

"Just thinking about Ralston," I explained. "It's going to be so weird going back. I mean, such different worlds."

"*Yo sé,*" Pablo said quietly. Of course, he would know. He had looked so out of place that day in January when he stood in front of our class. "We are—what is it Jake and all of you call yourselves? The border people?"

"The borderliners."

"*Sí, los* borderliners." Pablo wove his fingers together. "We hold the worlds together. Without us"—he drew them apart—"everything falls apart."

"I guess," I agreed, smiling at the thought of "*los* borderliners"—Jake, Em, Dylan. I couldn't wait to see them! This year, we were going to be the new leaders of our class. Maybe we could work our own little revolution, why not? I mean, look at everything that had happened to me since the day Pablo leaned across the lunch table and asked where I was from.

Thinking about it now on the observation deck, I felt such gratitude toward everyone and everything that had somehow brought me to this moment in my life.

"Thank you, thank you," I whispered, closing my eyes. It would have shocked Tía Dulce to know this is the way I pray.

The roar overhead grew deafening. The plane was coming in for a landing. *"Vuelo de Nueva York,"* the voice over the speaker blared. Flight from New York. Ten minutes early!

Down on the runway, everyone was in motion. The jetway wasn't working, so stairs were being rolled forward by several workmen. Small carts buzzed around like bumper cars at the county fair. In a totally time-warp moment, a donkey with two baskets of flowers strapped to its saddle—like those ornaments people put on their lawns—was led out on the runway by a man wearing a *sombrero*. They were followed by a combo of musicians in colorful peasant costumes. "What's going on?" I asked Pablo.

"It's for *los turistas*." The country was trying hard to draw tourists after twenty or so years of being a war zone. Our own flight hadn't gotten this kind of reception because we had made a connection through Puerto Rico and weren't targeted as tourist material.

The musicians broke into a lively tune as the passengers began deplaning. The donkey guy bowed to each female passenger and handed her a flower. It was a little much, but that's what I loved about this place. Stuff that was over the top in the States was no big deal here.

As each person stepped out of the plane, I felt a rise of anticipation, then a dip of disappointment when it wasn't a member of my family.

But this time, the boy in the Boston Red Sox cap was

Nate! He was looking around excitedly, probably thinking he was back in Disney World—the palm trees, the costumes, the little donkey. I waved, but he didn't see me. Behind him came Kate looking oh-so-cool in a pair of snappy sunglasses and black capri pants with a hot pink belly shirt—stuff she'd probably gotten on her shopping spree with Grandma in New York. Mom and Dad followed, looking wonderfully like the same old Mom and Dad! I waved and hollered. But of course, they couldn't hear me above the noise of luggage carts and the musicians playing.

That was it for my family, or so I thought. But then Dad turned to a familiar-looking woman emerging behind him. She was wearing a long, flowered caftan I had seen before. A pale, skinny man in an outrageously colorful Hawaiian shirt followed, a hand on her elbow.

Happy?! Eli Strong?! My hand froze in midair. And just then, Happy looked up and spotted me. She must have called down to the others, because suddenly my whole family began waving.

From the noisy reunion outside Customs, you'd think we hadn't seen each other for months, not just under two weeks! So much had happened that we couldn't wait until we were all in the van to tell each other about.

The biggest, immediate surprise was Happy's presence. I guess Dad had called to confirm they were all leaving (on

234

Happy's credit card!), and Happy had invited herself along, adding that she was bringing someone special.

"That's all she told us," Mom said, picking up the story where Dad had left off. "We meet up with her at Kennedy this morning, and there she was with Mr. Strong."

"Eli, please," Mr. Strong corrected her. He really looked odd in his wild parrot-and-palm-tree shirt. Like the Mona Lisa with a mustache or something.

"And they're gonna get married here!" Nate could not contain himself.

"Where?" I asked, though really the question could just as well have been why? when? what for?

"I've always wanted a wedding on a tropical island," Happy said in a dreamy voice. I guess by number five she was entitled. She glanced over at Eli, whose fair complexion was already blushed under the sun. Did she really bat her eyes at him?

Pablo looked over at me. I knew what he was thinking. We knew the perfect place for a tropical wedding, our cove.

Somehow, with so much news to exchange and luggage to load, we managed to get everybody in the van. Now I could see why Dad had chosen such a big one. We actually ended up strapping some of the suitcases to the luggage rack on top. Happy was not one to travel light—certainly not to her own wedding!

First stop was the new hotel in the center of the old city. The Bolívars had insisted we stay with them, but even if all the Bolívars moved in with friends and relatives, which is what they were planning to do to make room for their guests—even so, their vacated house would have been too small for all of us. I mean, Happy was used to a whole mansion just to herself!

Besides, Happy wanted the whole family to be together. It turned out that Aunt Joan and the girls would be arriving tomorrow, without Uncle Stan, who unfortunately was recovering from a hemorrhoid operation. (Thank you, Aunt Joan, for the details!)

Although my family ended up declining the Bolívars' invitation, I asked to be allowed to stay with them until we left the city. Mom must have seen the glance that passed between Pablo and me, because before Dad could start in that this was a family trip and we had to stick together, she spoke up. "I think it's a good idea. That way, the Bolívars won't be completely offended by our not staying with them. Besides, I sure hope we're not going to all stick together *every* minute. It'd be kind of nice to have a little . . . tropical time alone." Mom flashed Dad a look not unlike the one Happy had given Eli. At least she didn't bat her eyes at him.

I wanted to tell Mom and Dad everything that had happened, but my heart was so full. I didn't know where to start.

I kept thinking about Ms. Morris's exercise where we

wrote down a couple of details that revealed our secret heart and soul. I had a hundred on my mind. The donkey on the runway, the squalling babies in the nursery at the orphanage, Riqui's infectious laughter, the sound of Doña Gloria's voice.

Someday, I kept thinking, I've got to write them all down!

I thought of these details as *milagritos*. That was the name given to the little medals Dulce had pointed out to me at the church in Los Luceros, pinned to the robe of the Virgin Mary. They were in the shape of tiny eyes or a foot or a heart or a house—a part of the body people wanted the Virgin Mary to heal or a symbol of some problem in their lives they needed help resolving. Each of these medals represented the *milagrito*, or little miracle someone was hoping would come about.

Just as my parents kept that box in their bedroom with my papers, I now had a memory box in my head. It was full of the little miracles that had happened to me in *el paisito*, the little country with the big heart.

One day, when I was ready to write, I would open that box.

Milagritos kept happening even after my family arrived.

My family's first night, the Bolívars invited us all over for a feast, a kind of repeat of my first night in the country—

237

hard to believe that had only been ten days ago! A huge spread was laid out in the open-air patio, including a roast pig on a platter with a mango in its mouth. "Awesome!" Nate exclaimed, but his little face got an I-think-I'm-going-to-throw-up look when he heard this was *dinner*. Dulce and Mrs. Bolívar absolutely refused help from anyone, except from Esperanza and me. We were allowed to serve, clear, and order anyone who stood up to help to sit back down or else.

"Wait till you taste Tía Dulce's *arroz y habichuelas*," I said, squeezing in beside Kate. Supposedly, rice and beans had been our favorite food when we were both toddlers. We'd share a plate, picking up a bean and a few grains at a time with our hands.

"Who's *Tía* Dulce?" Kate made a face, as if to say, *I don't know about you, but I don't have an aunt named Dulce.*

Pablo glanced over at me, a slight lift to one eyebrow. He must have noticed, too. Kate had been especially quiet since she arrived—not her usual parading of her Spanish expertise. A couple of times, I tried asking her about her trip to New York. *Fine* was as much detail as she seemed to want to share with me.

Before we ate, Mr. Bolívar offered a toast to his wonderful friends from Los Estados Unidos. He was so "emotioned"—as he called it—that after a few words in English, he just automatically started speaking in Spanish. What he said would have been corny if it wasn't so totally true—how families

238

were made with the heart, how out of incredible tragedy had come the miracle of understanding and love, how we were all a *familia* now. Kate glanced over at me uncertainly, then looked away, tears in her eyes.

I almost started to cry a few times, too, but then Happy or Eli or Nate would ask me, "What's he saying?" and my emotioned self would go out the window. Translating corny stuff was like when Em had to explain a dirty joke to me.

Meanwhile, Pepito began calling out swear words— which Mom wouldn't let me translate for Nate at the table. In the middle of the meal: a crack of thunder, lightning— then rain began to pour on our dinner party, which was quickly moved into the small living room.

Nobody said a miracle had to be perfect.

There we stayed until late, finishing our meal, and drinking *cafecitos*. After a few shots of rum, Riqui and Camilo began talking in broken English about their revolutionary experiences. The Truth Commission. The hopeful but painful process of rebuilding the country. Nate had fallen asleep on Mr. Strong's lap; otherwise, I think my parents would have insisted on leaving. Nate really was too young to listen to all this. As for Mom and Dad, they looked exhausted after getting up at four this morning in Vermont to make their New York connection. But this wasn't exactly the kind of conversation you could walk out on. Kate was intent on listening, and turning and turning the new necklace I'd gotten for her on my first day here—a portable lazy Susan, at last.

239

I figured it was a good sign she was even wearing it. At one point, I couldn't stand the distance between us. I reached over and took her hand. She didn't squeeze back, but at least she let me stay holding her hand.

Meanwhile, Happy sat at the edge of the sofa, shaking her head. "I had no idea," she kept saying over and over. "Why, it's like what my mother's people went through in the Holocaust!"

"When we get back, we'll have to call Senator Barney. He chairs the foreign relations committee," she informed the Bolívar brothers. "I've given a lot of money to his campaign. Don't you think that's a good idea, Eli?"

"Indeed," Mr. Strong agreed. "Terrible, terrible thing," he added, I guess to show he had been listening.

Another *milagrito*.

It started out as the worst day. August 15, my family's first full day in the capital, just so happened to fall on my "birthday."

I *hated* my birthday. Was I really supposed to celebrate the day I was given away by someone who was obviously not celebrating having me be born? And it wasn't even *the* day I was born! Every year, I'd always get wicked PBS, pre-birthday syndrome, which reached its awful climax on August 15. Honestly, I didn't know why my family insisted on celebrating the day I was at my worst.

Since we were so far from home and away from our usual routines, I was hoping—against hope, I know—that everyone would sort of forget my "birthday." But, of course, Mom and Dad told the Bolívars, and that morning I woke up to my whole family *and* all the Bolívars singing "Happy Birthday" and *"Las Mañanitas"* (a birthday serenade song) on the patio just outside my window.

I pulled the sheet over my head. Maybe if I pretended to fall asleep, they'd go away.

"Yoo-hoo! Milly!" Mom finally called. She knew I couldn't sleep through the phone ringing on the first floor in Vermont. For sure, I was awake.

"Hey, sleepyhead," Dad joined in. Then someone was tapping at the window.

Grrrrrr! If I hadn't been a guest staying at the house of the parents of the love of my life, I would have used some of the swear words I'd learned from Pepito this past week.

But I tried to be gracious when I came out and all my family, Kaufmans and non-Kaufmans, broke out into yet another round of each song. Pablo threw me a helpless look. He must have tried to stop this. Meanwhile, Kate was cheering like crazy. Great, I thought. Finally, Kate was being friendly, doing something I detest.

When I got a moment alone with Mom and Dad, I whispered that I wished they hadn't spread the news around.

"Oh, honey! It's your birthday. We want to celebrate *you!*"

241

"But it's not my birthday. It's not even close. Sor Arabia at the orphanage said I was probably four months old when I got left on their doorstep."

"We told you that, honey," Dad reminded me. I knew they must have, but it was funny how sometimes you didn't register something your parents told you over and over until someone outside the family mentioned it once.

Meanwhile, Mom was all curious about the orphanage. "Sor Arabia? What orphanage? You mean the one you mentioned on the phone?"

That was how the idea got started of visiting CRI. First, it was just Mom and Dad going, but the visit soon turned into a group outing. Everyone, including Grandma, wanted to see the place. On the way, we stopped at the bakery and bought the biggest cake on hand, a sheet cake with coconut frosting. "No, it's not a birthday cake," Mom assured me. "Just a treat for all the kids." We also ordered a wedding cake to be picked up in a week. It turned out that Happy and Eli would not be getting married until the end of the trip because the paperwork took that long, even with Camilo, a lawyer, helping us. Happy winked at Eli. "We get to live in sin, darling."

Eli blushed the color of the hibiscus on another one of his loud shirts. How many Hawaiian shirts had Grandma bought him? I wondered.

We arrived at El Centro de Rehabilitación Infantil with the cake and a carton of sodas and a big bag of ice we picked

242

up at the *supermercado*. Sor Arabia was beside herself with gratitude and welcome. She claimed to remember Mom, who said that of course she remembered Sor Arabia. I could tell Mom was just being polite, and later in the van, she admitted that the only nun she remembered was Sor Corita, and that was only because over the years she'd been able to refresh her memory with the pictures in my box. "I was so in love with my two little babies, I'm afraid I didn't pay much attention to anyone else. You know how it is when you fall in love with someone. . . ." Mom's voice trailed off. She could tell something was up between me and Pablo, but we hadn't had a private moment, just the two of us, to talk.

Meanwhile, Sor Arabia couldn't get over Kate. "You haven't changed a bit!" she exclaimed. Oh, come on! Kate had been less than a year old the last time Sor Arabia could have seen her, right before my parents left this country. I thought nuns weren't supposed to lie. "Those same beautiful brown eyes and that sweet smile." Sor Arabia looked fondly at Kate, who was eating it up.

They hooked arms, and finally, Kate's Spanish was unleashed. During the ensuing tour, Kate asked all sorts of questions about the orphanage and whether they accepted interns. I felt that old gnawing of jealousy and competition in my gut. I tried reminding myself that this was Kate's way of showing interest in my past. A first step. But still, the heart feels what it feels, as Pablo might say. Ms. Morris once said basically the same thing when we were reading Anne

Frank's diary, and someone said something like, "Jeez, there's a Holocaust going on and this girl's complaining about her mother?!" Well, here I was in the middle of an orphanage, having an attack of sibling rivalry.

Kate sidled up to me. "Do you remember any of this?" she whispered.

"Of course not," I told her.

"Phew." She sighed. "That nun had me half believing that I remembered her." We exchanged a knowing grin.

Another step, I thought.

In the dining hall, the kids were waiting, super excited by the American visitors. The little guy who once ate up my cake was especially taken with Nate. He kept staring at this boy: his white skin, his blue eyes, and as it turned out, his baseball cap! Nate let him try it on, but then the little guy wouldn't take it off. Nate was too afraid to ask for it, but some kids were quick to point out to Sor Arabia that the cap hadn't been returned, and she made the little guy give it back.

After the introductions, the cake was brought in. The kids clapped. I beamed my family a *don't-even-go-there* look when I sensed the birthday song wafting through their brains. This time they actually gave me what I wanted and didn't sing it. We all sat down to eat cake, and this little guy wiggled in beside Nate. There goes Nate's piece, I thought.

But the little guy didn't ask for Nate's cake. Instead, he nudged his own serving over and gestured toward the cap lying on Nate's other side. Nate didn't get it and shook his head, meaning *I don't want more cake*, which this little guy took to mean that a serving of cake was no trade for a Red Sox baseball cap. So he dug into his pocket and out came a half dozen metal jacks to add to the bargain. What an outcry! The little girls at the table went wild. So that was who'd been stealing their jacks! I hated to think what awaited this little guy once we left. But I was so proud of Nate. As we stood up to go, he took off his cap and set it on this little guy's head.

Meanwhile, Happy pulled out her checkbook and wrote out a donation. She handed it to Sor Arabia, who turned pale with disbelief.

"You always bring *milagros* when you come," she whispered to Pablo and me as she bid us goodbye, adding, "New plumbing for the nursery."

This *milagrito* almost didn't happen.

There was a revolution—in the family—about plans.

After Aunt Joan and the cousins arrived, we stayed one more day in the capital. Next, we were supposed to head for the mountains. But it turned out that most everyone wanted to bypass the mountains and go directly to the beach resort.

We put it up to a vote. Only Mom and I raised our hands for the mountains. Dad was undecided because he was worried about driving conditions in the interior.

245

"We're overruled," Mom said cheerily, like she wasn't that sorry to lose. By now, Dad had gotten her worrying about the bad mountain roads he had never been on.

But Happy—yes, Happy!—read the disappointment in my eyes. She came up with a new plan. Why didn't she hire a driver to take me and Mom and whoever else wanted to go along on a mountain outing? Then we could all meet back at the beach resort. "We old folks need to rest up for our honeymoon." This time, she winked at me.

"Where are you going to find an experienced driver?" Dad challenged. I had noticed he stood up to Happy a lot more now. "It's not like we can just call up Roger."

"This is not a problem," Pablo explained. "You can hire a driver where we rented the van. They are very reliable. All the international agencies arrange for their transportation there." How could Dad argue with that?

But when he had Mom and me alone, Dad tried a new tack. "I just think it would be nice for us to all be together. You know, a *family* vacation."

"This is about . . . my family," I said, coming clean. And then I told them why I wanted them to see Los Luceros, how it was likely my birth parents had come from there. I worried that all the stuff about the eyes was going to seem over the top to them. I mean, in the States, if you claimed that everyone from a certain town had the same eyes, people would think you'd been watching too many Spielberg movies. But Mom wasn't that surprised. It turned out Mrs. Bolívar had

246

told her about Los Luceros when Mom noticed that Dulce and Esperanza had "Milly's eyes."

But Dad was nonplussed. "Let's get this straight," he said, hands on his hips. "You *did* go on a search for your birth parents—" He stopped just short of saying "after you assured us you wouldn't."

My eyes filled. "I didn't mean to," I tried explaining. "It just happened." The visit to the orphanage had led to meeting Sor Arabia. The trip to bury Daniel had led me to Los Luceros.

Mom was nodding, like she understood. But Dad still had a problem with my story. And I didn't blame him. It wasn't just Kate, I could see now, it was everyone in the family having to rearrange the puzzle pieces so that all our stories fit in. What if we couldn't get the pieces back together and be a family again? That girl, Pandora, popped into my head, how after she opened that box of trouble, the world was never the same. Suddenly, I was the one feeling scared.

"Honestly, Mil, I don't know where we failed you." Dad looked frustrated. "I thought you felt you could come to us."

"It's not like I went sneaking . . . it just kind of . . ." Soon I was sobbing too hard to even try to explain.

And this was how I knew my parents and I, anyhow, were going to be okay. When Dad saw me sobbing, he hurried over and put his arm around me. He remembered to be my father before he remembered to finish his lecture.

"I'm sorry, Dad," I said between sobs. "You've got to

believe me. You didn't fail me. The whole reason I could even go to Los Luceros is that I have you guys." It sounded lame, like I was blaming them for what I'd done.

But Dad was really listening, head bowed. Like maybe this was making sense to him.

"And I want you to know that I actually found what I was looking for."

Dad's head snapped up, his eyes a little worried. Mom looked surprised.

"No, no, I don't mean I found my birth parents. I mean . . ." How to explain this feeling that I'd touched bottom in my heart? How did I say that to anyone? How did I say it to my parents? "It's like . . . I found . . . Milagros. I mean, I'm still me, Milly . . . but now, I'm more me." How could something so simple sound so confusing?

But Mom and Dad were nodding as if to encourage me as I stumbled along. When I was done, Dad said, "We understand," which caught me totally by surprise. That was usually Mom's line.

"We would love to go see this place with you." Mom was smiling, her eyes soft and moist.

"Ditto." Dad nodded. My good old eloquent father! My sweet mom! I couldn't help throwing my arms around them. It felt so good for a moment, but then sort of embarrassing when we pulled apart and we all had red eyes and stupid grins on our faces.

We hired a driver with a jeep—Dad did insist on a four-wheel-drive vehicle. Pablo came along as our guide. Before we set out for the interior, Dad made a last-ditch effort to make this a family trip. But there was no budging Nate from Grandma's side after she mentioned making reservations for a whale-watching excursion. Meanwhile, Kate was back in her angry mode, still refusing to accept the fact that I had a birth family at all. "We *are* your family!" she insisted. Before we left, I scribbled a note. "Remember, no matter what, sisters *for life*. I love you and always will." I just hoped the cousins didn't find it first. Something I only thought about *after* I slipped the note under the door to their suite.

So the *milagrito* that almost didn't happen happened, but it turned out different from what I'd planned. Our first stop in Los Luceros was the little church. Mom bought a *milagrito* medal in the shape of a heart for Happy and Eli, then bought one for our family, and some for all the friends who were now a part of our circle of family. Dad bought a car—he was still worrying about road safety! I found this *milagrito* of two figures with joined hands, a medal to protect twins. For Kate and me, I thought. The other one I picked out was a tiny ring. When I turned to show Pablo, he was holding one up, too.

"What's that one for?" Dad asked the old lady selling them at the back of the church. While she explained that the ring *milagrito* was for weddings, for anniversaries, for vows made by a young novice before she became a bride of

Christ, Pablo and I headed for the statue of the Virgin at the front of the church.

"*Tu y yo*," Pablo said, pinning his tiny ring to the Virgencita's skirt.

You and I, like the flower. I smiled, remembering my first morning on the island. So many memories since! I pinned my ring next to his.

Then, while Mom and Dad were snapping a photo of the old lady and her panel of *milagritos*, we sealed our wish with a kiss and a thank you to the Virgencita.

The main reason for coming to the mountains was for Mom and Dad to meet Doña Gloria. But that first night with Dulce's family, the whole town came over to greet the special visitors. It turned out they thought Mom and Dad were here from yet another Truth Commission to collect testimonies. Everyone had a story about some missing son or murdered father or brother or husband. Mom couldn't stop crying. Meanwhile, Dad hardly talked, which is what he does instead of crying when he's really upset. It wasn't that Mom and Dad didn't know this stuff had gone on, but now, because of me, they felt intimately connected to it.

After Mom and Dad went to bed, Pablo and I took a walk around the square. I told him that I was having second thoughts about taking them to Doña Gloria's.

He had noticed, too. "Your parents feel responsible."

"It's like they've benefited from someone's tragedy. I mean, our happiness as a family comes out of somebody else having had a horrible life. It doesn't, I know," I added when Pablo looked like he was going to protest, "but then again, it does."

"But you wanted so much for them to meet Doña Gloria, no?" Pablo's voice felt soothing, like Mom's hand on my forehead when I had a fever.

"I know." I sighed. "But tonight, when I looked at Mom and Dad, they seemed so sad and helpless. I felt like, well, like *they* needed a mom and dad."

Pablo smiled sadly, as if he was thinking of his own parents and what they had been through. *"Pobrecitos,"* he agreed.

"I haven't exactly been easy to live with for the last eight months. No, seriously," I said before Pablo tried to defend me again.

Pablo put his arm around me and squeezed. "The truth is, your parents are so *especial.* They are people who spread more light."

I wondered how I could have missed it! It seemed so obvious now. Mom and Dad didn't have to come to this country; they didn't have to adopt some sick little orphan. In some ways, they weren't that different from Dolores and Javier and Tío Daniel and Pablo's brothers. Why make it any harder for them now?

"Ever since Doña Gloria, I've been thinking what big

251

heroic thing I could do with my life," I admitted to Pablo, who nodded as if he entertained these thoughts, too. "But it's like how in Spanish everything is a little this and a little that." I had pointed it out to him: how his mother and aunt were always talking about our little meals, our little appetites, our little outings in the little afternoon.

"Well, I'm not the big-hero, capital-letters type person," I went on. "I'm more a lowercase type. Milagritos, not Milagros." I had to smile, thinking how my nickname did fit me. "And here's a chance to do a little something. I can choose to spare my parents more grief. And it's not just them. Oh, Pablo, you know what'll happen if we take them up there. Doña Gloria will want to share all the stories she told us, and then probably some others she's thought about since. And like you saw, it's so hard on her to talk about all that stuff."

"Milagritos, Milagritos." Pablo rocked me in his arms. "And I was worried Doña Gloria's stories would be too much for you. But this country has made you strong!"

I crumpled in his arms. "Who, me? Strong?" I thought of telling him what Ms. Morris had said about stories saving your life, stories helping you find yourself when you got lost. But I thought it was something Pablo and his family already knew. Why else had they sat for hours in front of that TV listening to those awful testimonies?

We walked in silence for a while, holding hands, pointing out the stars. "Looks like the sky is keeping Doña

252

Gloria's promise. . . . To make more light," I added, though I doubted Pablo had forgotten. It seemed like there were twice as many tonight as before.

Maybe it was from looking at their light that I got the idea. "It'd be great for Doña Gloria's great-granddaughter to go to school. You think maybe we can talk Tía Dulce into arranging it?"

Pablo looked doubtful. "You know how Tía Dulce is about girls leaving home. But the truth is that Doña Gloria is becoming too frail to live so isolated. She should move to town. That way, her great-granddaughter can have an opportunity. I think it's a brilliant idea."

"I got it from on high," I joked, pointing at the sky.

"Then Tía Dulce will approve for sure." Pablo laughed.

I looked up and caught myself wishing on stars again.

The next morning at breakfast, Mom and Dad looked wasted. It turned out that they hadn't slept a wink all night.

"I think we should head back today," I suggested. "We can be at the resort by tonight."

They both tried not to look too eager. After all, they didn't want to wimp out on our side trip. "Didn't you want us to spend a couple of days here?" Dad asked, swallowing a yawn.

"I just wanted you to see this place," I explained. "Next time, we can all come up together and stay longer. Now, it's probably better if we get back." I didn't have to tell them about the tension between Kate and me. They could see it.

"Well, if you're sure?" Mom asked.

"Totally," I assured her.

Mom sighed with relief. "Then I think it probably is best, honey."

We made plans to leave after lunch, stopping on the way to visit Abuelita. Pablo wanted my parents to meet his grandmother, and of course, he welcomed the opportunity to see her one last time. After all, he probably wouldn't be back for another year.

"Is she the Doña Gloria you spoke of?" Mom wanted to know. "Or was that Dulce's mother last night?" I couldn't blame poor Mom. So many names and stories and people had come at them since they landed.

"Not really," I said, hesitating. If I went into too much detail, Mom was going to feel she should visit Doña Gloria. And I was more and more convinced that I'd made the right choice by not taking my parents up to see her.

"Doña Gloria is one of the oldest inhabitants of this area," Pablo stepped in. But I could see he didn't know where to head with his explanation. "She knows many more stories."

"I think we've heard enough stories for now," Dad said grimly.

* * *

We rolled into the resort late that night. But no one was in their rooms, not even Nate, who was supposed to have a little cot in Aunt Joan's room until Mom and Dad returned.

"What on earth?" Dad said.

"They are watching the stars," the man at the front desk explained. He gestured toward the back of the hotel. "There is a shower of light," he added, bowing politely as if he were announcing a special on the menu. We had heard about the meteor shower from Pablo's brothers in the capital.

We walked down some steps to an outdoor courtyard that hung above the sea. I could hear the waves crashing on the cliffs below. Torches were flaring around the perimeter, like this was an episode from some *Survivor*-type show on TV. And this was the little miracle we found: my family, in all their splendid, complicated, ornery glory, sprawled on those lounge chairs that you can slide back to the exact degree you want to tan when the sun is showing. The cuzzes were arguing with Aunt Joan about what a meteor shower actually meant. Meanwhile, Nate was snuggled beside Happy, who sat next to Mr. Strong, holding his hand across the space between them. Off to the side, her towel wrapped around her like a protective cocoon, I spotted Kate.

Everyone twisted around to look at us.

"*What* are you doing *here*?" they all seemed to ask at the same time.

While Mom and Dad explained and Pablo went off to hunt down some more lounge chairs, I headed for Kate. It

255

took her a second to acknowledge I was there. "What're you guys doing back?" she asked, like she didn't care.

"We missed you too much," I said. So she wouldn't think I was teasing her, I added, "It's not the same without you, you know." No response. It was like a Shakespeare soliloquy talking to my sister these days. Sometimes I'd ask myself, why keep trying? But then I'd hung in there with Happy, and Kate was like Mother Teresa in comparison. "So, can I scoot in beside you, sister-for-life?" I invited myself.

She didn't say anything, but she did make room for me.

"Has it started yet?" I asked, glancing up. The stars looked pretty awesome already. I couldn't imagine a meteor shower topping this sight.

"Not yet," she murmured. "Though Nate keeps screaming every few minutes that he's seen *something*."

"Ah, family," I sighed.

"You said it," Kate sighed back, like she *was* Mother Teresa. But she was smiling. I was sure of it, even if I couldn't really see her face in the dim light. She was my sister, I knew her moves. I could tell a smile from a scowl. I could sense she was starting to trust that love was going to hold us together after all. Give or take a few bumps.

Suddenly, attendants were hurrying around, snuffing out the torches. We looked up.

"Hey!" we all seemed to cry out at once. The light show was starting.

One Last Milagrito

A WEEK LATER, late afternoon.

The wedding party is standing in my favorite cove, which has turned into a wind tunnel. All day, the weather has been sunny, mild, and glorious. But by midafternoon, the wind picks up. Grandma's white caftan blows out dramatically behind her, suddenly looking a lot like the train of a wedding gown. Poor Eli's hair, the little he has that he plasters down over his bald spot, is standing straight up. He looks like an overgrown baby with a cowlick on top. We can barely hear each other talk above the howl of the wind. When we try to light candles, they're blown out. Instead of rice, we are pelted by droplets of water as the waves crash to shore. I start to feel this panic feeling, like the time

Happy came to Vermont and I worried she'd blame the cold weather on us.

But here is a little miracle. Camilo is serving as our justice of the peace—despite Dulce's fervent prayers that Happy will have a last-minute conversion and be married by a priest. Just when we're about to mutiny and take this party indoors, the wind dies down enough for us to hear Camilo pronounce in his broken English that Eli and Happy are man and wife.

"So what are we gonna call you now?" Nate pipes up. As always, out of the mouth of the baby in the family comes the question no one else can get away with asking. We're all assuming Eli will now be Mr. Kaufman.

"What do you mean?" Happy swoops down and hugs her precious grandson. "You keep calling me Grandma!"

"No, Ma," Aunt Joan explains. "Natie means, are you going to keep your name or what?" From the depths of her big purse, her cell phone starts ringing.

"What on earth!" Grandma's mouth drops open in disbelief. "I didn't think that I needed to make an announcement at my own wedding for cell phones to be turned off."

"Hello! Hello!" Aunt Joan is hollering into the tiny mouthpiece, but she can't pick up a voice. "It was probably Stan wanting to congratulate the bride," she explains, folding up her phone and putting it away. Grandma can't get mad at that. "Anyhow, Ma, are you going to be Mrs.

Kaufman or Mrs. Strong?" Good old Aunt Joan, all-around bigmouth and family troublemaker.

"I actually like your Spanish way of doing things," Happy says, smiling graciously at the Bolívars. "The woman keeps her name but then adds her husband's name, right? Katherine Kaufman de Strong. Sounds like a title, very European. Don't you think so, sweetie?"

"Indeed," Eli agrees. I guess he's Grandpa Eli now.

I decide to speak up. "While we're talking names, I want to make an announcement."

"Are you going to get married, too?" Nate cries out.

If I weren't so tanned and Pablo so dark, everyone would see us both blushing.

"Silly!" I dismiss such an incredible thought. "I just want you guys to know that I'm taking back my original name, Milagros. I mean, everyone who wants can keep calling me Milly, but I'll also answer to Milagros."

Kate lets out one of those breaths like a fire-breathing dragon in a cartoon. Here we go again, I think.

"I'm calling you Milly, period," she states, folding her arms. "That's. Your. Name." Each word is like the gavel of a judge in court.

I fold my arms right back at her. "It's actually up to *me* to decide what my name is, Ka-ther-ine." I draw out her name, which I know she dislikes, though with her namesake present, she can't act too disgusted. If all these people weren't around, I'd go on to tell Big Sister for Life that she can stop bossing me around. We're probably the same age, as it turns out.

"I'm really sick of you disowning us!" Kate starts to cry. How did this get started? Even if it's sort of crazy for my grandmother to be getting married by a former revolutionary on a windy beach in a Third World country, this is still supposed to be a wedding.

"Any other announcements?" Dad tries to joke. But no one laughs.

"I've got an announcement," Nate pipes up again. "Anybody got a knife or a safety pin?"

"A knife?" Happy looks surprised. "A safety pin?"

"Yeah!" Nate is too caught up with his idea to explain.

It turns out Happy has a safety pin on her corsage, and Mrs. Bolívar has a stash of anything you can think of in her purse. Soon we have half a dozen safety pins.

"We can disinfect them with the candles," Nate goes on excitedly. He is a boy possessed. On his sweet, freckled face I see the same wild look as in our inventor grandfather's portrait that hangs in Happy's living room. "This summer in camp we all became blood brothers. It's a Native American tradition. An ancient Native American tradition." Nate's voice is growing desperate. He can tell from the looks he's getting that his great idea is not going to get patented here. His bottom lip starts to tremble. "Come on, everybody, it doesn't hurt, really!" Tears form in the corners of his eyes. "I mean, that way we can all be blood family."

"Oh, sweetheart," Mom says, hugging Nate. She glances helplessly at Dad, then over at Kate and me. Our baby brother doesn't miss much. He has obviously picked up on all the tension lately, the talk about adoption, birth parents, blood family, disinheritance. How can we refuse him?

Besides, his doting grandmother is totally won over. "I absolutely insist that we close the ceremony with this ancient tradition."

Dad's a little worried. I can tell what he's thinking. The safety pins can be disinfected, but what if someone's blood is carrying an infectious disease. Camilo and Riqui are young men, and this culture is not exactly known for male chastity. "We assume everyone's clean?" He makes a joke. "If anyone knows any reason we should not be blood family, speak now or forever hold your peace."

No one confesses to anything. I'm sure most of the people here don't even get what Dad's worrying about.

And so we do it, but in a wimpy, reformed Native American fashion, so as not to have to prick ourselves however many times. The safety pins are distributed, one pinprick each, a droplet, which we pass around the circle. Eli starts. He touches Happy, who touches Nate, who touches Dad, who touches Mom, who touches Kate, who turns to me. It's the moment I've been dreading as I followed the touch going around the circle.

"Hey," she says, touching her finger to mine, "sisters forever?"

262

I answer her by bursting into tears just as she bursts into tears. We look like we're mirror images of each other. When we pull apart, I can tell from her runny mascara that mine has probably smeared, too. The cousins are full of glances. It is kind of hard to have a reconciliation in front of your whole family.

When I turn, Pablo lifts his hand to meet mine. I feel my whole body tingle, as if he were touching all of me. Finally, Pablo pulls his gaze away and turns to touch his mother, who passes it on to his father, to Aunt Joan, to the cousins, then on to Riqui, Camilo, Dulce, finishing with Esperanza—a lucky sign, I think, seeing as her name means hope.

Actually, in my head the circle doesn't stop here at all. The spark gets passed on to Em and Jake and Dylan and the kids at Ralston this fall who'll raise enough money so that Doña Gloria's great-granddaughter can go to school and learn to write down the stories of Rosa and the colonel and Alicia and Manuel and Javier and Dolores. On and on, the spark gets passed, person to person, to the tune of Alfie singing, "May the circle be unbroken." The way I figure it, with six-plus billion people in our human family right now, that many sparks sure could make a whole lot of light.

"We're blood family!" Nate proclaims. Everybody cheers.

The tide is coming in. The waves have already soaked the hem of Grandma's caftan. Time to go. Dinner and cake at their house, the Bolívars insist! But before we leave the beach, Pablo and I look at each other. We have one more thing to do. We climb quickly before everyone starts to holler that we're going the wrong way. Hurry! Hurry!

At the monument, we stand for a minute, looking out at the sea. Tomorrow I'll be leaving this country with some of my family. The Bolívars will follow a few days later. But even when they join us in Ralston, part of me will always be here in the little country where so many *milagritos* have happened.

"Pablo! Milly! Milagritos!" Everyone is calling for us to come.

Before we go, we read the inscription: *"On this spot, the noble martyrs fell and with their blood gave birth to a new nation."* But also on this spot, Grandma got married. Pablo and I fell in love. Little moments, dark and light, to put in the box. Someday, I'll write them down in a story—one way to keep my promise to Doña Gloria!

I close my eyes. *"La bendición,"* I whisper. I'm not sure to whom or to what. All I know is I need a blessing to take home with me.

The sun's going down fast, but just before it sets, there's an angle where it hits the sand and the water. For a moment, when I open my eyes, there is a little more light on the beach.

Acknowledgments

Over the years, I've been blessed with the light of so many children! Among them, my two stepdaughters, Sara and Berit. Your faith, patience, perseverance, and tolerance have been a blessing, have made us all into a family.

To my nieces and nephews, from your *tía* who loves you like a second *mamá*. And to my first grandchild, Naomi. I can't wait till you start reading, so we can share books!

To my godchildren from the motherland, Quisqueya, *la bendición:* Estel, Anamery, Rosmery, Miguelina. And to my *comadres,* whose hard lives make raising these children so difficult! *Gracias* for the honor of allowing me to help you.

To Lizzi, what a gift you have been to me! Your example and your story have been an inspiration. And to you, Marisa Casey, *gracias* for your wonderful emailed notes and anecdotes! And special thanks to your *mami*, Filis Casey, and the work her agency, Alliance for Children, has done and continues to do to help connect children with families in which they can flourish.

To my teenage consultants, Tori Vondle, Ellie Romp, Geetha Wunnava. And to my advisor on eight-year-olds, Nicolas Kramer, who is already ten but "remembers being eight." Thanks for the video game info.

To my helper, Amy Beaupré-Oliver, thanks for finding needles in haystacks, and for threading them for me, too. And to Marianne Doe, and the teachers and principal of Middlebury Union High School, who let me hang out in your classrooms and ask questions. How do you do it, day after day, year after year? Your tireless devotion to the young people of this community enriches us all.

To my favorite librarians, Fleur Laslocky, Carol Chatfield, and Joy Pile, willing to help me find the answers to the little questions my characters ask.

To my editor, Andrea Cascardi, *madrina*/godmother of this book, always believing I can do more and, somehow, bringing it forth. To Erin Clarke, for being the second *madrina*, ready to step in and help. To my cousin, Lyn Tavares, always so willing to proofread *mi español*. And to my guardian agent, Susan Bergholz, who puts in more hours than any agent or guardian or angel I know! *¡Gracias de nuevo!*

Without my *compañero*, the house of words would be built on the shifting sands of loneliness and self-doubt. *Gracias*, Bill, for the life together that makes the writing flower.

In Spanish the word for raising children is *criar*, just a vowel away from *crear*, to create. To raise compassionate, peace-loving children is a creative and loving labor. To the mothers *y madres*, fathers *y padres* who struggle to master this art. May all our children find their own stories so that they can create lives of meaning, purpose, and promise.

Always *y siempre*, for you, *Virgencita de la Altagracia, madre*, nurturer, and helper to all who struggle to *crear y criar* and, thereby, fill the world with a little more light. *¡Mil gracias!*

Finding Miracles

JULIA ALVAREZ

A Reader's Guide

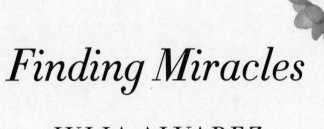

Questions for Discussion

1. In the novel's opening chapter, Milly claims to be allergic to herself. What does she mean by this? Give some examples of moments when this allergic reaction occurs and explain what causes it.

2. Early in the novel, Milly confesses, "The point is: I totally pass as 100 percent American, and as un-PC as this is going to sound, I'm really glad." Why do you think Milly is so afraid to reveal that she's adopted? How would you react to such news from a classmate?

3. When the Kaufmans go to the Bolivars' apartment to watch the election results, Pablo is noticeably troubled, leading Milly to comment that she's never seen anyone her own age so distraught over politics. The most important election in her life so far is the one for Ralston's student government. Do you feel similarly shielded from political worries? Do you follow

271

elections: locally, nationally, or globally? Are there political issues that affect your daily life?

4. In chapter five, Happy reveals to Milly that she, too, is a kind of orphan. What does she mean by this? Is Happy making a valid comparison?

5. During her stay with the Bolivars in her birth country, Milly gets a vision of family life—especially in terms of extended family—that is very different from her own. The easy affection of Tía Dulce, for example, is a far cry from Happy's reserve. What other differences do you notice in the family routines and attitudes?

6. Why is Kate so negative about Milly's trip with the Bolivars? Are her concerns justified?

7. The importance of names—both the ones we are given and the ones we choose—is central to the novel. How is this theme reflected in the stories of both Milly and Happy?

8. At one point, Pablo tells Milly, "Some say let us forget the past and build the future. Others say we cannot build the future without knowing the past." Kate—and, to some degree, Milly's parents—seems to advocate the former strategy, but Milly isn't convinced.

What do you think? Is it always better to know the historical truth, or does a focus on the past keep us from moving forward? Does Milly find what she's looking for in her birth country? Is it worth the worry it causes her family in Vermont?

9. What do you think Doña Gloria means when she tells Milly and Pablo that she's counting on them to "bring more light"? Do they fulfill this request? How?

In Her Own Words—
A Conversation with Julia Alvarez

Q. Most of your previous novels deal with immigrants from or residents of the Dominican Republic. In *Finding Miracles*, though, you choose to leave Milly's birth country unnamed. Why?

A. I really did not want to specify Milly's birth country.

My point was to underscore the fact that throughout the second half of the twentieth century, Latin America was rife with dictatorships, police states, horrible repressive regimes. (In the late 1970s, for example, only three countries in Latin America had freely elected governments.) Thousands upon thousands of people lost their lives, and the verb form "to be disappeared" entered our vocabulary. People who protested, many of them young students, were rounded up, tortured, killed. Many children were left orphans or lost their childhood altogether. By not specifying the country, I thought I would make it harder for readers to dismiss how pervasive this situation was. ("Oh, that only happened in Guatemala or Chile or El Salvador.") This was mass genocide, not over in Nazi Germany or Saddam Hussein's Iraq, but right here in our American hemisphere, with dictators and regimes often put in place and supported by our very own United States. A dark period in our American history that we have still not fully faced.

What was hard was inventing a geography and culture that could be any number of Latin American countries but none specifically!

By the way, at first my editor felt it would not work to leave Milly's birth country unnamed. Most times I listen to her (and she is usually right!), but this time, I held fast to my original notion. It just so happened that as I was working on *Finding Miracles*, I read Ann Patchett's wonderful novel *Bel Canto*, which takes place in an unspecified Latin American country. It turned out to be one of my favorite novels. I mentioned it to my editor as proof that it could be done. Of course, by then she was convinced that I could pull it off.

This, too, I've learned as a teacher and mentor of young writers when they ask me, "Can such and such be done . . . ?" or "Is it okay to . . . ?" I tell them: anything is possible in a story if you can pull it off, if you can get away with it!

Q. Throughout the book, Milly feels simultaneously detached from and drawn to her birth country. Having left the Dominican Republic for the northeastern United

276

States at a young age, did you experience a similar sense of conflict over which place was your "real" home?

A. I certainly did experience very strong homesickness when I arrived in the United States at the age of ten. Although I had been born in the U.S., my parents had returned to their birth country when I was three months old, so the Dominican Republic was my home; my extended *familia* were all there; Spanish was my native tongue. That first year in New York, I couldn't get used to the cold, the English language, the prejudice of some of my classmates at school who chased my sisters and me around in the playground, calling us spics and telling us to go back to where we came from.

What happened, though, was that slowly I began to adapt to my new country. I learned English. I became a reader. I dreamed of writing my own stories down. When I went back "home" to the Dominican Republic for vacations, I no longer totally belonged there anymore. I had changed, become Americanized. But then, once I was back on USA soil, I also didn't feel like I was totally American. In a sense, I was a person without a country, which made me seek the company and community of books. Every writer, I believe, feels that through story we are all connected, all one human family.

Milly's case is a little different from my own experience. She wants desperately to feel one hundred percent U.S. American so as not to be different from her brother and sister, Kate and Nate, who are biological siblings and children of Milly's parents. But she feels the absence of a part of her story that she has kept locked in her heart and that keeps tugging at the edges of her consciousness and prickling her skin in rashes! Like me, Milly is a hybrid, and she needs to include both parts of her story in order to be fully herself. But unlike me, Milly does not have a full-blown childhood experience of her birth country to give her a sense of what she is missing. Hers is a bigger blank than mine ever was.

Q. You originally found success in the world of adult fiction. What prompted you to begin writing for young adults and children? Do you approach the writing process differently for your juvenile work? Do you find yourself exploring the same themes?

A. About twelve, thirteen years ago, my husband, Bill Eichner, and I got involved in a project in the Dominican Republic. We visited a community of small farmers up in the mountains of the interior who were growing their coffee organically, under shade trees, in order not to deforest the countryside and poison the rivers. We wanted to help them out, so we joined their cause and bought up some abandoned farmland and started planting trees and coffee. We called the place Alta Gracia, after the national protector of the country, the Virgin of Altagracia, whose name means "High Grace." We thought this appropriate for a place high in the mountains, a place that we hoped would bring grace to our local impoverished cooperative of farmers and all those who visited or who ended up buying our coffee.

So far, so good—we were taking care of the land. But soon we realized that no one in the community of small farmers knew how to read or write, not the old people, not the middle-agers, not their children, not even the mayor and authorities. Human nature needed caretaking as well. So we decided to start a school on the farm to teach basic writing and reading skills.

What better "textbooks" for new readers than children's books, with their simple, straightforward stories, their eye-catching pictures? And so, as part of teaching literacy at Alta Gracia, I began reading a lot of children's books. Many were translations of books originally written in English about USA experiences. I thought, why not write stories based on old legends popular among my neighbors? And so I wrote *The Secret Footprints*, about a tribe of women, *ciguapas*, who come out at night to hunt for food. Most recently, I wrote *A Gift of Gracias: The Legend of Altagracia*, about the Virgencita Altagracia, after whom our farm project, Finca-Fundación (Farm-Foundation) Alta Gracia, is named.

I don't approach the writing process any differently when I am writing for young readers of all ages (the term I prefer to *children's books* or *juvenile literature*). Good writing is good writing and hard work, no matter what age reader is going to read what you write. What I can say is that writing for young readers (of all ages!) raises the bar in terms of succinctness, clarity, story pacing. Children and busy *campesino* farmers aren't going to sit still if your writing is long-winded or unclear or if the plot drags with too many asides or needless abstractions or cluttering distractions. So writing these books for young readers has actually sharpened my writing skills.

As for themes: storytellers are all part of the human family. That said, we come from our different cultures and landscapes, and we bring our tribe's experiences and songs to the long table of literature to which everyone is invited. And so there will be certain themes that will be common to any particular writer because of his specific place and time and tribe. Think of Robert Frost and his New England landscapes. Mark Twain and his bustling Mississippi River towns. Willa Cather and her Nebraska roots.

So, whether I pitch my singing voice to a story for young readers or an adult novel or a poem or an essay, it will undoubtedly reflect my tribe's adventures, which is a way of saying that certain themes will recur, a certain flame tree will crop up again and again, a wise older woman who tells wonderful stories will show up, book after book, sometimes called Chucha, sometimes Tía Lola, sometimes Doña Gloria. . . .

This is not to say that a writer can't use her imagination to write about people and places that are different from her very own background. The imagination has amazing powers!

But then that writer will have to do very good research so that, in a way, she becomes a native of that world she is trying to put down on paper.

Q. What made you want to be a writer? Did you consider any other career path?
A. I always say that I would never have become a writer had we not immigrated to the United States when I was ten years old. I admit it, prior to our arrival in New York, I was a terrible student. I was not a reader. Part of the reason was that my home culture was an oral culture. People told stories—and they were terrific storytellers, believe me! But it was not a literary culture. People just weren't seen reading. Remember, too, that our government was a dictatorship. Books from which people might get ideas were banned. Readers were immediately targeted as intellectuals, dangerous individuals. So there were no incentives for being a reader.

In my own family, I knew of two readers. One was an aunt who was an "old maid" in her twenties, and this was blamed on her reading. The other reader was my cousin, Juan Tomás. My grandmother, who herself never went past fourth grade, would worry that Juan Tomás was going to get sick because his nose was always in a book.

I took the healthy route! No one could catch me with a book, not that there were any books around except for dull textbooks and my father's medical books, with their disgusting pictures of skin rashes and oozing sores and organs that needed fixing.

When we arrived in New York City, I felt homesick and alone. Thankfully, I had some wonderful English teachers and librarians, who put books in my hand and encouraged me to write down stories from my childhood that would otherwise have been lost. I discovered that while I was reading a book, I felt less alone. I had the company of all kinds of people of all ages from all over the world. Here was a world where no one was barred, no one was told on the first page: "Stop! Go back to where you came from!" Instead here was a portable homeland, and we were all welcome! I really think that is what set me on the path to being a writer: becoming a reader.

I have often entertained fantasies of other professions, being a nurse (taking care of those who are ill, alone), being a farmer (growing things that nurture folks), being an activist for social justice (making the world a better place for us all). But what I've found, and why I love writing so much, is that I can pursue all these professions on paper. I can comfort people who feel alone, with what I write. I can nurture hungry minds and thirsty hearts. I can make the world a better place by changing, ever so slightly, the way a reader looks at the world.

Q. What books inspired you as you were growing up? And what books inspire you now?

A. I was not much of a reader growing up. (See above!) But my "old maid" aunt who was a reader did bring me back a book from a trip she took to the United States. It was *The Arabian Nights*, which is the story of a girl, Scheherazade, who lives in a kingdom where the sultan, who is full of hatred for women, takes a wife every night and then beheads her in the morning. Scheherazade's father hides her in his library, where she reads all his books and learns thousands of stories!

When she learns about what is happening to all the women in her kingdom, she decides she wants to help them. And so she begs her father to let her visit the sultan's tent and see if she can change his mind. At first her father refuses, but finally he relents.

And so, that first night when Scheherazade (I always did wish she had an easier name to spell and pronounce!) is taken before the sultan, she asks him if he'd like to hear one of her wonderful stories. "Sure," he says, "it's a while before sunrise." But wouldn't you know it, just as the sun is coming up, Scheherazade is smack in the middle of an exciting tale. She laments the fact that the sultan is going to miss out on the satisfying ending, since it's her time to die.

But no way is he going to let her die now. "You must finish your story tonight!" he commands. So Scheherazade is granted another day of life. The next night, she finishes her story, but it's still not daylight, so she begins another one, which, of course, she is still telling when the sun comes up again. The sultan again grants her a dispensation—and this goes on for one thousand and one nights. By that time, the sultan has fallen in love with Scheherazade because of her wonderful stories, and his hatred has been transformed into love. He is a changed man. Scheherazade has not only saved the women in her kingdom and herself, but she has managed to change the sultan through the power of her stories.

I loved this story. I was spellbound by Scheherazade's ability to spin tales: Ali Baba and the forty thieves; Sinbad the sailor; Aladdin and his magic lamp. . . . These are just a few of the thousand and one stories Scheherazade tells the sultan to save her life.

Back in the Dominican Republic, I had a tall four-poster bed. I used to love to sit on that bed under the mosquito net or crawl under the bed with the bedskirt all around me and pretend that I was in the sultan's tent and I had to think up a great story, or else. No pressure I've ever experienced as a writer can match the pressure I felt as a young girl of nine or ten to tell a good story to save my life.

As for favorite books now, I have so many! I love poetry, novels, nonfiction books—anything well written can engage my attention. It can be a story in a cookbook or a poem about a snake or a tale about a girl who saves her life by telling stories. I'm not picky when it comes to good books. But if a book is not well written, I don't care who wrote it—*poof!* It's transformed into a doorstop or a coaster or an item in the recycle box!

Q. As both an author and a longtime teacher of writing at Middlebury College, what advice do you offer young writers?

A. What advice can I offer young writers? Most important of all is to be a voracious reader. How can you learn to swim without getting in the river? I'm astounded sometimes when a young student writer tells me that he is not into reading! How can you be a writer without being a reader? That's like being a horseback rider but not really being into riding horses. Read, read, read. The best books are your best teachers!

Another piece of advice is to develop the habit of writing. If I decided to write based on whether or not I felt like it on any given day, I would end up writing maybe only a handful of days a month. All kinds of things would get in the way: an invitation to lunch at a favorite restaurant, a beautiful day tempting me to go out on a bike ride, a cold that makes me feel under the weather. Most people I know have no problem with my being a writer, but they often feel annoyed when I am actually writing, because I'm not answering their phone call or going to the movies or going shopping with them.

The point is that it's hard just to get yourself to sit down and write. Like any other skill, you've got to practice it to become good at it. In fact, even after you become good at it, you've got to practice to stay in shape. I often compare writing to dancing. Say a dancer only did her floor exercises when she felt like it. Say a week went by when she did not feel so inclined. Then the day she does feel inspired, she tries to do a jeté and she pulls a muscle or she falls flat on her face. Writing also requires daily exercise of your "writing muscles." If you don't write for a week, when you sit down to write, you just don't have the same agility as when you are at it every day, even if it's only for an hour. Once you have developed the habit of writing, you don't have to think about whether you are going to do it today or tomorrow or the next day. It's just something you do, like having breakfast or brushing your teeth or watching TV.

One of the ways to do this daily writing is to keep a journal. In other words, you don't have to try to write a prizewinning poem or a chapter of a novel every day. Just write an entry about whatever happened to you today. Practice putting the adventures of your life into words, the little things you notice, the way people around you talk, the view out the window, the smells after a rainstorm, the taste of your mom's apple crisp. Practice making your sentences reflect the rhythm of a scene. Imitate a paragraph you admire from your favorite book.

And here's a third piece of advice, a must for any writer: pay attention! Writing begins before you ever set pen to paper or put your hands on the keyboard. It's a way of life, of being awake to the little things around you that you would otherwise miss. I do agree with Henry James's advice to the young writer, "Be one of the people on whom nothing is lost." It's a great way to live, not just for writers, but for anybody: smelling the flowers—as the cliché goes—and touching them and tasting them, and even listening to them.

Haiku are great little "finger exercises," by the way. In order to write one, you have to pay close attention to the tiny things in your life. Not only that, but you have to choose the just-right word, since so few are allowed. It also helps that haiku are easy enough to compose even if you are far from pen and paper. Here are two favorites from the eighteenth-century Japanese poet Buson. Try a few yourself.

> *That wren—*
> *looking here, looking there.*
> *You lose something?*
>
> *Asked how old he was*
> *the boy in the new kimono*
> *stretched out all five fingers.*

*Read on for a chapter
from another modern classic
by Julia Alvarez*

I

The Eraser in the Shape of the Dominican Republic

"May I have some volunteers?" Mrs. Brown is saying. We are preparing skits for Thanksgiving, two weeks away. Although the Pilgrims never came to the Dominican Republic, we are attending the American school, so we have to celebrate American holidays.

It's a hot, muggy afternoon. I feel lazy and bored. Outside the window, the palm trees are absolutely still. Not even a breeze. Some of the American students have been complaining that it doesn't feel like Thanksgiving when it's as hot as the Fourth of July.

Mrs. Brown is looking around the room. My cousin, Carla, sits in the seat in front of me, waving her arm.

Mrs. Brown calls on Carla, and then on me. Carla and I are to play the parts of two Indians welcoming the Pilgrims. Mrs. Brown always gives the not-so-good parts to those of us in class who are Dominicans.

She hands us each a headband with a feather sticking up like one rabbit ear. I feel ridiculous. "Okay, Indians, come forward and greet the Pilgrims." Mrs. Brown motions toward where Joey Farland and Charlie Price stand with their toy rifles and the Davy Crockett hats they've talked Mrs. Brown into letting them wear. Even I know the pioneers come after the Pilgrims.

"Anita"—she points at me—"I want you to say, 'Welcome to the United States.'"

Before I can mutter my line, Oscar Mancini raises his hand. "Why the Indians call it the United Estates when there was no United Estates back then, Mrs. Brown?"

The class groans. Oscar is always asking questions. "United Estates! United Estates!" somebody in the back row mimics. Lots of classmates snicker, even some Dominicans. I hate it when the American kids make fun of the way we speak English.

"That's a good question, Oscar," Mrs. Brown responds, casting a disapproving look around. She must have heard the whisper as well. "It's called poetic license. Something allowed in a story that isn't so in real life. Like a metaphor or a simile."

Just then, the classroom door opens. I catch a glimpse of our principal, and behind him, Carla's mother, Tía Laura, looking very nervous. But then, Tía Laura always looks nervous. Papi likes to joke that if there were ever an Olympic event for worrying, the Dominican Republic would win with his sister on the team. But lately, Papi looks pretty worried himself. When I ask questions, he replies with "Children should be seen, not heard" instead of his usual "Curiosity is a sign of intelligence."

Mrs. Brown comes forward from the back of the room and stands talking to the principal for a minute before she follows him out into the hall, where Tía Laura is standing. The door closes.

Usually when our teacher leaves the room, Charlie Price, the class clown, acts up. He does stuff like changing the hands on the clock so that Mrs. Brown will be all confused and let us out for recess early. Yesterday, he wrote NO HOMEWORK TONIGHT in big block letters above the date on the board, THURSDAY, NOVEMBER 10, 1960. Even Mrs. Brown thought that was pretty funny.

But now the whole class waits quietly. The last time the principal came to our classroom, it was to tell Tomasito Morales that his mother was here for him. Something had happened to his father, but even Papi, who knew Señor Morales, would not say what. Tomasito hasn't come back to school since then.

Beside me, Carla is tucking her hair behind her ears, something she does when she's nervous. My brother, Mundín, has a nervous tic, too. He bites his nails whenever he does something wrong and has to sit on the punishment chair until Papi comes home.

The door opens again, and Mrs. Brown steps back in, smiling that phony smile grown-ups smile when they are keeping bad news from you. In a bright voice, Mrs. Brown asks Carla to please collect her things. "Would you help her, Anita?" she adds.

We walk back to our seats and begin packing up Carla's school-bag. Mrs. Brown announces to the class that they'll continue with their skits later. Everyone is to take out his or her vocabulary book and start on the next chapter. The class pretends to settle down to its work, but of course, everyone is stealing glances at Carla and me.

Mrs. Brown comes over to see how we're doing. Carla packs her homework, but leaves the usual stay-at-school stuff in her desk.

"Are those yours?" Mrs. Brown points at the new notebooks, the neat lineup of pens and pencils, the eraser in the shape of the Dominican Republic.

Carla nods.

"Pack it all up, dear," Mrs. Brown says quietly.

We pack Carla's schoolbag with everything that belongs to her. The whole time I'm wondering why Mrs. Brown hasn't asked me to pack my stuff, too. After all, Carla and I are in the same family.

Oscar's hand is waving and dipping like a palm tree in a cyclone. But Mrs. Brown doesn't call on him. This time, I think we're all hoping he'll get a chance to ask his question, which is probably the same question that's in everyone's head: Where is Carla going?

Mrs. Brown takes Carla's hand. "Come along." She nods to me.

Mrs. Brown leads Carla up the side of the classroom. I follow, afraid I'll burst into tears if I catch anyone's eye. I look up at the portrait of our Benefactor, El Jefe, which hangs above the classroom, his eyes watching over us. To his left hangs George Washington in his white wig, looking off into the distance. Perhaps he is homesick for his own country?

Just staring at El Jefe keeps my tears from flowing. I want to be brave and strong, so that someday if I ever meet the leader of our country, he'll congratulate me. "So, you are the girl who never cries?" he'll say, smiling down at me.

As we cross the front of the class, Mrs. Brown turns to make sure I'm behind her. She reaches and I take the free hand she is holding out to me.

We ride home in the Garcías' Plymouth with the silver fins that remind me of the shark I saw at the beach last summer. I'm stuffed in the back with Carla and her younger sisters, Sandi and Yo, who've been taken out of their classes, too. A silent and worried-looking Tía Laura sits in front next to Papi, who is driving.

"What's happening?" I keep asking. "Is something wrong?"

"*Cotorrita*," Papi warns playfully. That's my nickname in the family because sometimes I talk too much, like a little parrot, Mami says. But then at school, I'm the total opposite and Mrs. Brown complains that I need to speak up more.

Papi begins explaining that the Garcías have finally gotten permission to leave the country, and they'll be taking the airplane in a few hours to go to the United States of America. He's trying to sound excited, looking in the rearview mirror at us. "You'll get to see the snow!"

None of the García sisters says a word.

"And Papito and Mamita and all your cousins," Papi goes on. "Isn't that so, Laura?"

"Sí, sí, sí," Tía Laura agrees. She sounds like someone letting air out of a tire.

My grandparents left for New York at the beginning of September. My other aunts and uncles were already there, having gone away with the younger cousins back in June. Who knows where Tío Toni is? Now, with the García cousins leaving, only my family will be left living at the compound.

I lean forward with my arms on the front seat. "So are we going to go, too, Papi?"

Papi shakes his head. "Somebody has to stay and mind the store." That's what he always says whenever he can't go on an outing because he has to work. Papito, my grandfather, started Construcciones de la Torre, a concrete-block business to build houses that won't blow over during hurricanes. When my grandfather retired a few years ago, Papi, being the oldest, was put in charge.

As we come up the driveway to the García house, I see Mami and Lucinda and Mundín waiting for us. Somebody must have picked up my older sister and brother at the high school so they can say good-bye to the Garcías, too. Behind them stands Chucha, our old nanny, in her long purple dress, holding my baby cousin, Fifi, in her arms.

As soon as the car doors open, I run to Mami, who puts her arms around me. She doesn't have to ask me what's wrong. A row of suitcases have been brought out and lined up, ready to be loaded into the car. Beside them stands Mr. Washburn, a tall, skinny man with a bow tie that makes his whole face look like a gift someone wrapped up real nice. Papi has explained that Mr. Washburn is the American consul, who represents the United States when Ambassador Farland is out of the country.

"Troops all here?" he asks cheerily. "Ready to go?"

"Where's Papi?" Yo asks. She and I are the Oscars of our family, always asking questions. But I don't always get to ask mine when Yo is around.

A look passes from one adult to another as if they are playing musical chairs with their eyes, trying to decide who'll be the one stuck answering Yo's question. Finally, Papi speaks up. "He'll be waiting for you at the airport."